The Angel Gateway

Jane Adams was born in Leicester, where she still lives. She has a degree in sociology, and has held a variety of jobs including lead vocalist in a folk rock band. Her ambition is to travel the length of the Silk Road by motorbike. She is married with two children.

The Angel Gateway is her sixth novel. She is also the author of *Bird*, a chilling ghost story, and a series of crime novels featuring Detective Inspector Mike Croft, most recently *Final Frame*.

In 1995 Jane's debut, *The Greenway*, was nominated for the Crime Writers' Association John Creasey Award for best first crime novel of the year and the Authors' Club Best First Novel Award.

Macmillan has just published the sequel to *The Angel Gateway*, entitled *Like Angels Falling* (hardback, £16.99).

By the same author in Pan Books

The Angel Gateway

Jane Adams

PAN BOOKS

First published 2000 by Macmillan

This edition published 2001 by Pan Books
an imprint of Macmillan Publishers Ltd
25 Eccleston Place, London SW1W 9NF
Basingstoke and Oxford
Associated companies throughout the world
www.macmillan.com

ISBN 0 330 48132 0

9 8 7 6 5 4 3 2

A CIP catalogue record for this book is available from
the British Library.

Typeset by SetSystems Ltd, Saffron Walden, Essex
Printed and bound in Great Britain by
Mackays of Chatham plc, Chatham, Kent

For my husband, Julian. Stay Crazy!

Prologue

February 12th, pale sun in a bright blue sky, unexpected after almost a month of rain. It was two thirty in the afternoon and the square in front of the courthouse almost deserted, the lunchtime crowds gone back to work and the rush hour still a long way off.

After most of the day in court, DI Ray Flowers was bored. He leaned against his colleague's car and scanned the square again, looking for distraction. A Victorian fountain stood centre stage circled by benches and trees that would hang with blossom later in the year. Today, a bitter north wind cut across the open area and no one stayed to sit on the wrought-iron benches. A woman and small child hurried by the fountain, the child momentarily distracted by the pigeons that pecked around his feet. A skateboarder, ignoring the prohibitive notices, attempted flips. An old man in a dark raincoat holding his hat tightly onto his head rushed past the other way.

Ray thought about getting into the car, the chill finally biting through his clothes and raising goosebumps on his skin. He glanced back over his shoulder to see if there was any sign of Guy Halshaw, the car's owner. He could see his colleague through the glass doors, chatting to a court official, a young woman with bleached blonde hair and bright red lips. A Halshaw special if ever there was one. Typical, Ray thought. You take Guy anywhere and he'd pull, it had always been the same. Like Ray, Halshaw was a big man, tall and rather less rounded with the years than Ray himself and Guy had the looks to go with it. Even in his younger days, Ray Flowers with his rather lumpy face and washed out blue-grey eyes had never been anyone's idea of an Adonis.

Amused, annoyed, prepared to settle down for the wait, Ray dug deep into the pocket of his coat for the car keys. He failed to see the man running from the main street and across the corner of the square. Soft-soled shoes deadening all sound, Ray didn't hear him either. Lulled by the unexpected brightness of the day the last thing on Ray's mind was pain, but a second later his mind was filled with it. There had been the sudden glimpse of the man out of the corner of his eye, his arm already drawn back. And then the flames burning against his skin, eating their way into flesh, searing tendons on hands that had been thrown up in last-minute defence. Ray's mind and body filled with agony and the silence of the bright blue day was broken by his screams.

She woke reluctantly, dragged from the heaviness of fever-laden sleep by some sound outside.

She had been dreaming. In her dreams, she walked again in her garden.

The beds were overgrown with weeds, but the air was fresh scented by a fall of rain. And she did not mind too much what others may call weeds. Much of what seeded naturally had their own virtues and their own uses.

Her feet trod something soft and yielding and the

sweet scent of thyme rose like the spirit of a dear, lost friend.

She heard a sound behind her and turned to look. Her roses had fallen, a summer storm sending them crashing to the ground. It seemed strange to her that they were still in flower so late in the season. But then, what dreams were ever truthful? The roses planted in her garden grew white flowers and bloomed for just some little time in June.

She slept then with her windows wide open to the world and let their fragrance fill the house.

In her dream, these September roses had a yellow flower that grew in clusters and cast a fainter scent. She remembered, when she woke, that she had seen a man tending to them. A man dressed somewhat strangely for a cottager, tying back the flowers, puzzling himself over the arrangement of every branch and stem as though the task were new to him.

Dear Lord, if all her dreams could be so real, so peaceful, then she would sleep out her time here and hope never to wake again.

Part I

Chapter One

September 2000

It was late evening by the time Ray turned the key in the old-fashioned lock and let himself into Mathilda's cottage.

He stood for a moment in the dim light and surveyed the tiny front room. It had changed little from the summer visits he had made here with his parents so many years before though the cottage, and this room in particular, seemed smaller than he remembered.

Perhaps, he thought wryly, he had just been much smaller himself then.

Ray turned and closed the stiff front door, then stepped the few paces it took to reach the centre of the room, ducking instinctively but unnecessarily under the exposed beams that slatted across the dull white ceiling.

The walls of the room were lined with book shelves filled mainly with neatly stacked, well thumbed paperbacks. Furnishings were worn, grown old with their owner, the most threadbare seats hidden by plaid rugs and coloured throws. And there were bare boards around the square of the carpet where it didn't quite spread to meet the skirting, the old wood stained almost black with age and years of polishing.

Ray smiled and, as he often did when he smiled, touched his cheek experimentally as though to see how the muscles reacted to the action.

Stiffly, that was how, but it was getting better. The scarring not as inflexible, or maybe it was just that these days he risked smiling a little more often.

He crossed the room to the fireplace. A fire had been lit earlier and heat still radiated faintly from the coals. The cottage had been empty for months but the solicitors had assured him they'd arrange for it to be cleaned and aired before he took possession. Ray wondered how much that consideration would be adding to his bill.

Two little tables kept guard on either side of the fire. These were the things Ray remembered most from his visits here. Two low, round tables cluttered with an assortment of odd and – so his mother was fond of saying – useless objects. As a child, being allowed to play with Mathilda's things was the only good part about otherwise boring adult visits. His mother had been right, he supposed, they were useless. Odd-shaped stones, a toy fire engine, a snow storm and a painted tin containing remnants of broken costume jewellery. Its twin, full of foreign coins, sat on the other table. He fingered the objects now, remembering the pleasure he had taken in trying to guess what Tildey had added to her collection since the last visit. Remembering the guilt, too, when he had purloined a couple of coins from Tildey's box. Three terrible months he'd kept them until the next visit, then slipped them back.

Ray went through to the kitchen and looked out of the crooked, cross-hatched window at what had been Mathilda's garden. It would have broken her heart to see it like this. Overgrown, trellises broken down by the spring storms and not mended, the yellow climbing roses fallen to the ground and muddied by yesterday's rain. He leaned wearily against the kitchen table and glanced around at the 50s-style cabinets that must have been the height of fashion when Mathilda had them put in. Was he hungry? He thought vaguely that he really ought to eat or should at least go back out to the car and bring in the groceries. Maybe he'd do that, then go to bed.

Impatiently, he jerked himself into action, inspected the state of the fridge and the larder and was relieved to find them clean and the fridge working, even if the must of long misuse still caught unpleasantly at his nose.

He went back out to the car, making two trips to fetch the luggage and the box of essentials he'd bought on the way. He thought again about eating but the weeks of inactivity in the hospital seemed to have sapped his strength and Ray decided that he really could not be bothered with that now. He left the cases where they lay at the foot of the stairs and climbed slowly, then along the short scrap of a hallway into what had been Mathilda's room.

Someone had been thoughtful enough to make up the bed. He blessed them, whoever they were, and sat down with an ungraceful thump on the edge of it. The windows were low, eye level now that he was seated. To his surprise he found that he was looking out between the top branches of the apple tree in Mathilda's garden. He could see the church spire still crowned by the lop-sided weathervane he remembered. Beyond that was Southby wood.

It was warm for a September evening. Very warm and Ray was deeply tired. The bed was almost unbearably soft.

Without being aware of the transition, Ray drifted into sleep.

She wished that she could see more than a patch of sky. More than just the glimpse of the sun she'd had as they dragged her from the wagon and into the courthouse. Even in those few moments, scenting the freshness in the air was like paradise.

It had rained. The gardens would need it, they had told her that the summer had been dry enough.

Who tends my garden? she wondered.

Did anyone take trouble with it? Or was it poison now because she loved it?

The scent of lavender and of sweet thyme. Of rosemary. Rosemary for remembrance and for virtue.

She wished that this thing could be over and she could sleep, sleep in some place where there could be no dreaming.

Chapter Two

Morning brought confusion. Where was he? Why was he sleeping in his clothes and with one leg dangling over the edge of the bed? It took several minutes for Ray to have the answer to those questions clear in his mind. Minutes more to realize, pushing himself reluctantly upright, that he had slept deeply and without the dreams that usually plagued him.

Just knowing that made him feel good, impatient to be on with the day. He dragged one of his suitcases from the foot of the stairs and up to the bedroom, a task made awkward by the lack of strength in his injured hands. Physio had helped a lot, six months ago he couldn't even have thought of driving the car, but he still had a long way to go.

He sorted fresh clothes and, with some difficulty, persuaded the old gas boiler in the bathroom to give him enough water for his bath.

The boiler was slow and stingy. He paced irritably between bathroom and bedroom, waiting for the bath to fill and finding homes for at least some of his clothes.

The cooker, surprisingly new considering it was in Mathilda's house, was somewhat more efficient and he dealt with breakfast quickly, boiling water for his coffee in a saucepan and telling himself that he must add a kettle to his list of 'Things Needed'.

By nine fifteen he had set the kitchen to rights and completed the unpacking, feeling energy flowing through his limbs and a clarity of thought he'd not experienced in a long time. Perhaps the doctors had been right. Make a fresh start, somewhere new. Well, he could think of worse places to be in and it wasn't beyond the bounds of reason that he could commute to work from here.

He stopped the idea in its tracks before it got anywhere. Thoughts about getting back to work had been what you might call unproductive thus far, he was trying not to give them too much of his time.

He went back into the bathroom and prepared to shave, staring at himself in the mirror. Shaving was never something he had enjoyed and these days, there was the added dimension that only parts of his face needed it. The network of scars laced his left cheek and part-way across his chin. The right side, by contrast, was almost unmarked. On the left, though, his beard grew in odd little clumps, like islands amongst the over-smooth scarring. He had experimented with the art of beard growing but given up, unable to stand either the itching or the patchwork effect. The twice daily ritual of the blade had been reinstated and he put up with it as best he could, added it to one of his other lists: the one headed 'Signs of Returning Normality'.

Back in the bedroom, he looked out once more at the tangled garden and the church beyond. Mathilda hadn't been buried there, just had her ashes scattered, the graveyard being full and it being unthinkable that she could possibly have left her remains elsewhere. The solicitors had told him that there was a small memorial stone though, and he supposed he really ought to go and find it. He supposed also that he ought to take some flowers, it seemed the proper thing to do.

Ray went back down stairs, let himself out into the garden and, with the help of a kitchen knife, cut seven of the least damaged yellow roses from the climber. It was awkward to cut them so that the stems were of a decent length. Not the cultivated, bred-for-the-florist's-shop affairs these. They had real scent and the slightly shaggy look of creatures not really tamed. They had thorns too. He sucked wounded figures and held the roses gingerly, looking for something else to add to his rough bouquet. Rosemary from the bush just outside the back door and bay. He tried to pull branches from the cushion of fragrant thyme threatening to overwhelm the garden path, but it seemed reluctant to let go without roots and all pulling free. Feeling guilty at just adding to the disorder, Ray patted it carefully back into place and took the rest of his finds inside, wrapping the stems in kitchen foil to protect his hands from the vicious thorns.

Ten minutes later found him in the churchyard searching for Mathilda's marker. It wasn't hard to find, a simple stone tablet set close to the church door, with an inset of brass inlaid wood. MATHILDA O'DONNEL. JUNE 1917–MAY 2000. That was all. No message, no formal regrets. Ray felt that he should be sad at there not being more but he couldn't. The plaque was so much like Mathilda, matter of fact and to the point, but still with a thought for the aesthetic. He laid his flowers down, lowering himself cautiously to his knees and allowed his fingers to trace the letters of her name. Mathilda

O'Donnel. Strange, but he'd rarely thought of her as having a second name, or, if she had, that it would be his own.

Awkwardly, Ray cleared his throat, glancing around to make certain he was unobserved. 'I'm a bit late,' Ray said softly. 'About four months too late, and I don't even know what you thought about dying, so I can't even think of any words to say.'

Unexpectedly, Ray felt tears pricking at the corners of his eyes. He wiped them away with the back of one large hand, then got to his feet hurriedly before any more should fall.

'Better to be busy,' he told himself, allowing his mind to drift on to other things, like what he would need to renovate Mathilda's garden and how he should find out who cleaned the cottage and that he should contact his solicitor and tell him whether or not he wanted to live in the cottage or to sell. The list went on and on.

Feeling impatient again, he turned sharply and walked back towards the village to buy the other things he needed, promising himself that he'd call the solicitor as soon as he got home and then make a start on the garden.

Home. It was funny but Ray found he was already thinking of the cottage in that way. He'd have to add that to his signs of normality list. It sounded like a good word to add.

It took longer than Ray had anticipated to get back through the village. Everyone he met seemed to know who he was and want to stop and talk. To ask if he planned to stay and how he was feeling now. It was both gratifying and exhausting. He answered them as best he could, told anyone who asked that he might well live in the cottage and tolerated their reactions to his scars. He had grown used, but not resigned, to the whole gamut of reactions from outright disgust to sideways embarrassment. People here were no different. Some made an obvious effort to look straight at him, as though overanxious to show that the way he looked didn't interest them. Others shuffled their feet and looked anywhere but directly at Ray, making him want to turn their heads forcibly so that their eyes met his.

It was almost eleven by the time Ray got back to his cottage. Someone was singing as he opened the front door. At first he thought it must be coming from outside the cottage, perhaps from the churchyard beyond. But, no. The ardent strains of 'Onward Christian Soldiers', sung with more gusto than skill, were echoing happily from his own kitchen.

Ray's first impulse was to creep silently to the fireplace and clasp the largest of the fire irons. He replaced it immediately. Burglars didn't generally announce their presence by singing in their victims' kitchens. Instead, he crossed the room, shouted loudly enough to register over the noise and opened the kitchen door.

'Hello. Who's there?'

The woman, busily arranging flowers at this kitchen table, turned with a bright smile. 'Well, hello there. You must be Ray.'

'Er, yes.' He felt more than a little taken aback at

finding himself on first-name terms with this unknown woman. He found his hands in hers, both of them being shaken enthusiastically and had the strong notion that he'd only just escaped an equally effusive hug.

'Evie Padget,' she announced by way of introduction. 'Used to clean for your aunt.'

'Oh,' he managed, beginning to make sense of the situation. 'You, er, you must be the one who cleaned the place up for me.'

She nodded, beaming. 'Not that it needed much doing, love, tried to keep it nice for you, we did. I've been in once a week, regular as ever since your auntie died. Be a shame, I said, really a shame to let the place go and you not fit to take over.'

She had released his hands now and was bustling about unwrapping his shopping and putting it away. 'Ah!' she pronounced with great satisfaction. 'You've got yourself a kettle. Now I'll just boil it out for you, then we can do it up again and have a nice cup of tea.'

Ray stared, knowing he'd been well and truly invaded, though the sheer enthusiasm with which she greeted him made it difficult to take offence.

Evie had filled the kettle, plugged it in and turned back towards Ray, who stood like a socially inept child lost at some grand occasion. She smiled beatifically, clucked her tongue at him and came over for a closer look.

'My, but you made a mess of yourself!' she said, contemplating the scarring on his hands and face, her tone and gestures just those she might have used for the same child when it fell down in the mud and spoiled its party clothes.

'Be able to do much more about it, will they?' She pulled out a chair, gestured Ray to sit down and began to take cups and saucers from the cupboard.

'They don't know yet,' he said, then more defensively, 'they've done a good job so far.'

She nodded, found the sugar bowl and filled it, making him unaccountably ashamed that he'd used sugar directly from the bag that morning.

'Hard things to treat, burns are,' she said as she unhooked the kettle and poured the water away before refilling it again. 'You should always boil the kettle out before you use it the first time. Yes, a hard thing to treat,' she went on before he had the chance to interrupt. 'I had a sister worked at the county general. Works in a typing pool out at Edgemere now.' She paused to plug the kettle back in. 'Took retraining,' she added and looked at Ray as though to ensure he understood the importance of that. 'Always said that burns were the worst thing to treat. You'd see people come in, half their legs hanging off and they'd be out again, all stitched up in no time. Burns though, take months, they do.'

Ray found himself caught between an impulse to tell her that he knew that already and a strong urge to laugh. Neither seemed appropriate. Instead he asked, 'She was a nurse, was she, your sister?'

Evie laughed. 'Dear me, no. She cleaned the wards, before she took retraining. She did one of these back-to-working courses and ended up fiddling with a VDU all

17

day. Wouldn't do for me, though. I've got enough to do to keep me busy here.'

It sounded like an invitation and Ray responded to it.

'What do you do then?' he asked.

Evie beamed at him and then got up to make the tea. 'Well, for a start I go on the school bus every morning. Closed our local one down, they did. Said there weren't enough children to warrant keeping it going.'

She paused long enough to set the teapot on the table and sit down once more. 'We keep the playgroup open, I help out there as well three mornings a week. It's supposed to be three to fives, but we let the younger brothers and sisters stay as well. I mean, most of the mums stay and help so why not?'

She looked at him as though expecting contradiction. Ray mumbled a response and Evie seemed satisfied enough to carry on. 'Then there's some of the old people can't get out as much as they'd like so I do a bit for them, and of course there's Mr Padget to look after, my husband, you know.

'You're pretty busy then,' he said. Her sudden switch to formality when speaking about her husband had taken him by surprise. It was something he associated with his parents' generation and he doubted Evie Padget was more than a dozen years older than himself.

She was telling him about her children – four of them – and their children, and Ray found himself caught up in the essential trivia of the various generations of the Padget clan. He hoped he was making all the right noises at all the right moments and he couldn't have been doing too badly because eventually Evie turned a smiling face towards him and invited him to return the compliment.

'You didn't know your aunt that well, did you?'

Ray shook his head. 'No, I'm sad to say, I didn't. Life seemed to get busier as I got older and I'm afraid Mathilda was one of those things I didn't make time for.'

She gave him a sympathetic look. 'It's a pity, that,' she told him solemnly. 'I think you two would really have liked each other.'

For a moment Ray thought she was going to probe more deeply and found himself frantically searching through his memories for anecdotes that would in some way match Evie's. He guessed her appetite for the scraps of other people's lives would be voracious. To his surprise, though, she got to her feet, lifted their teacups and placed them in the sink and began to gather herself together ready to leave.

'Well,' she said, 'I must be going.' She smiled at him again as though to assure him that she bore him no malice for his neglect of Mathilda.

'We'll keep the same arrangement I had with your aunt, shall we? Just a couple of hours, two mornings a week. You'll find her account book in the right-hand desk drawer. I've already made out a new column for myself, just the way I used to. Had to up the rate a little bit of course, but you'll still find me very reasonable.' She bent towards him confidentially. 'Don't feel you have to discuss it now, just do what your aunt did and leave what you owe me on the table in an envelope.' She smiled again, her pale blue eyes crinkling happily. 'So nice to have someone living here again.'

Feeling somewhat relieved and not a little confused, Ray escorted her to the door. She turned on the way out and laid a plump freckled hand on Ray's arm. 'She wasn't lonely, you know. She had a lot of friends, a lot of interests. Mathilda wasn't the kind to hang around waiting for people to come to her.' She patted his arm and departed, marching briskly down the street, calling her good mornings to anyone in sight.

Ray withdrew gratefully into the tiny living room, looking around him again at Mathilda's domain, not certain whether he felt comforted or saddened by Evie Padget's last statement.

Chapter Three

Ray had exhausted himself in the garden that afternoon, weeding out what he hoped were weeds, digging up the more open patches of ground and tying the yellow roses back onto hastily patched-up trellis.

Evening should have found him wanting his bed, but it hadn't. The unaccustomed exercise had woken his body to an extent he knew he would pay heavily for later, stimulated a mood of restlessness that made it hard for him to settle.

He'd switched on the television – Mathilda had never bothered with anything more than a badly tuned portable – and spent the best part of an hour trying to coax a less than snowy image onto the small screen. Then having produced something watchable, lost interest and looked for yet another diversion.

He'd found it in Mathilda's desk.

In one of the drawers were receipts, bills and the like from the two years previous to his aunt's death. Ray fingered them thoughtfully, noticing that they were kept in date order and clipped carefully together, like with like. He'd never thought of Mathilda as being finicky, visits to her had always been relaxed affairs. But ordered, yes, there had always been the sense of that. It was strange trying to get to know her like this.

A search through the other drawers discovered letters,

a few photographs, postcards and other oddments. Ray skimmed these briefly then put them aside, feeling like an intruder. He'd spent his working life poking about in other people's concerns, strange that this should feel so odd, so different.

The centre of the desk hinged down to provide a writing table and revealed an assortment of pigeonholes and tiny drawers. Briefly, Ray allowed himself the childish pleasure of wondering about secret drawers and hidden recesses. His fingers probed and poked excitedly at anything that looked at all likely but he found nothing but assorted stationery and out-of-date stamps. He gave up, turned his attention to the larger cupboards that flanked either side of the central drop-down panel. Both were locked. Keys? He'd seen them somewhere. One of the tiny drawers. He found the right key at the third attempt and opened the cupboard. Formal papers, deeds to the house, solicitors' letters. Making a mental note to have a proper look at these later, he turned his attention to the second door. The key turned smoothly and the door swung back. Ray reached inside and withdrew the top one of about a dozen identical red volumes.

Mathilda's journals. He'd forgotten about them, though he'd seen these little red books often enough on his visits here. He remembered asking her about them, what they were, why she wrote in them. Remembered her answer.

'So that I can keep things fresh in my mind.'

Possessed of that subtle arrogance of childhood that needs no help to recall the important things, he hadn't understood then. Now though, as an adult, for whom selected lapses of memory had become part of his daily conditioning, he thought he did.

Reverently, feeling something like a thief, he took them out and laid them on the rug in front of the fire. Then sat, staring uncertainly at them as though daring himself to look inside, poke around in the private thoughts of this woman who had, he felt, already given him so much more than he had ever earned.

He put off the inevitable by making coffee, standing in the doorway and staring at the bland, unadorned red covers while waiting for the kettle to boil. He made his coffee strong, then, on impulse made himself a flask of it for later. He had the feeling that it was going to be very late before he took himself to bed. He added a shot of whisky for good measure, then sat down and began to read.

The man's sandy hair was stained a brassy yellow by the sodium light. He had been standing on the towpath for the better part of the last hour and his coat collar was turned up against the increasing chill coming off the water. Ten minutes ago it had begun to rain. Light rain that seemed like nothing and soaked through everything. It had set the man shuffling and fidgeting, made him hunch his shoulders and dive his hands deeper into his pockets. Sitting in the warmth of the unmarked car, Josephs made a bet that their man would soon give up his vigil and head for home.

'Who do you think he's waiting for?' Peterson asked for the fourth time in the hour.

'Buggered if I know. Whoever it is, they've a crap idea of timekeeping.'

Peterson nodded and poured black coffee from a Thermos flask. 'Want some?'

'God, no. I'm sloshing.' Josephs shifted awkwardly to ease the pressure on his overfull bladder. 'I bloody hope he moves soon.'

The factory car park backed onto the towpath, giving them a clear view of the sandy-haired man. They had parked up in the deep shadows close to the factory wall, their outline broken further by the chain-link fence and winding stems of late bindweed that clambered through it. A gap in the fence, fifty yards away, gave access to the canal and further down they could just glimpse the lock gates and the North Gate pub that stood on the bridge above. Their man had his back to them, gazing fixedly at the bridge as though expecting someone to leave by the back door of the pub and come down the path towards him. Only occasionally did he glance the other way towards the new restaurant and the Victorian warehouses, now redeveloped as expensive flats, set beyond the twin bridges where the river curved and almost joined the canal.

It was, Josephs thought, a grim place to be standing alone at night.

'He's moving,' Peterson said. 'Must have decided his friend is a no-show.'

'Thank fuck for that.' Josephs lifted the radio to his mouth, ready to alert those on the bridge that their target was headed towards them. Then he stopped.

'Where the hell did he come from?'

Their target seemed as surprised as they were. The second figure wore a full-length raincoat and was more heavily built. He must have come from the direction of the Weir Head restaurant, their view of that section obscured by the corner of the factory wall.

'Recognize him?' Peterson asked.

Josephs shook his head, mentally reviewing the pictures in the file. 'Something familiar about him, though.' He radioed the watchers close to the bridge who might have a better view.

'Our man doesn't look happy.'

The two of them were arguing, the man with sandy hair raising his arm and gesturing angrily. The man in the raincoat was more impassive, his demeanour quieter. He placed a hand on the other's arm as though trying to calm him down.

'Wish we were close enough to hear.'

'We move now, they'll spot us.'

The two men had begun to walk away towards the Weir Head, disappearing from view behind the factory wall. They were still arguing.

Josephs radioed those on the bridge. 'Do you still have them in view?'

'That's a yes. They're walking slowly towards the restaurant.'

'We'll wait until they get to the bridge over the weir then we'll follow them,' Peterson said.

Josephs nodded. At that point the two men would be just out of sight of those watching from the North Gate bridge and far enough ahead not to notice anyone following. He relayed the instruction to the other team, then got out of the car and waited for the go. When it came, the radio seemed overloud in the still air.

'Target has been joined by a third man. Repeat, a third man. He's standing in shadow, but it looks to be an IC1 male, medium height, wearing a dark jacket. Damn, we've lost them at the bend.'

'Roger that.' He nodded to Peterson. 'Come on.'

The two men walked silently along the towpath. There were no lights on this stretch, but here, close to the heart of the city, it was never truly dark and they moved confidently enough, pausing only at the bend where the canal diverted away from the river at the second bridge. It was here that the second team must have lost sight of the three men.

The towpath narrowed beneath the bridge forcing Josephs and Peterson to walk in single file and duck beneath the arcing brickwork. Up ahead, the towpath was empty. Peterson pointed at the flight of steps beside the road bridge just beyond the Weir Head restaurant.

'Must have gone up there.'

'Bloody shifted then.' Josephs scanned the bridge. There were a few pedestrians, a group of four crossing towards the restaurant and a second, larger group headed for the student flats. He had a clear view perhaps a quarter mile further up the towpath, that section being redeveloped and better lit, but no sign of anyone. Then, 'Shit!'

'What?' Peterson followed his gaze. 'Bloody hell. I'll go in.'

'Like fuck you will. The canal's choked with weeds and there's six foot of mud at the bottom of it.'

'But what if he's still alive?'

'You looking for a posthumous medal? I've seen you swim. He's floating better than you do.'

Peterson took the point. He stood, helplessly, on the towpath while Josephs lifted the radio and called in, staring at the turned-up collar of the light blue jacket and the sandy hair, blackened by the filth of the canal.

Chapter Four

> Kitty came to me again last night. I feel so sorry for the poor girl.

Frowning, Ray skimmed the brief reference again. The clock told him that it was three a.m. and he should be sleeping. He stretched wearily, ready for bed now, but reluctant to move.

Kitty? Who the hell was Kitty?

He'd read through three of the books, skimmed others, but could remember no other reference to Kitty amongst the enthusiastic accounts of the visits to friends, to the theatre, to shop in Edgemere or whatever else Mathilda had taken it into her head to record.

She had an odd way of making her entries. A few lines recording the bare facts of the day from rising to late evening. Then a fuller account of some aspect of her day, chosen with the randomness of someone sticking a pin into a list.

But Kitty. Who was Kitty?

He picked up one of the, so far, unread volumes. Flicked through the neatly written pages in the hope of finding some new reference.

There seemed to be nothing, though tiredness, merging with coffee-soaked alcohol, probably wasn't helping.

He reached down and scooped up one of the others.

Halfway through, one more note about Kitty. He looked at the date, it was 30 September three years before.

> Kitty came again last night, she spent a long time just sitting in my room as though she found it a comfort just to have me there. Poor soul. Will she ever find real peace?

This second reference, so like the other. Mathilda had been a kindly soul. Ray could well imagine all kinds of waifs and strays coming to her attention. Wearily, he put the book down, conscious that he couldn't even think straight any more.

He pushed himself to his feet, a sudden attack of vertigo forcing him to grab the desk for support. He must have really overdone things today, or rather, yesterday. He glanced at the clock again, the slow-swinging pendulum mesmerizing as it caught the light. Three thirty. God. No wonder he was tired.

On impulse, as he passed the telephone, perched precariously on a low stool at the foot of the stairs, he picked up Mathilda's address book, flopped down on the bottom step and squinted sleepily at the alphabet decorating the page edges.

Kitty what? He didn't even have a last name to look for. Hopefully, he looked under 'K'. No luck. He began to read through page by page. Still nothing.

He dropped the book down beside the telephone once more, used the newel post to haul himself to his feet and began the slow climb up the stairs to bed. This time at least, he managed to crawl out of his clothes and under the covers before falling into a deep, alcohol-aided sleep.

The next three days passed more swiftly than Ray could have imagined. He'd spent most of them just getting himself organized in the cottage. Working in the garden, driving into Edgemere, the nearest large town, for supplies he couldn't get in the village and fending off what seemed like an endless stream of visitors who had come to see how he was settling in.

At least, he thought wryly, the natives were friendly. He guessed he had the influence of Evie Padget to thank for that. She was evidently the first line of village defence.

Her second 'couple of hours' had him tidying up in a kind of frenzy beforehand and then taking the opportunity to shop while she did whatever she did. He arrived back in time for the obligatory cup of tea though, and found that she'd been entertaining a stranger in his absence.

The young man sitting at the kitchen table and listening with courteous interest to Evie got up as Ray entered the room. He looked to be in his early thirties, with a shaggy head of unruly sandy curls and amused grey eyes. His mouth seemed created for expressiveness, at the moment it was twisted into a wry smile, which expanded rapidly into a broad grin as he stepped forward to greet Ray.

Mrs Padget made the introductions.

'This is John Rivers. He's our curate, you know.'

Ray shook his hand. 'Curate? That's a sort of trainee vicar, isn't it?'

The man laughed. It was a warm, welcoming sound. Ray found himself disposed to like him.

'Something like that,' he admitted. 'None of the privileges of rank and twice the amount of work.' He moved back to allow Ray access to the table.

'Can I offer you some of your tea?'

'Thank you.' Ray smiled, then noticed that Evie seemed to be about to leave.

'Er . . . you're going, Mrs Padget?'

Evie nodded enthusiastically and gave him one of her broad smiles. 'I've done for the morning. John will tell you all you need to know.'

'Need to know?'

'Yes, dear, about what you asked me. You know. I bumped into you out shopping the other day and you asked about your aunt's friend. Well, John will be able to tell you, nothing's more certain. Spent hours with her, John did. He'll know all about her friends.'

She took her leave with her usual effusiveness, leaving behind an almost tangible void.

John Rivers sat down with a relieved sigh, and picked up the teapot. 'Shall I pour?'

Ray nodded, knocked a little sideways by Evie Padget's announcement. He remembered now, the day after he'd found the mysterious entries in Mathilda's diaries, he'd met Evie and asked her, in passing, if she knew a friend of his aunt's by the name of Kitty. He'd forgotten all about it until now.

'Shall we go through?' he suggested, picking up his cup and indicating the living room. John Rivers smiled and nodded.

'You mustn't mind Evie,' he said, 'she always means well. Look, I didn't mean to barge in on you like this. It was just a courtesy call really, but Evie was here . . .'

'And you found yourself Shanghaied.'

John laughed again. 'Something like that.' It seemed to be a pet phrase of his. They settled themselves, like firedogs, in opposite chairs either side of the fireplace.

'So you knew my aunt well?' Ray asked. 'I wasn't aware that she was especially religious.'

'I don't know that she was,' John said, 'but, yes, I think I got to know her fairly well. I lodged here for a while when I first came to the area; in fact, I was here right up until the time she died.'

'Oh,' Ray said. 'I didn't know that.' He frowned and covered his confused emotions by sipping his tea. So this stranger had been with Mathilda, closer than he had been. Knowing her better, spending more time with her. The mixed emotions of guilt and jealousy, both, he realized, completely needless, took him somewhat by surprise.

'Evie said you were asking about a friend?' John said, offering Ray a bridge to cross the awkward moment.

Ray eased himself slightly in his chair. He'd done more walking and more physical work in these last few days than he'd done in months and a dull ache seemed to permeate his entire frame.

'It was a note I found. Well, not a note really, an entry in one of her journals.'

John's smile was non-committal. 'She was as precise about that as she was about everything else. Every night, last thing, just before she wound the clocks. What was the friend's name? You'd probably find them in the address book, the one by the telephone.'

'No, I looked there. Her name was Kitty. I don't know Kitty what, but from what my aunt said about her, she seemed important.'

John was looking at him curiously, a slight frown creasing between his eyes. Puzzled, Ray went on. 'It could be short for something, I suppose. Katherine, perhaps. To tell the truth I'd given it no thought, not since asking Mrs Padget.'

John placed his cup and saucer carefully on the floor beside his feet. 'What exactly did your aunt say about Kitty?'

'Well, I could show you, I suppose.'

Ray crossed to the desk and rummaged for the right books. It took him some time to find the passages. He'd been too tired the night he'd read them to think of marking the pages and too busy to think of it since. He handed them over to John, who read them in silence. 'Did you notice the dates?' John asked. 'That they were the same, I mean?'

Ray hadn't, only that the text was similar.

Carefully, John closed the books, laid them on the arm of the chair.

'Yes,' he said, 'I know who Kitty is and,' he laughed lightly, 'why she isn't in the address book.'

'Oh?'

John gave him a speculative look, as though wondering

just how to express what he had to say. 'The thing is,' he said slowly, 'I should say, I know who Kitty *was*.'

'She's dead then?' Ray guessed.

'Oh yes,' John said. 'She's well and truly dead. The fact is,' John Rivers went on, 'Kitty's been dead for the last three hundred and fifty years.'

Chapter Five

The Video Wall was preparing for its grand reopening. The refurbishment of what had been the Sphinx until two months before was all but complete and it was up to the cleaning crew to put the final polish on the place.

Alex Pierce was reported to be well pleased with the results and no doubt Mark would be just as happy when he finally got out. Brother Mark was still on remand, but the evidence was getting thinner by the day. If something wasn't pulled out of the bag soon Mark would be back in business and eighteen months of investigation would be down the drain.

And, so far, the Video Wall was legit, straight down the line.

Peterson watched the entrance. Three of the girls were just going off shift when Alex Pierce himself came out and called out to one of them. 'Hey, Sally, you got a minute?'

Peterson watched as Alex Pierce talked to the girl. He wasn't shouting now and Peterson couldn't hear what had been said, but he could see the girl preening, relishing the attention from her boss.

Pierce held a purple envelope in his hand, the kind that might have had a birthday card inside. Peterson could just make out a line of silver writing on the front but he was too far away to see more. Peterson saw the girl giggle and then turn away after awarding Alex a brilliant smile and a glimpse of cleavage. He watched her walk to the T-junction and go left. Alex Pierce had already gone back inside. Peterson got out of his car and began to follow the girl.

Chapter Six

'Her name,' John said slowly, 'was Katherine Hallam, but, as her mother's name was also Katherine, the family generally called her Kitty.'

'How do you know about her?' Ray wanted to know. 'And what's her connection to my aunt?'

'Well, the main connection is this place, this cottage. Kitty lived here for a while. Early 1640s that would have been.'

'I'd no idea this place was so old.'

John nodded. 'Oh yes. This whole row dates from earlier than that but most have been altered. New windows put in, that sort of thing.'

'So, how did my aunt become so interested? And the entries in her journal. What the hell did she mean, Kitty came to her? Mathilda was the last person in the world I'd have said believed in ghosts.'

John smiled wryly at that. 'I take it you dismiss such things then?'

'Yes, of course. Don't you? Haunted houses belong at the funfair, there's no truth to them.'

He spoke somewhat more harshly than he'd meant. The truth was, he was not so much a disbeliever as someone who had, on occasions, come very close to believing and was far from comfortable with it.

He frowned again, rubbing the scarred side of his face

reflectively. The new skin still had a tendency to dry out quickly and become sore and itchy.

'I don't think Mathilda thought of herself as being haunted,' John said. 'More, that she had an occasional visitor of a slightly unusual kind. She thought of Kitty more as a bewildered foreigner having problems with the local language than a ghost.' He pulled the shaggy curls back from his forehead. 'Kitty was certainly real to your aunt and, as you've seen from her journals, someone she felt very sorry for. I was interested enough to do a little poking around. Kitty was quite infamous in her time, poor woman.'

'Infamous? Why?'

'I'm sorry to say that one of my distant predecessors took exception to her.' He smiled a little sadly. 'Kitty Hallam was accused of witchcraft, tried, and found guilty. She was sentenced to hang. It's all in the parish records if you're interested. I had bits and pieces photocopied for Mathilda, they're probably around here somewhere.' He pushed himself to his feet. 'I should be going now,' he said. He smiled again, a half-shy, half-embarrassed smile that made him look more like a small boy than a grown-up priest. The jeans and overlarge sweater he was wearing doing nothing to amend the image.

'Do you have to go?' Ray found himself asking. 'Look, I was about to have lunch. If you'd join me . . .'

'And sing for my supper?'

Ray returned the wry smile. 'Something like that,' he said.

*

'Her name, as I told you, was Kitty Hallam and until she was eighteen life must have been pretty good. Her father was well off, ran an apothecary's shop over in Edgemere, and had plans, it seems, to open a second once Kitty finally married. He'd taught her a good deal of the business. We tend to think of women in those days as having low status, and in some ways they did. But for a family business to survive, I suppose everyone had to pitch in. Anyway, by all accounts, Kitty was pretty and clever, and certainly not short of prospective husbands. The world must have been sweet for Kitty. Then, well, it all went terribly wrong.'

'What happened to her?' Ray prompted him.

'There was a fire. It started in the kitchen and spread rapidly. The house was one of those half-timbered affairs. I'd guess it went up like kindling. The alarm was raised and everyone ran for their lives, all except Kitty who'd been ill and was sleeping in an upstairs room. The fire had devoured the stairs before anyone could reach her. Her father wrote a letter to relatives, telling them about it. Kitty climbed out of her bedroom window. They saw her standing on the sill, the flames from the burning room rising up behind her. Before she had the nerve to jump, her nightgown had caught fire and her hair was blazing.

'It must have been a terrible sight. And the pain . . . Well, against all the odds, Kitty lived. She broke her leg in the fall and it never really set properly. She limped for the rest of her life and the scarring on her face and hands saw off her one-time suitors. It must have been a horrifying thing for a girl like Kitty. She must have felt she'd lost everything.'

'It's a horrifying thing for anybody,' Ray said quietly. He touched the side of his face. He might not be an eighteen-year-old girl but he could still relate to the scars.

John went on. 'The fact was, Kitty survived, lived to prove that she was made of sterner stuff than anyone gave her credit for. To my mind, her esrtwhile suitors didn't know what they were missing. From all the accounts we have, she was quite some lady.'

He rose from the table, began to clear away the remnants of lunch. 'She moved then, to this village.'

'To the cottage? Here, I'll put that away.'

'No, not to the cottage at first. Where do you keep the washing-up liquid? Ah. No, she moved in with the rector, Matthew Jordan, a cousin of the Hallams, and became his housekeeper. His friend too. He thought a great deal of her, even spoke up for her at the trial, which must have taken some courage under the circumstances.' He paused to gather the rest of the pots and dump them into the foaming water. 'It was a good arrangement. Kitty had a home, a place in the scheme of things, and the skills her father had taught her made her a valuable member of the community. I understand she even ran some sort of informal school. Then, when she'd been here about six or seven years, the Reverend Jordan became ill. Ill enough to force him to retire. He went off to live with his niece and Kitty moved here. The new man arrived, complete with wife and household, and took up residence in the rectory – that's gone, of course, it was where the village hall is now.'

He gave the plate he was holding another dunking in the water, scratched ineffectively at a fault in the glaze.

'Then Kitty's problems really started. That was in 1642, the summer. The Civil War hadn't quite got under way, but there was enough turmoil for no one to be in any doubt that big changes were on the way. Jordan was what you'd call a High Church man. A real traditionalist. This new man, Randall, was Puritan to the core. A real fire and brimstone Bible thumper. He and Kitty didn't exactly hit it off, and Randall's wife, well, it was her testimony really that ensured Kitty's conviction.'

'Her testimony?' Ray wiped the plates thoughtfully, and replaced them carefully in the cupboard.

'Yes. She claimed she saw Kitty consorting with the devil in Southby wood. Testified that Kitty had bewitched the village children as well, that they followed her around, whispering the devil's secrets or some such thing.'

'Superstitious nonsense.'

'That may well have been so, but she was believed. You'd have to go and look through the court records, if they still exist, to get details. That would have been my next port of call, but Mathilda fell ill and it sort of lost its importance.'

Ray nodded slowly. 'I might just do that. So, your information – where did you get that from?'

'Ah, now there I was lucky. You know, maybe, that there's no resident here any more. There's a pool of us serving about six parishes. When the residency ended here, all the records and a quite extensive library were transferred to Edgemere and a lot of it was then sent off to the records office. I was asked to help with the cataloguing, and, lo and behold, the Reverend Jordan kept journals, recorded just about everything he ever did.

For some reason, when he died, his personal papers were sent back here together with some church properties. That was my starting point.'

He emptied the sink and dried his hands. 'I really do have to go now,' he said, 'but I've enjoyed this. Maybe we can return the compliment?'

'We?'

'Me and my wife, Maggie. I'll give you a ring, OK?'

Ray nodded. 'That would be nice. Thank you.'

'No problems. But you'll have to put up with the dog and the kids climbing all over you. I'm afraid they're all three convinced that any visitor to our house wants to play.'

Ray laughed a little uneasily and touched the scarring on his face again. He wasn't used to children.

'The kids'll want to know how you did it and the dog will probably try to lick you anyway,' he said. Then extended his hand and clasped Ray's briefly, the broad grin back on his face. 'Now,' he said, pulling at the tangle of curls falling forward into his eyes, 'the boss – Maggie to you – tells me I can't come home until I've had some of this cut off and its my turn to help out at the local Gingerbread group.'

He made his exit soon after that, leaving Ray thoughtful and a little lonely.

He wandered back into the living room, turned on the television and flicked restlessly through the blend of afternoon soaps and quiz shows, and sat down to watch, though with most of his mind elsewhere, plucking gently at the threads of Kitty's story. He felt a sympathy with her for their commonness of injury, if nothing else. He recognized as his own, the pain she must have felt, knowing that his own hurts, well treated and healing, still caused him discomfort to say nothing of the emotional strain it had placed upon his life. He'd been lucky, his hands still retained most of the normal range of motion. He just had to be a little more concentrated on tasks requiring dexterity. What was harder to overcome was the variety of reactions that his injuries invoked.

Ray stared harder at the television, suddenly annoyed with himself for becoming so involved in something that could no longer matter.

It had mattered to Mathilda. He sensed also that Kitty had come to matter to John Rivers. In the end boredom and curiosity won. He gave up on the television, got up almost hurriedly and went over to the desk. John had talked about photocopies. If Mathilda had kept them – and what didn't she keep? – then the most likely place would be the desk.

He opened the door to the other cupboard, the one housing the more official correspondence, and began to rummage through the assorted, carefully ordered papers, not, this time, for clues to his aunt's life, but for that of a woman who'd been dead three hundred years before Ray had even been born.

Chapter Seven

It had rained in the night but the sun had risen fierce and early. Ray stood barefoot on the garden path, bathed in the sea of fragrance that rose from wet earth and rain-drenched plants.

He had been up late again the night before, reading what he could find of the photocopies John had made. It had been a frustrating task. John had not really known what to look for and had copied only parts of documents, fragments that must have looked relevant to Mathilda's search. Reckoning up the cost of photocopying, Ray could understand why he had been so selective. To say nothing of the time he must have spent even to get as far as he had.

Even so, Ray had found himself irritated by the half story that these patchwork records told. He wanted to see the real thing. To know the rest. He went back inside the house and made his morning tea.

John had copied pages from the Reverend Jordan's diaries and bits and pieces from the parish records, mainly relating to the trial. The journals were couched in the most cautious of terms as though Matthew Jordan had been afraid to commit too much to paper. The omissions showed, even to the stranger that Ray was. His instincts told him a great deal about Matthew Jordan and Ray was deeply saddened by what he thought he saw.

Matthew Jordan had seen Kitty not just as friend and housekeeper. He had loved his young cousin with far more than familial emotion and the thought of her death was tearing him apart.

Searching for more, Ray drove into Edgemere.

The young woman at the records office was friendly and sympathetic, but she was less than helpful.

'I'm just a student,' she said. 'This is my holiday job and I only do mornings.'

She had gone off to consult with someone in another room and came back smiling. 'You want to see Miss Gordon,' she told him. 'She's not in today and it's half day closing anyway, but Miss Gordon knows the catalogue back to front and inside out, she'll be able to sort you out in no time.'

Somewhat put out, Ray had to settle for an appointment for ten o'clock the following morning. He left a list of the sort of documents he wanted to see, the Reverend Jordan's diaries, any court records that might be held, then went back into the sunlit street and wondered what to do next.

He'd noticed a cafe earlier and went to get himself a cup of tea. He sat in the window with tea and toasted teacakes, watching the world go by. Edgemere was an attractive little town. The main street was very wide, leaving room for the market still held there twice a week, and the new bypass had taken the bulk of through traffic away to the south. A butter cross stood opposite the cafe and a flower seller had set up in its shade. Half-timbered buildings formed a backdrop. The lower floors of some had been converted to shopfronts and Ray wondered if any dated back to Kitty's time. Her father's house had been like this, he recalled. Half-timbered and with the shop below. But it had burned down long before.

The tourist information centre told him about the battle that had taken place not three miles from Edgemere. It had been a decisive one for the Royalists, early on in the Civil War but was not well known even locally having been overshadowed by the similarly named Edgehill only a month or so after. From there the King had barely escaped with his life. Ray pocketed the free leaflets on offer – maps of the old town and the battlefield and guides to local museums and places of interest. On impulse he asked if they had anything more detailed and bought a guidebook full of colour pictures and what looked like not a lot of text. He asked, but no one had even heard of Kitty Hallam.

Chapter Eight

The following morning, Ray was awake with the birds. He had fallen asleep reading the pamphlets he had collected the day before. In the night they had slipped from the bed and lay scattered on the floor.

He lay watching the sun rise above the church and filter through the green leaves of the apple tree, thinking about Kitty. Had this been her room? What had it been like? Mathilda had furnished it simply, whitewashed walls complementing the exposed beams running across the ceiling. A brass bed and worn rugs on a bleached wood floor. Would it have been so different in Kitty's time?

Ray turned on his side, the better to watch the slowness of the sunrise, shafts of light striping the blue quilt and turning white walls to primrose. Had she lain here, so long ago and watched the sun rising over the church tower and the tall trees of Southby wood?

Ray laughed at himself. He was beginning to obsess. What was it about Kitty Hallam that had drawn him so powerfully? It was more, he felt, than the mere coincidence of injury and some oddly placed regard for his aunt's interest.

Ray rolled onto his back, the sun now above the level of the apple tree and the light too bright for his eyes. He found himself thinking about his life and what he had done with it so far. A career copper with the almost obligatory broken marriage to a woman he'd known at college and whose face he could barely recall. He still owned the marital home, the man his wife had left him for too rich for her to bother depriving Ray of his half share, though now, even that was up for sale. He had his hi-fi equipment and collection of CDs and direct cut vinyl, safely – he hoped – in store and a Volvo estate that he kept planning to replace with something more dynamic, but he had never been a great one for possessions.

And there were a few, a very few people, that he called friends. He could number these on the fingers of one hand as distinct from the 'people he knew' that must run into hundreds.

Not, Ray thought morosely, one hell of a lot to show for forty-five years.

Irritated by this threatened dive into self-pity, Ray hauled himself out of bed and started to run his bath. Breakfast was early and he left the cottage far too soon for a ten o'clock appointment. It was only eight thirty-five when he crested the hill outside the village and looked back across the valley. Ray pulled the car onto the verge and stood, leaning against it, examining the patchwork of fields and scattered houses. Loose spokes radiating from the centre of the village itself, circling the hub of the churchyard. A small development of 'executive homes' had sprung up in what had been an orchard about a quarter-mile from the village proper, and the village hall now stood where the rectory would have been. Other than that, Ray thought, Kitty would have known the place.

A narrow path crossed the fields from the road where he had parked the car and led to a stile and a plank bridge before turning towards the church. The path had been there when Ray was a child and on occasions they had walked it, Mathilda and his mother up ahead, his father, generally lost in thought, following on behind and Ray, with a big stick to beat the nettles back, bringing up the rear.

It was an old track then, old perhaps even in Kitty's time.

Ray stood quite still, gazing down into the valley, feeling the early morning sun already tightening his skin, impatient to be getting on with the day, but holding back, waiting for something. Then as Ray watched, a flock of birds rose from the thicket of crack willows standing beside the river, as though a hidden someone had disturbed them passing by.

Part II

Chapter Nine

June 1642

Kitty got awkwardly to her feet and pulled herself back onto the bank holding the roots of the large crack willow for support. She hurried back towards the village carrying the watercress she had been gathering.

Tomorrow, the Reverend Jordan would leave for his niece's home and Kitty's duties to him would be over. This afternoon, Matthew Jordan's niece and her husband would arrive and the evening meal, Kitty was determined, would be a celebration among friends, not a precursor to the sad goodbye that would follow.

The kitchen door stood wide open. It was already warm outside but the heat from the cooking fire made a furnace of the room. A covered bucket, water fresh drawn from the well, stood by the kitchen door, a wooden dipper hanging from its handle. Kitty drank from the sun-warmed water, its taste honeyed with sunlight, then she kicked off her shoes and cooled her feet on the flagstone floor.

'Mistress Hallam, mistress. Master Jordan has been calling for you this last quarter-hour.'

Kitty smiled. 'One moment, Ellen, and I will be there.'

She dropped the basket of watercress on the board next to the stone trough used for washing vegetables. Later it would be chopped with parsley and green onions to stuff a chine of beef that would be salt-crusted and slow-cooked in a Dutch oven close to the hearth. The larger joints of meat already hung on the spit, slow turned by the 'jack', the dripping of their juices into the basting tray hissing a soft accompaniment to the clatter of pots and the crack of the wood on the open fire.

Ellen, five years old but already useful, stood on a stool to help her mother with the bread. Three loaves had already been set to prove on the scrubbed table. And Mim, who had been in the household since Ellen's mother had been a mere babe, sat close to the open door, a rough cloth cast across her lap as she plucked the last of the birds that would be stuffed with chopped fruit and sweet herbs to be eaten cold on the journey of the following day.

Another day, Kitty thought with a sharp stab of sadness, and this place would change for ever. The household broken into so many parts as the servants left to work elsewhere and Kitty herself moved to her new home in the village.

'I'll go and see what Master Jordan wants,' she said, 'then I will be back to help.'

'There's sugar needs to be broken and searced,' Mim told her, 'and the Jumbals to be made. If you would do that, Mistress Hallam, since you have a lighter hand.'

Kitty smiled and nodded, then went through to the hall that divided the kitchen from the remainder of the house. She paused a moment to glance in the small mirror hanging by the door, tucking a loose hair under her cap. She had grown so used to the sight of herself that she no longer hid from the looking glass as she had in the early days, when the scars on her face were peeled and raw and she had hated every casual glimpse. These days, Kitty had learned to be valued for other things and to see virtues in herself beyond the story a few scars could tell.

Matthew Jordan was calling to her from his study.

'Ah, Katherine, there you are.' He paused, looked wearily around the little room he used as his study, now all but packed away and ready for his departure. 'Oh, but I'll miss this place. It looks so bare with my books gone from the shelves and everything so unnaturally . . .'

'Tidied?' Kitty laughed. 'I'll miss this too but it is for the best, we both know that.'

She crossed the room and opened the desk drawer, taking Matthew's reading glasses from beneath a stack of papers.

'Oh, there they are. Kitty, sometimes I think you read my mind.'

'No, I just know you well. Seven years of playing lost and found with your spectacles has me well trained.'

'I will miss you, Katherine. I'll have someone else to train over again. But, you will visit with us.'

'I will, I promise you. And now, Master Jordan, I must be on with the day. There is food to prepare and sugar cakes to make.'

'Sugar cakes, Jumbals. Excellent.' Matthew Jordan smiled like a satisfied child.

'And the sugar won't pound and sieve itself any more than the salt will come off the butter without washing and I promised Mim I would be back to help.'

Matthew Jordan smiled gently at his cousin. 'I will miss you, Katherine, I mean that, you know.'

'I know. But tonight we should celebrate. Thomas

and Margaret will bring news of how things pass with the King and Master Eton will be here to argue with you. Let the rest go until we have to think of it.'

The old man nodded. 'You are right, of course. And you might well find, Katherine, that the new incumbent and his wife value your presence as I have done. You might not even notice I am gone.'

Kitty laughed at the obvious fishing. 'I will notice your absence,' she said. 'No matter how great a friend Master Randall and his wife become you will never be replaced.'

Chapter Ten

Ray had arrived fifteen minutes early for his appointment with Sarah Gordon and she'd kept him waiting the full time. He got instinctively to his feet as the woman strode into the lobby. Miss Gordon, he thought immediately, was not someone you would want to greet sitting down. She had an air about her of something more bossy than authority, a woman not used to having her time abused.

She assessed Ray at a single glance and offered her hand. 'Sarah Gordon,' she said. 'I've ordered the documents you asked for, they're being brought up for you. Come on through.'

Ray followed her behind the barrier of the front desk and into the cool of the library beyond. Sarah Gordon was a tall woman, almost matching Ray for height, and she carried it well, with a military precision. Her thick red hair was pinned tightly into a businesslike chignon and she wore heavy framed glasses that exaggerated the size of her grey-green eyes.

Nice bones, Ray thought to himself, and a good shape to go with them. He was still smiling at the thought when Sarah Gordon turned to him.

'The documents you wanted,' she said, indicating books and papers stacked neatly on a long table. 'There are a few that can be copied, others have to be scanned into the computer and you can have printouts. There's a charge, of course. Photocopying damages them. Handling does them very little good either so we ask you to keep it to a minimum. Others are too fragile to copy or scan so you'll have to make your own notes.' She looked suspiciously at Ray. 'You've brought a notebook, I take it?'

'Oh yes.' He patted his pocket. 'A pencil too.'

'Right, well, I'll leave you to it.' She took a few steps away from the table, then turned and indicated a smaller desk at the other end of the room. 'I will be over there should you need anything.'

She gave Ray a long last suspicious look and walked away. Ray sat down, laughing to himself. Obviously, he didn't look like someone able to handle historic documents or capable of doing research. He surveyed the books and documents laid out on the table in front of him with a feeling of great satisfaction and not a little awe. These things had survived more than three hundred years and had probably hardly been looked at in all that time. He reached out for what he took to be one of the Reverend Jordan's notebooks, one of a dozen, leather bound, yellowed pages foxed with age. The pages crackled as he laid the book open on the table, their faces covered with a tiny spidery hand set in impossibly close lines as though someone had been eager to save space. The ink had been protected from the light in the closed books and was remarkably unfaded considering the age. Ray bent over the first page and began to read, frowning in his effort to make out the words, conscious that he really was gazing directly into the past.

*

It was lunchtime before Sarah Gordon's curiosity finally got the better of her and she came over to see what Ray was doing. He sat, pen poised over notepad, squinting hard at a paragraph of Matthew Jordan's close scripted entry.

'Problems?' Sarah asked him.

Ray sighed. 'I used to have a sergeant who specialized in deciphering the impossible. Failing that, there was always some young probationer looking to earn a few brownie points.'

Sarah raised an eyebrow at him, then grabbed a chair and tucked in close by, peering in turn at the paragraph Ray pointed to.

'Sergeant?' she asked. 'A military man then?'

Ray laughed uneasily. 'Police,' he said. 'Detective Chief Inspector Ray Flowers at your service,' he told her. 'Twenty years in Her Majesty's service, for all the good it's doing me.'

'A policeman. Run out of modern criminals, have we?'

Ray glanced sideways at her. 'I wish.'

'Not an amateur historian either, are we?' she said. Then smiled, a revelatory smile that took the harshness from her words.

Ray smiled back. 'No, I'm on holiday. Well, actually, I've just come to live round here and I'm sort of semi-retired. Well, actually I'm still on sick leave.'

Sarah's eyebrows raised above the thick frames of her spectacles. 'Do I choose any or all from those options?' she asked him.

'Any and all I suspect. I've not decided yet.' He

sighed. 'I thought this would be easy, but it's taken me all morning just to read through June 1642. It's going to take me weeks at this rate.'

'And you are in a hurry?' Sarah asked him. 'Is there a time limit? Because if there is it might be good to choose the retirement option rather than the holiday one, you know.'

She got up as though suddenly making a decision. 'It's my lunch break,' she said. 'I've got an hour and the pub next door does good sandwiches and Theakston's Old Peculiar on draught. You can tell me what it is you're searching for in 1642 and I'll tell you where you ought to look.'

Ray returned to the cottage at six that evening to find messages on his answerphone.

One was from his solicitor. The estate agent had called. Someone had made an offer on Ray's house. And there was a message from an old friend who was thinking of leaving the force and setting up on his own. He wanted Ray to join him. Ray listened to his messages, then dumped his notes and the bundle of copies Sarah had made for him on the sofa and went through to the kitchen. Unable to face cooking that night he'd picked up fish and chips on the way home. He filled the kettle and switched on the radio while waiting for it to boil, stamped around the kitchen finding a plate and cutlery and buttering bread. It had been Evie's cleaning day and he'd left her money as instructed, in a small brown envelope on the kitchen table. She'd taken it and made up the account book for him, leaving a little note that he could do with more milk and also something to clean the mildew off the back door, if he could pick it up in Edgemere.

He turned up the radio, fiddling irritably with the tuning. He should get his music out of storage and brought here, then at least he'd have something decent to listen to. The television rarely held his attention for long and sometimes the evenings could be lonely.

It was a thought that led him back to Sarah Gordon. Now, there was a woman worth making an effort for. He had been hesitant at first to explain to her about Kitty, but she had listened well, a spark of interest in her grey-green eyes.

'You're a detective,' she said to him. 'If this were a criminal investigation, how would you begin?'

Ray laughed. 'With the witnesses,' he said. 'But unless you've got a Ouija board handy I can see problems with that. That's why I thought, you know, if I read the diaries, my aunt's and the Reverend Jordan's, I might get a handle on things.'

'And what have they told you so far?'

'That my aunt felt she was being haunted. Not that it bothered her, I think she felt the ghost was quite benign. And that the Reverend Jordan really didn't want to leave his home in 1642. It wasn't the thought of moving in with his niece. I gather he was going back to the family home because when she married, her husband took over a place that had been in Jordan's family for generations. It was worry about leaving Kitty. Jordan saw himself as her mentor and her protector and I get the feeling that he'd have liked to be much more, if he'd thought it proper, which he didn't.'

Smiling, Ray took his supper through to the living room and plonked himself down in an armchair. He'd rather like his relationship with Sarah Gordon to be 'more' if she saw it as proper, and Ray very much hoped she did.

Chapter Eleven

Ray ate fish and chips with his fingers and read about the last meal Matthew Jordan had shared with Kitty.

The old priest had taken great pleasure in describing the food, which seemed to have landed on the table all in one course, a mixture of sweet and savoury. Of roasted meats and stuffed fowl. A 'fricassée of rabbit and chicken flavoured much with wine' and something referred to as a 'sallet' of fresh herbs decorated with figs and preserved oranges, which the Reverend described as 'being served very prettily' but which he did not eat. Not being a salad man himself, Ray could appreciate the sentiment.

Matthew Jordan had a taste for sweetmeats, though. He went to great lengths to record the candied fruits and the 'jumbals', which seemed to be some kind of biscuit, and some kind of rice pudding that he had described in exact detail, so that his niece could make it for him when he moved to her home.

Ray sat with a piece of battered fish fast growing cold between his fingers as he tried to figure it out.

The rice, sugar and milk was fine, the addition of so many spices together with eggs and something called barberries, he could accept, but adding beef suet and stuffing the whole lot, haggis wise, into a prepared stomach sounded bizarre.

He bit into his fish and wondered if Matthew Jordan's

niece ever made this favourite pudding for her uncle, and if she did, had he complained that it was not as good as Kitty's. That there were too many spices, or the sheep's stomach had not been boiled for long enough?

There had been five people at that last supper: Matthew, his niece Margaret and her husband Thomas Stone, Kitty herself and someone Matthew referred to as Master Eton, who was not explained, but was enough of a friend to be debated with, something Matthew Jordan had enjoyed as much as the food.

It appeared that they had talked of politics. Of the tension between the King and Parliament and whether or not it would finally lead to outright conflict.

Ray had only an approximate idea of the history of that time. He had a Hollywood notion of dashing Cavaliers and puritanical Roundheads and Oliver Cromwell having his portrait painted warts and all, but he realized, reading through the record of Matthew's debate with his friend, that he knew very little at all of the real effects the war must have had upon the ordinary people.

The Reverend Jordan's niece and her husband lived in Leicester, twenty miles or so away, in the Belgrave area. Ray had driven through the city. Belgrave Road, he remembered, was now referred to as the golden mile, full of saree shops and Asian restaurants. When he'd been there, preparations for Diwali had been in full swing and the Belgrave Road illuminated with pre-Christmas lights. He found it hard to visualize as it might have been in Kitty's time. Most of the buildings were Victorian. Rows of terraced houses leading off the main drag. Nothing he had noticed had seemed older.

In June 1642, Leicester had been sitting on the fence, hoping that the problems threatening the country would resolve themselves before the town was forced to become involved. Careful not to take sides, they had elected and sent two members to Parliament from opposing sides. Lord Grey of Groby, a committed Parliamentarian, and Thomas Cooke, a supporter of the King.

'And it seemed to me,' Matthew Jordan had recorded in his journal, 'that this could only lead to conflict. That it will please no one, simply make equal enemy . . .'

Ray pushed his plate aside, he had skipped the rest of the debate and moved two pages on to Matthew's entry of the following day. It was brief, but, to Ray's eyes, poignant. It concerned Kitty.

> *watched her waving to me, running along beside the path as a child might until we reached the tight bend in the road and she was gone from my view. And I felt great heaviness of heart that I had lost the best and truest friend, outside of any wife, that any man might have.*

Morning brought the post and a package redirected from Ray's old address. He opened it to find the gas bill and a plain brown envelope with a Middleton postmark.

Ray tugged impatiently at the flap. Inside was a single piece of paper, a clipping from a newspaper, folded in half. He unfolded it and laid it on the table.

'River man named' the headline told him. Puzzled, he scanned the text. A man's body had been pulled out of the Soar close to a bridge and moorings just outside of

Middleton. There was no doubt that he had drowned but a blow to the head added complications. Had he hit his head falling into the river? Or was it the blow that had caused him to fall?

Ray sat down and read the text again. The man was described as a petty criminal with a history of violence. His name was Frank Jones, it was an ordinary enough name and it meant nothing to Ray, surprising if, as the paper stated, he was a persistent offender. Less surprising perhaps as it described him also as a Leicester man.

So, what was he doing in the Soar at that point, miles away from his home patch?

Ray turned the clipping over and examined the envelope. There was no separate message, but scribbled at the foot of the clipping was a date and a location, Middleton Magistrates' Court, 12 Feb, the place and day that Ray had been attacked.

Ray drew his hand slowly across his face, tracing the ridges and hollows of the scars that crossed his cheek, trying not to draw the most immediate of inferences. There had been more than one officer who had sworn to get the man that had attacked DI Flowers, though Ray, more concerned with the pain and whether or not he would lose his sight, had taken little notice of their angry promises. He had heard that the investigation had stalled and they were no closer to knowing who had attacked him than they had been in the first days. The thought, however small, that someone suspected what they couldn't prove and might actually resort to murder on his behalf was something he had never considered and it sickened him. He threw the rest of his breakfast in the bin and got ready to leave.

When he had been injured, the papers had been full of Ray Flowers. Rubbish about the hero cop injured in the line of duty. But he'd been spared the impact of it, too badly hurt to be aware of anything more than drug-eased pain. Not knowing what to think, but afraid that it must be the worst, he got into his car and drove to Edgemere, hoping to find refuge in the records office and the older story of Kitty's life. Once there, concentration eluded him. He stared hard at Matthew Jordan's words, trying to make sense of them, but his mind was filled instead with images of that unknown man, glimpsed so briefly before the red pain eating its way into his face had driven everything else from his mind.

Ray sat in the cool, dim section of the records office, watching the dust motes swirling in a shaft of light, his mind telling him that it was all ended, that he was alive and safe, while his body sweated fear.

'This might be useful to you,' Sarah Gordon said, dumping a book on the desk in front of him and pointing to a couple of paragraphs halfway down the page. 'It gives you a bit of background.'

Ray thanked her vaguely.

She stared at him. 'You look ill,' she said and pulled the book away as though he might contaminate it.

'I'm all right.'

'Sure you are.' She sighed. 'Look, I'll summarize this for you if you like?'

Ray fought to give her full attention. 'Please do,' he

said. 'I mean, I am getting to grips with bits of this Civil War stuff. I've figured out it's more than Cavaliers and Roundheads.'

'So I should hope.' She glared at him. 'The main thing to remember is that King Charles was a fool. He thought that every decision he made had to be the right one, regardless of sense.'

'Divine right of kings,' Ray said.

He was rewarded with a little smile. 'So you are learning something. We were a rich country by then, trading links all over the world. Colonies in the New World and Jamaica and, of course, in Ulster. We'd already abolished Irish law and religious rights and we were doing our best to do the same with Scotland. By 1637 Charles had a rebellion on his hands up north by his forcing High Church liturgy on a proudly Low Church population. By 1640 contingents of the revolutionary committee, they called themselves the Covenanters, had already crossed the Tweed. Charles had war with Ireland, an uprising on the Scottish borders and Parliament threatening another on his own doorstep . . . Are you listening to me?'

Ray jumped. 'I'm sorry,' he apologized. 'Yes, of course I am. You were saying?'

She scowled, but gave him the benefit of the doubt and carried on. 'That Charles was beset by problems. He'd ruled without Parliament since 1629 and only called them back in 1640 when he ran out of money. Look, Ray, you're not listening to me, are you? I'm not used to people tuning me out.'

Ray managed an apologetic half smile. 'I don't suppose

many people dare. No, you're right. And I'm sorry, I just can't seem to get my head into gear today.'

Sarah Gordon gathered up her book and used it to tap Ray smartly on the shoulder. 'Come along,' she said.

'Come along where?'

'Early lunch. You're buying. Consider it punishment for non-attention. And you can tell me what it is that's on your mind.'

Chapter Twelve

She had known that it would not be pleasant, showing strangers around the house that had been her home. And these strangers were not initially prepossessing.

She had been watching for them since just after dawn, but it was almost noon when the Reverend Randall and his family arrived, accompanied by an entourage of servants and baggage carts. The master of the house rode a fine bay gelding and the mistress seated pillion behind a young male servant. Two children sat beside the driver of one of the carts, one fast asleep despite the jolting on the hard bench seat, the other, a girl about eight or nine, looked about her with an air of disbelief.

They had come from Nottingham. Kitty wondered how they would settle into village life after the bustle of the town.

She left through the back door, and raced to get to the vicarage before them. She arrived as the first of the wagons trundled into view. The smell of fresh baked bread wafted from the kitchen. Mim had promised to light the kitchen fires and bake bread and she had left cold meats and cheese to break fast after their journey.

The head of the household was the first to arrive, breasting the slight rise at a canter and pulling his mount to an abrupt halt before the door. He stared down at Kitty.

'Mistress Hallam?' His gaze searching her face and examining her scars with an expression that barely concealed distaste.

Then he followed her inside.

'It is a pleasing view,' Randall commented, looking from the study window.

'The Reverend Jordan found it so.' She pointed. 'The sun sets beyond those trees and when the snow falls in winter, the whole valley looks to be aflame.'

A noise in the hallway drew them back outside. The children thundering into their new home and calling for their father.

'Can we look upstairs? Can we go outside?'

'Which is to be my room?'

Their father smiled fondly. 'Go outside and explore the gardens,' he told them. 'But keep clear of the men unloading the carts.'

Through the open door Kitty could see the Reverend Randall's wife directing the unloading of their furnishings. Heavy chests were being lowered to the ground and Turkey carpets spilled from the back of the cart and into the dust. She could hear the woman scolding.

'Mim, who was cook here for the Reverend Jordan, she has baked fresh bread and left cold meats for you. She will return tomorrow if you still have need of her. Will you need aught else?'

Randall shook his head. 'No, the servants can make themselves of use and my wife will direct things as she pleases. I understand that you kept house for your kinsman. How do you keep yourself now he is gone?'

'A small allowance from my father,' Kitty told him,

surprised that he should ask. 'He is a man of business and has enough to provide for me. In any case, I took no pay from the Reverend Jordan. He gave me home and protection and that was enough.'

The man nodded as if satisfied, then he held out his hand. 'If you would please to give me the keys, mistress, then we need trouble you no further.'

It was, she thought, strange to be treated as a servant in this house where she had been all but mistress for so long, but she handed him the ring of keys, telling him briefly which belonged to the outer doors and which locked the stores and cupboards before turning to leave.

'I wish you good health, sir, and happiness in this house.'

'And I thank you kindly. Oh, Mistress Hallam, there is one small matter. The land about these parts seems fertile and well tended. You could tell me perhaps, who it is collects the tithes?'

'That would be Master Eton's man, sir. Master Eton, he owns much of the village and surrounding land.'

He thanked her with the briefest of nods, then went outside to assist his wife in ordering the carts unpacked.

She left them, barely noticed by anyone and walked back into the village towards home. She must make allowance, Kitty told herself, for the long journey. He must be tired, and not up to the niceties that she had come to expect from Matthew Jordan. But even so, his dismissal of her as though she barely mattered had, Kitty felt, been harsh.

Though, then again, he had smiled at his children and spoken to them kindly and there had been pride in his expression when he'd looked at them. That must count for something.

But she found herself unable to shake the heaviness from her thoughts. Nothing would be the same. That, of all things, was certain.

Chapter Thirteen

Ray poked at the food on his plate. Sarah had recommended the lemon sole and he wondered if he dared put ketchup on it. She was waiting for answers and he was unsure of what he could tell her. 'I had a letter today,' he said finally. 'I suppose it brought it home to me what I'm giving up. It's hard to imagine another life.'

'Enjoyed the chase, did you? Thrill of pitting your wits against the enemy?'

Ray looked sharply at her, then realized she was winding him up and grinned. 'It was rarely like that,' he said. 'Someone once described policework as ninety per cent boredom and ten per cent panic.' He glanced again at the little packets of tomato sauce in the basket at the centre of the table. 'I'd argue with the ratio, but . . . well, you get the picture.'

'So why stay with it?'

'I enjoyed the ten per cent.'

Sarah smiled at him, then reached across and passed the ketchup. 'Go ahead,' she told him. 'I won't think badly of you.'

'How did . . .?' He smiled wryly. 'You ought to have been a bloody copper.'

'Good cop or bad cop? Seriously though, Ray. This . . . letter. What did it say to upset you so much?'

'Are you always so direct?'

'Only with the people I respect.' She took advantage of his surprise. 'Hard, isn't it? Facing your own mortality.'

'What would you know!' He said it harshly. Far more harshly than he'd intended.

'Oh, I beg your professional pardon! I didn't realize you had to be one of the boys in blue to understand that stuff.'

Ray shook his head. 'That wasn't what I meant,' he said. 'Or maybe it was, I don't know. I'm sorry, Sarah, I don't know how I feel about any of it any more.'

'Oh yes you do, Ray. You know very well and that's the problem. It's not easy when you're used to being in control, to running the show, to admit that you were scared half out of your wits and totally unprepared for all the rage and pain and sheer humiliation that comes with knowing you're human and very vulnerable.

'Ray, I may not have been through what you've been through but I've been scared and I've been alone, regardless of how many people there were making sympathetic noises. I don't know what happened to you, how your face and hands got into that state, but it must have been pretty bad. I understand what it's like to know that you might be going to die or at the least maimed for life and the sheer relief, yes and the guilt, when death points the finger at someone else and not you.'

Ray glanced at her cautiously, then stirred his tea, playing with his spoon.

'Five years ago,' she went on, 'I found a lump in my left breast. It wasn't very big and it wasn't very impressive.

You know, not at all the way you think that death should be. But it was there and it wouldn't go away however much I wanted it to. Finally I went to my GP and before I knew it I was in hospital having bits of me removed by a surgeon whose only interest was that he'd saved my life, nothing about the kind of life that I'd be living afterwards.

'Ray, I was devastated. Not because I've ever been that vain about the way I looked, or that I was even in a relationship that might be affected. It was something more fundamental than that. I'd gone from one moment in my life when I'd felt secure and certain of myself, to an instant later when my life was threatened and I was anything but certain and secure.'

'What did you do?' Ray asked her. 'I mean . . .'

Sarah laughed a little harshly. 'I paid to have myself rebuilt,' she said. 'Like the Six Million Dollar Man, only not quite so expensive. I went to another doctor who told me that, if I'd gone to him in the first place, most of my left breast could have still been there and his job would have been a hell of a lot more simple. But, anyway. I paid for Humpty-Dumpty to be put back together again and while he sorted out the physical stuff I tried to do something about the rest of me.'

'I thought, I mean, I've heard there are support groups and that sort of thing nowadays.' He stared at her, suddenly embarrassed. 'I'm sorry, I'm pretty ignorant.'

'Aren't we all, until you're faced with it. Yes, there are support groups and I joined one for a while. A couple of the women I met I still keep in touch with, but it wasn't me. I'm too much my own person to go joining things.'

There was more to it than that, he knew, but Ray didn't push. She picked at the remainder of her food and then she asked, 'How long before you could look in the mirror and see yourself and not just that mass of scars?'

'I shave every morning,' Ray said. He tried to make a joke of it, but the laughter stuck in his throat. He tried again. 'It's not the scars. It's not the fact that people look at me in the street. It's not any of that. It's . . .'

'That you feel guilt every time you want to complain,' Sarah said softly. 'Because, after all, you're still alive, no matter what your scars are like. You're still alive, so what right do you have to complain?'

He looked at her, stunned. He'd never put it into words like that, not even in his most private thoughts.

'You've every right. Every right to complain and shout and rail against all of it. Against every little scar and every minute of pain. Every right, Ray, and don't let anyone tell you that's not so.'

'And you declare that right, do you? You stand on the rooftops and proclaim your hurt to the world, do you?' He didn't know whether to be amused or outraged. The spot she'd touched was still too tender.

'Damned right I don't!' She smiled a little sadly at the expression in his eyes. 'No, I do what you do and I hide it all away. Easier for me than you, I guess, unless I wear a transparent swimsuit.'

'That I'd like to see.' He looked away, suddenly uncertain as to whether he should have said that.

Sarah reached across the table to touch his hand. 'Keep talking like that, copper,' she said, 'and you might get lucky.'

She dreamed of the strange man again, the one she had seen in her garden. This time, he was inside the cottage, moving slowly from room to room, searching as though for something lost. And it seemed to Kitty that the furnishings had changed in her little house and that a Turkey carpet covered the floor that had once been bare boards scattered with woven rugs.

In her dream she followed this stranger, walking a pace or two behind him up the stairs and into her own room.

She could not see his face, only his back. She could see that his hair was short, cut neat against his neck and curling a little about his ears. He was big, this man. Big about the chest and waist and tall. He filled the doorways and felt it needful to dip his head as he passed beneath the lintel.

Her own room, of all the cottage, was the least changed, the walls still white and the boards still bare but for a bright strip of carpet laid beside the bed. A washstand had been placed against the wall opposite the window and a mirror above, but neither jug for water nor basin for washing stood upon the marble, just an assortment of men's things. A comb for his hair and keys and coins and other things she did not know. And she stood quite still, just inside the door, and watched this man as he placed his hands upon the marble stand and bent his head to peer into the glass.

How long before you could look into the mirror and see yourself and not just that mass of scars? Sarah Gordon had asked him.

Ray looked now, defiantly. Stared straight into his own eyes reflected in the mirror and asked himself the question Sarah made him ask.

'I see myself,' he said. 'I can bloody well see myself.'

And he touched his scars, feeling the lineage and extent of every one, still gazing with a fixedness at his own grey-blue, bloodshot eyes.

And then, Ray Flowers cried, standing there with his hands gripping the washstand and his gaze still fastened on the glass and he let the anger and the pain rip through his body in harsh, wretched sobs that made his six-foot frame tremble and his eyes blur until he could no longer hold his own gaze.

It looked so easy in films. You just squeezed the trigger and there was a big bang. That was it.

He'd always known it wasn't really like that. Basic training, even just the target range, had taught him it was never just like that. Sometimes he'd imagined it. Shooting someone. But he'd always thought that if it happened there'd have been some purpose in it. That he would have saved a life, maybe, and not just taken one.

He'd almost pulled out and in the end it had been fear of not doing it. Fear for his wife and kids and for himself that made him squeeze the trigger and fire off the first shot. And then he couldn't stop. Kept on and on until the clip was emptied and someone took the gun away.

They gave him whisky. A bloody great tumbler full of the stuff that burned his throat as he drank it down. It didn't even touch him. He was still stone cold sober and the man he'd shot was still stone cold dead.

Chapter Fourteen

John Rivers phoned on the Friday morning and invited Ray to lunch after church on the Sunday.

'I don't expect you to come to the service,' he said. 'Not unless you want to, of course.'

'Oh.' It seemed graceless to go to lunch and not to see his host in church. 'Of course. Look, I haven't been to a church service in years, so you'll have to forgive me if I don't know the form. But of course I'll come to that too.'

Not well put, Ray told himself. He could hear John Rivers chuckling at the other end.

'I don't mean to impose, John, but could I bring someone with me? Um, she's a friend.'

'Of course. That would be nice. I hope she likes kids.'

Ray had no idea. He tried, unsuccessfully, to visualize Sarah playing with children. They agreed a time and John rang off, on his way to a meeting. Ray replaced the receiver thoughtfully, wondering what Sarah would say to dinner with the vicar.

He told Sarah as soon as he got to the records office. She was less than impressed at Ray's invitation.

'I can't say I'm that keen on vicars.'

'Neither am I, but this one's not your usual kind.'

She smiled at him. 'Seriously though, I'd love to come.'

Ray took a deep breath. He'd done a lot of thinking overnight and come to an important decision.

'A friend of mine. He's just about to leave the force and is trying to set up his own security firm. He wants me to join him and I've decided to tell him yes. Someone's made an offer on my house and if the sale goes through I'll have the capital.'

'Is this a sudden decision?' Sarah asked. 'Or has it been fermenting for a while?'

'For a while I suppose, but I made the final decision on the way over here.'

'It sounds like a good idea. You should be useful, not just content to sit around.'

Someone called her from across the office and Sarah left him. He delved once more into Matthew Jordan's diaries. An entry for the August of that year intrigued him. It spoke of a letter received from the mysterious Master Eton who, Ray learned, went by the name of James, concerning events at the beginning of that month.

It saddens me that the new incumbent thinks so little of our customs that the Lammas doll should be so slightly cast aside. Superstition it might well be but to the local people it is a great matter. I will pray for him that the harvest still be good. A poor harvest will further reduce the people's faith, however misguided such a reaction might be. I have written to James Eton and suggested that I intercede with Master Randall, but I would guess mine is the last voice he would listen to.

    It troubles me that Katherine has become involved

in this quarrel. James Eton promised me that he would watch over her now that I am gone, but she is a headstrong woman and will be right as much as Master Randall will be right.

Ray made a note to ask what Lammas was. He figured it was vaguely religious. And what was a Lammas doll?

Whatever it was, it looked to Ray that this must be where the trouble began for Kitty. Matthew Jordan gone for less than a couple of months and the conflict already there.

Sarah dumped a slim booklet on the desk in front of him.

'You'll find this relevant,' she said. 'It's something published by a local history group. 1616, 18 July, nine women were hanged for witchcraft on the evidence of a little boy. He claimed they tormented him with their familiar spirits, which caused him to have fits.'

Ray read the passage she had pointed to. It was taken from a contemporary letter written by one Robert Heyrick of Leicester to his brother William.

We have been greatly busied this four or five days past, being assize time, and a busy assize, especially about a sort of woman, witches, that nine of them shall be executed in the forenoon for bewitching a young gentleman of the age of twelve or thirteen years old, being the son of one, Mr Smith, of Husbands Bosworth.

He looked up sharply at Sarah. 'Nine of them,' he said.

Sarah nodded. 'Read on.'

Sir Henry Hastings had done what he could to hold
him in a fit: but he, and another as strong as he, could
not hold him. If he might have his arm at liberty, he
would strike himself such blows on his breast, being
in his shirt that you might hear the sound of it the
length of the whole chamber – sometimes fifty blows,
sometimes a hundred, yea, sometimes two or three
hundred blows, that the least of them was able to
strike down a strong man; and yet all he did to
himself did him no harm.

'And these women were actually tried for this?' Ray
questioned. 'What other evidence did they have against
them?'

'None as far as we know. In fact, later in the year
James the First visited Leicester. He was fascinated by
witchcraft and a true believer if ever there was one. He
interviewed the boy and practically got him to confess
that he made it all up.'

'So the women died for nothing. Some kid's fantasy.'

'It wasn't that uncommon, Ray. Millions died, all
over Europe. In fact, in parts of Europe, denouncing your
neighbours as witches was a profitable business. If they
were found guilty, and most were, you and the Church
got to split their property between you.'

Ray was silent for a moment. 'These women,' he said,
'would they have tortured them?'

Sarah frowned. 'Officially torture wasn't used in Britain, but it's all a question of definition. We didn't go to
the lengths the Inquisition went to, but certain things
were allowed. You could swim a witch. Tie her hand and
foot and chuck her in the nearest pond. Mostly, if she

sank then she was innocent, but not everywhere. In some places it was said that the water was God's creation and would bear the innocent on its surface. I suppose they figure that since Christ walked on water . . .'

'A truly innocent woman would do the same. Sarah, what about the ones that sank, did they leave them to drown?'

'Some must have drowned. We don't have figures. There are records of others dying of shock and pneumonia, but again we just don't have the numbers. As for actual torture, well, sometimes what we'd call torture was allowed. Burning with irons, that sort of thing.'

'And presumably, Kitty would have known that.'

'Ray, most people believed in the power of witches in those days and what was done with them was widely publicized. She would have known.'

'She would have been terrified of that,' he said.

Sarah snorted rudely at him. 'Who wouldn't be? Look, I've only ever burned myself on the oven door, but I know that it hurts. Faced with that, I'd have thought she'd have been half out of her mind before they'd even started.'

'You seem preoccupied this morning.'

'Master Eton. A pleasant day to you.'

He swung down from the back of his horse and walked beside her towards the cottage.

'Something troubles you, Mistress Hallam? Your thoughts were so far away you did not even hear me approach.'

Kitty laughed. 'I'm sorry, I meant no insult.'

'I know that. I only meant . . . Mistress Hallam, Kitty, I have known you since you moved to Matthew's house, and now he's gone, well, I promised him that I would watch over you. If you have troubles, Kitty, I hope that you should be able to bring them to me.'

'Did I look so worried? No, really, my thoughts were elsewhere, but truly, nothing was wrong.'

'What then?'

She hesitated. 'It will only amuse you and I would not be a jest in your eyes.'

'You would never be that. I regard you as highly as my friend Matthew. I hoped you would be aware of that.'

She had hurt his feelings. Kitty had no wish to do that.

'Do you believe in spirits? In hauntings?' she asked him.

'In spirits? I'm not certain that I understand.'

'No more do I.' She sighed, then decided to tell. 'The first night I moved to my new home I saw a man, standing in my garden.'

'A villager.'

'No, I know everyone here. This was a stranger. I went out to speak to him, I thought he looked for someone, but by the time I had unlatched my door the man was gone.'

'Was it dark? Perhaps you mistook yourself.'

'Not so dark, but I have seen him again. Twice more. A glimpse only, as if in the corner of my eye. But I have dreamed of him, Master Eton, and the dreams are so vivid they are like nothing I have ever known.'

He was silent for a moment, thinking of what she had said. 'Kitty, you are the most rational person I know and with the most sense of any woman I am like to meet but these are fancies I would expect to hear from Mim, or some other simple soul.'

'I know it and you are right. I cannot explain myself and that troubles me.'

Eton nodded thoughtfully. 'There has been much change in your life,' he said. 'I think that perhaps the answer to this lies there, in an unsettlement of mind, more than one of spirit. Kitty,' he said more seriously, 'I am honoured that you trust me with this and I am glad that you do, but you should be careful. There are many who would be suspicious of such fantasties and read far more into them than there should be seen.'

'I know this too,' Kitty told him. 'But you have been a good friend.'

Eton nodded. 'And hope always to be.' He sighed. 'I have just been speaking with Master Randall over the business of the tithes. Who collects them and what records should be kept.'

'The records have always been kept well enough.'

'So I thought, but he wants all things itemized to the last detail and accuses me of being lax in my collection of them.'

'Lax? How?'

'That I let the poorest work off what they might owe instead of demanding pay in money or in kind. Lord as my witness, Kitty, such demands should have been lost with the feudal lords. I cannot and will not demand payment from those who would starve if they should give it. They work enough hours for the Church without Randall seeking more.'

Kitty smiled. 'It seems you like him as much as I.'

'Oh, probably a good deal less, though it doesn't do to say so.'

He halted and prepared to remount his horse. 'I must be gone. Take heed, Kitty and put these fancies aside. They come merely from anxiety of mind and all things being unsettled.'

She nodded. 'I am sure that you are right,' she told him, but as he rode away she could not shake from her mind the image of the man in her room, bending to look into the glass. A mirror that she did not have, showing scars so like her own.

Sarah had got tickets for Tollethorpe Hall and the performance of *A Midsummer Night's Dream*.

'You may not be into Shakespeare,' she had told Ray, 'but this is something not to be missed. They perform outside in the grounds of the manor house and it's just beautiful.'

'What if it rains?'

'Then we'll get wet.'

There seemed no argument against that and, Ray had to admit, the setting was beautiful and the evening magical as they watched the Dream enacted against a backdrop of English woodland in the slow-gathering dusk.

A light mist was rising as the heat of the day was drawn out of the earth and neither seemed in any hurry to be home. As they drove beside Rutland Water on the

Oakham Road, Ray pulled the car over onto the verge and they leaned against the dry stone wall to look out over the water.

'I remember this before the lake was here,' Sarah told him. 'It was all little villages and rolling farm land. I saw it when the lake was still half filled. The tops of walls poking out through the water. It seemed to take time to look right here.'

'Did you live out here?' He still knew so little about her.

Sarah shook her head. 'No. My dad delivered drawing office equipment. Peterborough and Oakham were part of his Thursday run and in the holidays he'd let me go with him. I liked it best in winter. Early morning, going out in the frost and fog, watching the sun burn through just before we stopped for breakfast. He'd have bacon butties and a massive mug of tea and I'd eat cornflakes. I'd never touch them at home, but eight o'clock in the morning when we'd already been on the road a couple of hours, they tasted wonderful.'

Ray laughed. 'Where was that?' he asked.

'I forget. There were transport cafes all over then, full of truck drivers and motorbikes.' She shook her head. 'It's all these chain franchises now that cost the earth and serve lousy tea.'

The light mist was thickening over the water and the air growing chill but Ray was reluctant to move. Sarah wore black trousers and a cream silk blouse. She had a jacket draped around her shoulders and she pulled it close.

'Are you cold?' he asked her.

'Yes, but I want to stay. It's a nice cold. Autumnal. I love this time of year when everything's on the change and the light is so wonderful.' She paused and turned to smile at Ray. She was so beautiful, he thought. Not conventionally, but in a way that was purely Sarah. She wore contact lenses out of working hours, showing off her grey-green eyes. Ray wanted to reach out and pull her close, but he dared not move. He stood still watching her in profile as the light faded and the mist drifted by and he held his breath, not wanting to do anything that might break the spell.

It was a long time since Ray had thought about love.

Chapter Fifteen

Ray drove to Middleton on the Saturday morning to check on the house sale and arrange for some of his more personal things to be taken out of storage. He picked up his hi-fi and his collection of CDs and vinyl and a few other items he felt he would like to have at the cottage but he was surprised at how little attachment he felt for most of his possessions.

He had arranged to meet George Mahoney for a late lunch at the Weir Head by the canal basin. Two o'clock saw him facing Mahoney across steaming plates of chicken curry and seafood pasta.

'You look well, Ray. What is it, country living?'

Ray laughed. 'I don't know,' he said. 'But I do feel better.'

He reached for sugar to put in his tea and absently pocketed a couple of packets spare. 'Actually, George, I've met someone. Her name's Sarah and she works in the records office in Edgemere.' He hesitated, stirred his tea. 'She's pretty special. I've never met anyone quite like her.'

George Mahoney raised an eyebrow at him. 'Romance in the air?' he asked. 'Well, I'm glad for you. You've been alone altogether too long.'

'It's not that serious,' Ray began to protest. 'I've known her only a few days yet. But,' he said smiling, 'I'm hoping. You'll like her.'

'I'm sure I will.'

'Come over to the cottage one weekend. There's a spare room.'

'I'll let you know when I can get free.' George Mahoney glanced around the dining room. 'Do you come here often?' he asked.

Ray laughed at the cliché. 'Time to time,' he said. 'The food's good and I like the location.'

Mahoney nodded. 'I'd like this place a lot better without the phoney beams.'

'My cottage has genuine ones. Bloody great black things that collect cobwebs the size of a small marquee. I told you the house sale looks set to go through.'

Mahoney nodded. 'Are you sure you want to do this? I have the capital we need to set things in motion and I would understand if you didn't feel ready to commit yourself.'

'I'm ready,' Ray told him. 'And it's better to have a reserve. I don't want us going to the bank cap in hand a couple of years down the line. I've never been one for owing, you know that.'

George Mahoney nodded again. 'I've been putting out feelers,' he said. 'Corporate security is where the money is right now.'

'And it's as boring as hell.' Ray gave his old friend a shrewd look. 'OK, I can buy that as bread and butter, but what else, George? You're not going to be happy spending the rest of your life installing fancy alarm systems.'

Mahoney took a sip of his drink. 'It makes money,'

he said. 'And making money is what we need to do if we want the freedom to do other things.'

'What other things? Come on, George, if you want me as a partner I'd like to know what I'm getting into.'

George Mahoney nodded slowly. 'I just need to talk to people first, finalize things. Trust me, Ray, if I pull this off, you'll be more than interested. There was talk, a couple of years back, of setting up an official Cold Case unit but funding wasn't available. As ever. They've got one going in the USA, jointly run by the FBI and the police. I did some work with them a couple of years ago. I was impressed.'

Ray looked dubious. 'Official, you said?'

'Well, semi-official. As I said, funding didn't happen. But there's been enough interest for us to think about doing it on a semi-official basis.'

'So we work our butts off on this corporate security lark and then take on extra work picking up dead files on the side?'

'That's about the size of it.'

'Just the two of us?'

'Well, I'll concede that we may have to bring others on board. But there'd be some official funding. Expenses, that sort of thing.'

'You're crazy, George.'

'Probably. But, Ray, you know you like the notion. I can see your eyes light up. And you've got to admit, it would make life interesting.'

Ray thought this over. George moved in different circles to the ones he was used to. Ex-army and soon to be ex-DPG, George Mahoney was a man with connections. He'd been a co-ordinator in the Diplomatic Protection Group for the last eight years and a field officer for five more before that. Ray was eager to know what more he had in mind but knew George of old. He would say nothing until all his facts were in order. 'All right,' he said. 'It doesn't sound altogether practical, but I'll admit it might be interesting.'

'Oh it will be.' George pushed his empty plate aside and leaned back in his chair. 'Now, what's on your mind? You said on the phone that you had something to show me.'

Ray reached in his pocket for the clipping. 'This came through the post. No message, just the date scribbled on the bottom.'

Mahoney read in silence. 'The date you were hurt,' he said.

Ray nodded.

'And you think someone is tying up loose ends?'

'It seems a fair bet.'

'I would agree. Have you spoken to anyone about this?'

'No. I called in to see my superintendent when I was in town today but he wasn't in. I'm reluctant to come out in the open about this.'

'It was sent to your new address?'

'Redirected from the old one. Only a handful of people know where I've moved to.'

'And your thoughts?'

Ray frowned. 'First off, that someone had done him in on my behalf. Last I heard they had no one in the frame for it. I was alone when the attack happened and witness reports of a man hurrying away were hazy at best, I don't know, maybe something broke but there was insufficient evidence to go through channels. Maybe I should have kept a closer eye on things recently but to be brutally honest the nightmares have been bad enough without poking at the wound.'

There were few people Ray would have admitted that to but George Mahoney merely nodded. 'And your second thought?' he asked.

'That someone else wanted me to know. Someone who'd organized the attack in the first place. The department worked on the assumption that it was mistaken identity. I was standing by Guy Halshaw's car. In a place I was not expected to be, and Guy Halshaw is similar in build to me.'

'And he was due to be chief prosecution witness in the Pierce case.' Mahoney nodded. Pierce had been the biggest drugs bust the local force had ever had. 'I always wondered,' Mahoney commented, 'if they wanted Halshaw not to testify, why they didn't just have him shot.'

Ray smiled, feeling the tightness pulling at his face. That had occurred to him as well.

'And now you wonder if you were the real target.'

'It's crossed my mind.'

Mahoney read the report again, thinking deeply. 'Do nothing,' he said. 'If someone is playing vigilante and they want a pat on the back they'll be in touch again. If it's a threat of some kind, then the same advice follows. Wait for them to make the next move. As you say, few people know where you are, best keep it that way.'

Ray looked doubtful. 'I thought I'd try to find out a bit more about the dead man,' he said, but Mahoney had his notebook out and was scribbling brief details taken from the clipping.

'Leave it to me,' he said. 'I can still access records without arousing interest. You'd have to bring someone else on board and, frankly, I don't like the feel of that.'

Reluctantly, Ray nodded. 'All right,' he said. 'I'll give you a few days on it. But I don't think I should let this go.'

They finished their meal, talking of more general things, then wandered out to walk along the towpath.

'The body was found close by here,' Ray said. 'Just before the lock gates. There's a backwater used for permanent mooring and a footbridge leading from the main road.'

Mahoney looked to where he pointed. 'Lucky it didn't get caught up in the lock,' he said. 'The sluices would've made a right mess.' He changed subjects abruptly. 'You're going to settle in this cottage of yours then?'

'I think so, yes. It's keeping me busy. I'm learning to garden.'

Mahoney laughed. 'That, I don't believe.'

'It's true. I've the scars to prove it. Roses have thorns, you know.'

'I had heard. Seriously though, what are you doing to fill your time? I know you, Ray. You've never been one to sit around.'

'I'm getting restless,' Ray admitted. 'I see Sarah every day. You could say she's helping me investigate something. What you might call a real cold case.'

His tone, the laughter in his voice, made Mahoney look sharply at him.

'My aunt,' Ray said.

'The one you inherited from?'

'Yes. She was convinced the cottage was haunted by a woman who lived there in the 1640s. She was accused of being a witch. I got interested and I've been looking at the history. That's how I met Sarah, rooting around in the records office.'

'Ah, I did wonder. It didn't seem like your kind of place. And have you seen this ghost yourself?'

'No. I don't think I'd know how. But it's keeping me busy.'

'Digging up the past.' Mahoney sounded disapproving. 'I'd have thought we had enough unsolved cases without having to go back that far.'

'Sarah said the same thing,' Ray agreed, but he knew the comment carried far more weight than Sarah's had done. 'Like Janine,' Ray added, recalling the case that had first brought them together.

Mahoney nodded. 'Like my Jan,' he said.

Chapter Sixteen

'Mistress Hallam? We thought we would come to say hello. I am Hope Randall and this is my brother, Samuel. I am eight and he is almost twelve. I've seen you often about the village but Samuel was afraid to come till now.'

The boy bowed awkwardly. 'My sister lacks manners. I am sorry for that.'

Kitty smiled at him, standing so awkwardly in her doorway when his sister seemed already so much at ease.

'Come in, both of you,' Kitty said.

'You used to live in our house, did you not?' Hope demanded. 'Do you like it here? It's rather small.'

'Hope!' Samuel gave Kitty an apologetic look and grabbed his sister by the arm. 'Hope, I mean, we both, thought we should make your acquaintance. It seemed only polite.'

He tugged at his sister's sleeve, trying to call her to heel but Kitty could see that this was a lost cause. Hope freed herself without even thinking about it and danced through to the kitchen, peering out through the back door.

'Oh, I like your garden.'

'Thank you,' Kitty said. 'It will look better in another year when the plants have had time to grow.'

'Do you grow these things for your medicines? Mim

says that you make simples and ointments for when people get sick. How did you learn to do all that? Can I learn?'

Kitty laughed aloud. 'One question at a time! First of all, my father taught me the virtues of plants and how to make use of them and yes I grow these things for making medicines and yes, if you wish to learn then I will show you how.'

'We should ask our father first,' Samuel said.

'Of course you must, but if he agrees, then it will be a pleasure to teach you. Both of you, if you wish.'

Samuel looked uncomfortable. 'I'm not sure,' he said. 'Our father may not approve—'

'You mean our *mother* won't,' Hope retorted. 'Our mother does not approve of anything.'

'Hope! You shouldn't talk like that.'

'Your brother is right, my dear. You should not disrespect your parents.'

'I'm sorry.' Hope pulled a face at Samuel. 'But our father says we should always speak the truth and it is the truth, our mother disapproves of everything.'

She pranced around the room, admiring and examining Kitty's home, while Samuel cringed at his sister's bad behaviour and Kitty did her best to look stern for his benefit.

'Mim says you were in a fire?' Hope said. 'That's why your face looks like that.'

Samuel shrank visibly.

'Mim is right,' Kitty said.

'Does it hurt you still? I should not want to look like that. Did everyone point at you?'

'Some people were rude and uncivil enough,' Kitty told her.

Hope stopped in her tracks. 'And I am being as rude and uncivil as they?' she said, her small face creasing with remorse. 'Oh, I am sorry, Mistress Hallam. My father tells me often I should know when to hold my tongue.'

Kitty just smiled at her. 'I am sure that you will learn in time,' she said. How on earth, she wondered, had the Randalls managed to produce a child as exuberant as this?

Chapter Seventeen

Church had been bearable, Ray thought. Mostly hymns and a mercifully short sermon. One of the congregation had read the lesson, something about a letter to the Ephesians, but Ray's mind had been wandering by then and he hoped that no one would ask him any questions. Sarah sat beside him, looking wonderful. She wore a blue silk dress that fell softly to mid-calf and her thick red hair hung loosely around her shoulders, kept off her face by two ornate combs. He felt a sudden surge of pride that she was with him, that and what seemed, given the location, like an inappropriate surge of very physical desire.

Service over, they waited for John to finish talking to his flock. He stood with his wife Maggie by the church door, chatting about the harvest festival and parish business.

'She's very pretty,' Sarah commented, looking at Maggie.

'Yes, she is,' Ray agreed. Maggie had soft blonde hair brushed back from her face and cut into a neat bob, very blue eyes and a smile as ready and open as her husband's. 'And you're very beautiful, Sarah.' The words were out before he could stop them. He tensed instinctively as though anticipating the worst.

'Not used to giving compliments to the ladies, are you?' Sarah squeezed his arm and smiled at him.

'No, no, I'm not, but I mean it.'

They walked together back to the vicarage. Maggie had explained that this was their home parish and that John did the service here one Sunday in three, his workload spread around three parishes all too small to warrant a full-time man. He was also on a rota, providing back-up to cover illness and holidays.

The children, Gareth and Beth, raced ahead. So far Ray had only heard them giggle and he wondered if they were actually capable of speech. He wasn't used to children. Wasn't even certain that he liked them, though he had long ago learned better than to say so.

The two women were already chatting, walking side by side and Ray fell into step with John.

'We're really glad you could come,' John told him. 'And that you could bring Sarah. It's great for Maggie having another woman to talk to. I mean one that isn't on a parish committee.'

'Has to be on her best behaviour then, I suppose. She's not what I would think of as a vicar's wife.'

John laughed. 'Well, thank the Lord for that! Actually, it's been tough on her. I grew up with the job. It's what my father did, but Maggie, well, I'm not sure she was even a believer until we met.'

'And now?'

John just smiled. 'I don't have theological discussions with my wife,' he said. 'She supports me in all I do. She's my best friend and my sharpest critic and, at risk of sounding trite, I really do believe that God knows what goes on in our hearts and that he wouldn't object to anything that goes on in Maggie's.'

The two women had waited for them by the gate and Ray was glad not to have the opportunity to reply. He was rather touched by John's words, but hadn't a clue what to follow them with.

'I've cooked lamb,' Maggie said. 'I hope that's OK with everyone.'

'Anything I don't have to cook is great with me,' Sarah told her. 'I'm a disaster in the kitchen, but if you're prepared to take the risk I'll give you a hand.'

'If you could make tea or coffee, that would be great. It'll be about another fifteen minutes.'

The house was Victorian – dark, carved wood on the curving banisters and polished block floors scuffed and scratched by years of feet. Lunch was served in the dining room at the back of the house. French doors led from there out into a long garden.

'We tell everyone that we're encouraging wildlife,' John said when he saw Ray looking out. 'But the truth is we don't have time to do it properly. I manage to cut the grass and Maggie's doing a good job of putting new plants in so I suppose we'll get straight sometime.'

The dining table must have come with the house, Ray thought. It looked too large and heavy to fit through any of the doors and the chairs were an assortment of Victorian, 1950s and modern pine. He had glimpsed a round pine table as they had passed the kitchen and guessed that they had come from there. Hastily packed-away toys stacked in the corner of the room and traces of crayon on the polished surface suggested that the dining room was more often used for the children's games than it was a place to eat.

He made himself useful, dressing the table with a cloth and laying cutlery while John chased the children around the garden and the dog, a lop-eared thing with a rough brown coat, chased him. The children, he noted, were still giggling but he had heard them shout a few words to their father so presumably they could talk. He took his time with the table, glad of an excuse not to join the game. He was relieved when the meal was served and everything called to order.

'You're a good cook, Maggie.'

'Thank you, Ray. I enjoy it. Beth, if you don't want that just leave it. It doesn't need spreading around your plate.'

'Ray tells me you met at the records office.'

Sarah nodded. 'I work there.'

'She's the boss lady.'

'Try and tell my staff that. No, but it's a nice job. I'm lucky, doing something I like.'

'And the research,' John asked, 'how is it going?'

'Pretty well,' Ray told him. He watched in fascination as Beth dissected a piece of cauliflower with the tip of her knife. 'She should become a surgeon.'

'Beth, I told you just leave it. She doesn't like vegetables.'

'Neither did I at that age,' Ray sympathized.

'She doesn't like meat either,' Maggie added. 'Sometimes I don't know what the child lives on.'

The dog, Ray decided, lived on table scraps. It had decided he might be a soft touch and sat at his feet begging. Ray resisted mostly, not certain what the house policy was on feeding dogs at the dining table. The children finished their meal first and were told that they could get ice cream and take it out into the garden. Seeing the size of Beth's portion as she dived past the French doors a few minutes later Ray thought he could guess what it was she lived on. Children out of the way and a more grown-up Dutch apple pie served to the adults, the talk moved back to the matter that had first brought them all together.

John had filled Maggie in on the background.

'Do you feel anything in the house?' she wanted to know.

'No. If I feel anything it's Mathilda's influence. She lived there for years and loved the place. I don't think I have what it takes to see ghosts.'

'I wish I did,' Maggie said wistfully. 'I'd love to see a ghost.'

'You're not supposed to say that, darling. You're supposed to talk pityingly about poor lost souls.'

Maggie laughed. 'Come off it, John. I spend enough time with poor lost living ones. A ghost would make a refreshing change.' She turned back to Ray. 'John says your aunt was very aware of Kitty but he didn't feel anything strange in the house either.'

'Maybe she's choosy, I don't know. Mathilda was an unusual woman.'

'You didn't move to the area at the same time as John?' Sarah asked Maggie.

'No, I was finishing my degree course. I'd gone back as a so-called mature student and I was in my final year when John got drafted. His predecessors hadn't got their new place sorted out at first so John found accommodation with Ray's aunt. The kids and I moved in with my parents until the summer.'

'What were you studying?'

'French and German combined honours. I want to do an MA on medieval French literature when time allows, but that's got to be put on hold until at least next year.'

'How did you meet Mathilda?' Ray asked John.

'I put a card in the local shop, Mathilda phoned me and offered me a room. Things worked out well and I really liked her. I stayed for something like eight months and moved in here just after she died, then I rattled around this place on my own for a couple of months until Maggie and the kids arrived.'

'I wish I'd kept in better touch,' Ray said.

John nodded sympathetically. 'Have you got any further with Kitty's story?'

'A little. I know that she was taken to Leicester after her arrest and that she was tried at the assizes there but I'm going to have to go to that records office to get any further. Sarah's faxed them and they're seeing what they have but apparently records for the period I'm looking at haven't survived too well.'

'What sparked the trouble?' Maggie asked.

'Well, it seemed to have begun in the August after the Reverend Randall arrived. Some quarrel about a Lammas doll that got the new vicar riled.'

'Lammas was like an early harvest festival,' Sarah told him.

'And the doll would be something like a corn dolly, I imagine.'

Ray nodded. 'I figured it must be something of the sort. The locals made a new one every year and kept it in the church. The old one was burned.'

'Very pagan,' Maggie commented. 'Nice, though. We always have a sheaf of wheat brought into the church.'

'Well, the Reverend Randall wasn't that open-minded. It caused a big argument and Kitty took the villagers' side.'

'She wasn't arrested then, though?'

'No, that was just the start of things. It was June the following year when things got really out of hand and I haven't read that far yet, so I can't tell you exactly what went wrong. But she was brought to trial at the autumn assizes and sentenced to death by hanging.'

'Poor woman,' Maggie said softly. 'I wouldn't have wanted to be alive then.'

She got up, poured more wine for everyone and then went through to the kitchen to make the coffee while the others gathered pots and cutlery and cleared the table. Sarah was thoughtful when they sat back down.

'When I was at school,' she said, 'we did something rather silly.'

'Didn't we all?'

She smiled. 'There was this rumour that one of the classrooms was haunted. That someone had died there. I mean, this was a 1960s concrete monstrosity so I think it was a bit unlikely, but we believed it. Or at least we said we did.'

'You held a seance,' Ray guessed.

'One lunch break. We were supposed to go outside at lunchtimes, but on rainy days we were allowed to stay in and two members of staff patrolled the corridors to make sure we weren't getting up to anything. Anyway, we'd worked out we had a fifteen-minute window and we'd got someone sitting by the door watching the corridor.'

'Did you have a Ouija board?' Ray asked.

'Oh no, nothing so sophisticated. Marjie Amos had pinched a glass from the dining hall and we'd spent break tearing up bits of paper and writing out the alphabet. And, if I remember right, we had scraps of paper with yes and no written on them as well. So we set this thing up on the teacher's table, there were six of us all crowded round with our little fingers resting on the glass and twelve minutes left on the clock, trying not to giggle.

'I remember *The Exorcist* had just come out at the cinema and we were all too young to get in, though one girl, Julie something, she tried and managed it. She had big tits and make-up put on with a trowel so I suppose that helped.'

John laughed. 'Some of the fourteen year olds at my youth club can get into the over-twenty-ones' nights at the local club.'

'I always looked about twelve,' Maggie complained. 'No curves. Nothing till I turned eighteen.'

'So what happened with this spirit stuff?' Ray questioned.

'Well, we scared ourselves senseless in the end. Talk

about hysterical teenagers, we were the archetypes. This Julie, she'd got a copy of the book *The Exorcist* and we all read it. I remember, she'd marked the pages with all the best bits on and we took it in turns to read them out. It was like a dare. You've got to remember, this was an all-girls grammar school, and we were all sex-obsessed fifteen years olds. Anyway, after a while, we moved everything into the big stationery cupboard at the back of the class, we had to leave the door open a crack to let some light in at first, then someone got more organized and borrowed a torch. Boy, it was scary and it was obsessive too. For weeks we couldn't think of anything else. My grades went down, I had nightmares, the works.'

'Did you get any messages?'

'Oh, yes,' Sarah told them. 'One from somebody's gran and a lot of fragmentary stuff from people claiming to be Napoleon or whatever we were doing in history at the time.'

'Speak perfect English, did he?'

'Immaculate. Not a trace of accent. But there was one thing that really upset us all. A whole series of messages from a little boy. His name was Tom and he was utterly miserable because he missed his mum and couldn't understand why he'd been taken away from her. He kept begging for her to come and fetch him and saying that he promised not to be naughty any more. It was pathetic really, but it got to us in a big way.'

'Did you try to find out about him?' Maggie asked.

'We tried. He gave an address that was fairly local and a couple of the girls actually went there, but the street was being demolished. It was one of these old rows of terraced houses they were so fond of knocking down in the 70s and that was that.'

'And what made you stop?' John asked.

Sarah frowned. 'It had started off as a bit of a laugh,' she said. 'Then it became something more. It was distressing, if you want to know the truth. We all of us began to take it seriously, to feel sorry for this child crying for his mother and we knew that there was no way we could help.'

'You felt that he was real,' John pressed.

'Are you about to condemn me for conjuring devils?' Then she nodded. 'Yes, he was real. He was in pain and he was lost and it gave us all bad dreams. Eventually one of the girls said that she'd been pushing the glass and made the whole thing up. We refused to believe her at first, then made out we were all furious to be taken for such a ride, but really, I think we were all relieved to have an excuse to stop. So, we didn't talk to her for a couple of days and we threw our bits of paper away, took the glass back and closed the book on that particular fad.'

She sipped her wine and there was silence for a moment until Ray asked, 'Did you try it again?'

Sarah nodded slowly. 'I did,' she said. 'Oh, not with scraps of paper and a wine glass. It was about five years ago. A close friend had just lost her mother and was very cut up about it. She felt that she hadn't had the opportunity to say goodbye. Anyway, she got it into her head to go to this spiritualist meeting and I went along with her as moral support. I'd expected some grey-haired, blue-rinsed Doris Stokes type but the medium was a young woman with a really kind and down-to-earth approach to it all. It surprised me.'

'And did your friend get her message?' John asked.

'Well, yes, she did I suppose. I mean I've no idea whether or not it was from her mother but this medium seemed to recognize what she needed. She said that my friend had someone who had passed on recently and that she felt she hadn't been as close to this person as she should have been.'

'Fair guess,' Ray commented, 'given the circumstances.'

'Oh, I agree. But she told my friend that the soul who had passed on understood. And loved her and that there was nothing to forgive. It was what she wanted, needed to hear, and I thought it showed great compassion.'

'I agree,' John said, accepting that her words were something of a challenge. 'But what else happened, Sarah?'

She laughed. 'You're as bad as Ray. But you're right. It was late in the meeting and this medium suddenly looked across at me. She said she had a message for me from someone who had been just a child when he had passed over. That his name was Tom and it was all right now, because his mother had come for him.'

'Oh my God,' Maggie said. 'That must have been weird.'

'It shook me badly,' Sarah admitted. 'I'd never forgotten about Tom. I still had dreams about him years later, but to have someone confront me with the memory, that really was too much.'

Ray looked across and met her eyes. Five years ago, he thought. That would be the same time Sarah had been battling with the cancer. To have such a shock added to an already stressed mind must have been devastating.

'And you never tried anything again?' John asked.

'No. I never did. Do you believe we can contact the dead?'

'I don't know, Sarah. I think maybe that the dead have better things to do with their time. But there are so many anecdotal stories that it would be foolish to discount the possibility of spirit contact and, of course, the Church never has. It just warns against tampering in realms that you cannot understand.'

'And what Mathilda was doing with Kitty,' Ray asked, 'you don't see that as tampering?'

'It's a difficult one,' John said as he got up. 'Would everyone like more coffee? I don't really think Mathilda had a choice, Kitty rather imposed herself. If Mathilda had felt threatened by her then I would have tried to do something or at least got some advice for her, but your aunt felt that Kitty belonged in the house and had as much right to be there as she had. And, well, you know already how sorry for her she felt.'

'And yet it was only when you came along that she actively did anything about it?' Maggie questioned.

'So far as I'm aware, but you have to bear in mind that Mathilda was a busy woman even after she'd retired. She was on parish committees and charity boards and she did voluntary work. It was only the last eighteen months or so, when her health began to decline, that she stayed at home all day or that she would really have had the time.'

John had returned with the coffee and talk became

more general as the children came charging back in, begging their father to come and play, then camping by the French door to wait when he told them five minutes while he finished his coffee. Ray listened as the women switched their conversation back to Maggie's prospective MA course, his mind drifting from the problem of Kitty and Mathilda and nagging instead at the news clipping he had received.

'Will you go back to your job?' John was asking him. Ray brought his mind back to attention.

'I've been giving it a lot of thought. I still have a lot of pain in my hands and I'm having physio to improve the mobility. A friend's offered me a partnership in a security firm he wants to set up. We're still thrashing out the details, but I think that's what I'll do.'

'Security?' John asked him. 'You mean like night watchmen or bouncers?'

Ray laughed. 'No, nothing like that. George is thinking in terms of corporate stuff. Surveillance equipment and alarms, that sort of thing, and he's been very involved in computer fraud this last year or so.'

'Preventing it, presumably.'

'You can never tell with George, but yes. It's big business these days and I figure it's time for a change after twenty-odd years. I've never really done anything else.'

The children were getting impatient and John went out to play. Maggie and Sarah, chatting like old friends, began to clear the table of the last few things and disappeared into the kitchen once again. Ray thought about following them, but the kitchen with its circular table was cramped and he wasn't that interested in the academic discussion the two women seemed to be enjoying. Courtly poetry just wasn't on his list. So he sat, sipping the last of his coffee and staring out into the garden, wondering if he should call home and see if there were any messages and knowing that would be a bad idea. If George had left him something then he'd want to get onto it straightaway and he didn't think Sarah would be appreciative of that.

The appearance of the child in the doorway startled him.

'Hello,' Ray said. 'I thought you were playing with your dad.' He felt a momentary pang of fear that John might have sent her to fetch him.

'He's looking for the ball. It's gone in the bushes.'

'Ah.'

Beth came over to him, studying his face with an expression of pursed-lipped concentration.

'What happened to you?' she asked him. 'Did you get burned?'

'Sort of, yes.'

'My friend Emily, at school. She got burned with a kettle. She's got scars all down her back.'

'Nasty,' Ray said.

'What happened to you?'

'Um, someone burned me.'

'Did they mean to?'

Ray nodded. 'Yes, they meant to.'

'Why?'

It was a question Ray had no real answer to. 'They thought I was someone else,' he said. 'It was a mistake.'

Beth considered this. 'Did they burn the lady in the church too?'

'The lady in the church?' He was confused. 'You mean Sarah?'

'Don't be silly. Sarah's pretty, she doesn't have that on her face. No, the other lady. The one sitting on the other side of you.'

Ray stared hard at the child. The space in the pew next to him had been empty. 'I'm sorry, Beth, but I didn't see any other lady.'

Beth frowned at him, clearly disbelieving. Ray decided he should try again. 'What did she look like, this lady?'

'She looked like you, of course. She had those lines.'

'Scars?'

'Yes, on her face. The same side as you do. And she was wearing a white hat and a white shirt and a black jacket and a long black skirt. I thought she was a friend of yours and she might be coming to our house as well.'

Chapter Eighteen

The sky was cloudless and an almost unearthly blue, glowing with the weak light of a winter sun. Ray could feel the chill of a north wind blowing through his clothes, cutting with a sharpness that promised snow. In his dream, a child ran through the open square, one chubby little hand clutching the string of a red balloon. The child laughed aloud, chasing through a flock of grey-flecked piegons that took to the air in a chaos of fluttering wings. In his dream Ray watched the child and laughed with him and there was no tightness and no pain from over-stretched skin and destroyed muscle to mitigate his laughter. And yet, even as he watched the boy run, the red balloon tugged by the bitter wind, Ray knew what was coming. The same dream, so many times before, ending in the same anguish as the child ran to him, growing and growing with every step, tugging at the string until, a full-grown faceless man, he stood before Ray with the red balloon clutched tight between his hands. Laughing out loud as he hurled pain into Ray's face and outstretched arms.

On the Monday evening, they had eaten together at the cottage. Ray had bought steak and made a passable job of cooking it, serving it with little potatoes glistening with butter and a salad he'd found ready-prepared in the local supermarket.

'Not much of a cook, I'm afraid.'

'Join the club,' Sarah commented. 'My mother and grandmother were brilliant. My sister's not bad either so I don't know what happened to me.'

'Do you think there's a gene for cooking?'

'Buggered if I know, but there seems to be one for everything else so I don't see why not.'

Ray laughed, but the dream, which had come as it always did just before the dawn, had tormented him all day. It soured his mood and left him feeling vulnerable.

'What is it?' Sarah asked him. 'You're not yourself tonight.'

The question had been asked with an un-Sarah like gentleness and he looked up suspiciously expecting to see pity in her eyes. Instead there was only considered thoughtfulness.

'Bad dream,' he said.

'About this?' she reached across and touched the scarring on his face. 'No, don't pull away. If I minded it I wouldn't be here with you, would I?'

'I mind it.'

'I know you do. You hate your scars as I hate mine, but we have to accept them for what they are. A part of us now whether we wanted them or not.'

'Yes,' he said quietly. 'It was about what happened. But it was different, you know the way dreams are.'

'I remember seeing you in the papers,' Sarah told him. 'You made the headlines, but I'm not one for reading that sort of stuff.'

Ray was amused. 'What do you read? Or don't you bother?'

'I read a lot, you know I do, but as far as the papers are concerned I read the reviews and I look at my horoscope and I might even scan the weather report. Oh, and I do the crossword once in a long while.'

'You're not serious?'

'Believe me, I am. I think maybe I prefer the past when it comes to news. At least you know how the past turned out. I don't like surprises.'

Ray laughed again, touching his cheek as he did so. He fancied it felt hot where Sarah's fingers had lain. 'I was waiting for a colleague,' he said. 'Standing by his car outside of the Magistrates' Court in Middleton. Do you know it? There's a big open square in front, with a fountain.'

Sarah nodded. 'I worked there for a while, across the road on Main Street.'

'Well, it was a bitterly cold day. Very crisp and clear and Guy was chatting up some woman in the lobby, so I knew I was in for a wait. I was just about to get into the car when it happened. He came from nowhere. I didn't even see him till the very last second. He had this aerosol in his hand. He sprayed it in my face and lit it with this stupid little disposable lighter. It acted like a flame-thrower and he kept it trained right on my face.'

It sounded so simple put like that, Ray thought, so why did his throat grow so tight and his hand shake when he reached for his glass?

'Is that the worst of it?' she asked him. 'That you

didn't see it coming? In that one moment you weren't alert or prepared and didn't even have time to fight back?'

She had done it again, he realized. Put her finger squarely on the deepest part of his pain and pushed hard. 'Yeah, I guess it is,' he told her.

They cleared the remains of their meal away, moving quietly around each other in a way that Ray found oddly soothing. He was rarely comfortable with silence, though at the same time always awkward when it came to making small talk and it was a relief that with Sarah neither was a problem. He wanted her so much. Wanted to lie naked with her in the big bed upstairs and feel the warmth of her body. Inhale the scent of her and feel the weight of the thick red hair loose in his hands. It was a long time since he had felt this way and he was uncertain as to what to do about it. He'd never been a man to rush headlong into things but to remind himself that he had only known this woman for a few precious days seemed an irrelevancy.

Ray reached out and touched her hair. 'Sarah, I . . .'

She took a deep breath then took his other hand. 'We're both far too old to play silly buggers, Ray. You want to go to bed with me and I want you too. So why don't we just get on with it?'

'Romantic to the last.'

'I don't think.' Sarah smiled at him, that slightly tight-lipped smile that belied the way it made her eyes sparkle if you took the time to look. He followed her upstairs, guiding her towards Mathilda's room, closing the curtains and switching on the bedside light, feeling like an awkward child in the company of an unfamiliar adult. He watched her as she unfastened her dress and let it fall to the floor, then pick it up and smooth the creases from it before laying it on the chair. 'Help me, Ray,' she said. 'I'm out of practice when it comes to this.'

He went over to her, eased the straps of her slip from her shoulders and kissed her gently. Her hair and her lips and then the curve of her neck. He couldn't place the perfume that she wore but it was warm and sweet with just the faintest tang of citrus and her skin was soft beneath his hands.

'Has there been anyone,' he asked, 'since . . . ?'

'No one. I tried, but somehow it never worked out.'

He moved the straps of her slip further down her arms, letting it slide down her body. This time she left it where it lay. His fingers were clumsy on the hooks of her bra. Naked from the waist, she would no longer meet his eyes. 'You're beautiful,' he said and meant it. She flinched when he touched the scars that quadranted her breast, his fingertips brushing lightly, uncertain just how far he could go. How fast.

'Touch me properly,' she said. 'Like you mean it. Anything that was going to break did so long ago.'

'Oh Sarah.' He pulled her to him and for a long time just held her, stroking her back, feeling the richness of her hair twisted in his hands until she pulled away and shed the rest of her clothes, pulling back the covers and sliding into bed.

Ray undressed quickly, the buttons on his shirt awkward beneath clumsy fingers and there was no way, he thought, to elegantly remove socks and shoes.

He was aware that his body, never particularly shapely, had suffered from the months of inactivity. That he was overweight and gauche. He was suddenly panicked that after such long abstention everything would happen far too fast and the moment be spoiled, never to return.

But it was better than that. 'We have all night,' Sarah told him. 'Nothing else matters right now.' And they made love gently at first, as though afraid to cause each other pain, only gaining in confidence when the expected hurt failed to arrive. And finally, when Ray fell asleep, it was with Sarah wrapped tightly in his arms.

Chapter Nineteen

Lammas had arrived with the promise of a good harvest later in the year. The first fruits had been gathered and the first sheaf of ripe wheat been cut from the top field where the sun always shone the longest and the wheat always ripened the earliest in the season. In the seven years since she had come to live in Oscombe, she had never known a time when there was not enough ripe wheat to make the harvest dolly on Lammas eve.

Kitty had been attending a birth, the woman being delivered with the Lammas sunrise. It had been an easy birth, the mother having born one a year for the past five years with equal ease had needed little help, but it had become accepted in the village that Kitty be there, despite her own lack of husband and babies. Her father had taught her well. She had a good knowledge of the herbs that could ease labour and improve the flow of milk or help cracked nipples or bring down the dreaded fever that plagued so many women after birth and so often killed. In six of these last seven years few children had been born within ten miles of Oscombe and she had not attended.

It was a state of affairs that did not best please Mistress Randall, the new reverend's wife. The thought of an unmarried woman having to do with details that only a married woman should know had outraged her sense of propriety. And she had been raised in town, where so often to call the midwife was a resort only of the desperate. Kitty had once witnessed the results of such a birthing when she had gone with her father to help a woman whose bleeding would not stop. A so-called midwife, eager to collect her next fee, had wrapped the cord around her hand and wrenched the placenta from the mother's body.

The poor woman had died. Kitty's father told that oftentimes such action led to the womb being turned almost inside out. Beyond an infusion of poppy to kill the pain, there had been nothing he could do.

This day though, Kitty had followed the rising sun home across the fields, impatient to be back in the village for the celebrations. She had a great liking for the Lammas worship, the taking of the first harvest for blessing, the making of the 'dolly' and the meal that the whole village shared on the green beyond the churchyard wall. The weeks following would always be amongst the busiest. Harvest stretching well into the autumn and that followed by the preparations for the winter planting and the laying down of the food stocks for the cold months to come. Lammas brought a breathing space. A moment of rest before the chaos and it was one that Matthew Jordan had whole-heartedly approved, for all, as he confided to her, that he was certain of its pagan origins.

This year though, her hopes for the festival were troubled the moment she entered the village. A small crowd had gathered by the church, the Reverend Randall at its heart and Master Eton standing close by listening to the quarrel.

123

'What goes on?' she asked him.

'The Reverend does not approve our way of worship.'

'Whyever not?'

Mim turned to her. She held the new made dolly in her hands.

'Mistress Hallam. Please will you explain. This is no sinful thing, it has been done since my grandfather's time and his before that.'

'A sinful thing?' Kitty asked him. 'I do not understand.'

'I have already told him, Mistress Hallam, that it is nothing but a country tradition,' James Eton said. 'But it seems we differ in the way we view these things.'

'Most certainly we do,' Edward Randall said, his face distorted by anger. 'The fruits of the field, I will bless,' he said. 'God's harvest I will welcome to this church, but that idol. That creation of the devil I will not allow to cross this threshold.'

'We told him that the idol had been kept within the church these many years,' Eton said. 'That each year the old one was taken from the church and burned and the new one welcomed in. Matthew had no quarrel with this.'

'What Master Jordan believed to be the truth,' Randall replied, 'and what I hold dear are different things. Already I have found a store of incense within the church. And candles to be lit before the Virgin's statue. Papish things that I have already disposed of. This "dolly", had I seen it within the church, I would have burned also.'

'What harm could come from a bundle of woven straw?'

'If that were all!' he said, jabbing a finger towards Mim. 'That woman, when she came to bring that thing into the church, said the spirit of the harvest was locked inside her dolly. This is a place of God, mistress, not the site of some pagan spirit.'

'It is a cocoon of straw,' said Kitty. 'It represents the hope of good harvest in the eyes of those who work the land. They depend on the harvest to feed and clothe them through the winter. Where else should they bring their hopes if not to the church?'

'It is a point well made,' James Eton said. 'Believe me, Master Randall, I have little patience with such supersititions, but I do not see the harm that can be done by what is a simple act of faith.'

But Edward Randall would have none of it, he straightened to full height and looked with pity on them all. 'I can see that there is much work to be done here,' he said. 'But I am disappointed. Simple folk, I could understand holding such beliefs and failing to see the harm, but you, Master Eton and Mistress Hallam, I had understood to be educated well beyond the commonplace. I have tolerated what could be seen as your strangeness, your healing and your meddling, yes, and even spoken for you, seeing much good in what you did. But this is indefensible.'

Mim was crying, unable to understand what was so wrong.

He demanded to know where last year's dolly was kept and was told it was in the bell tower lodged above the bells.

'Then I will send my man to fetch it down,' Randall said, his anger seeming to dissipate then. 'This afternoon, bring the harvest and I will bless it. God will see the rightness of the act and will forgive such superstition.' Then he nodded briefly at Master Eton and took his leave.

'He is convinced of his own righteousness,' James Eton said. 'I believe we should view him as sincere, if a little zealous. And his views, it must be said, differ from Matthew's greatly.'

He bent and picked up the straw dolly that Mim had left beside the gate. It seemed wrong just to cast it aside. 'Perhaps you should take charge of this,' he said to Kitty. 'At least the village will know that it is kept, and maybe he will mellow a little as the year passes and will allow his mind to be changed.'

It was in Kitty's mind that this would not be so, but she said nothing. Mim and the others departed and left Kitty to walk back towards her cottage with Master Eton.

'This is bad, Kitty, but it is all of a piece with what is happening everywhere just now.'

Kitty nodded. Her father's letters regularly brought her news of what was happening in the country. There had been fighting the month before in Manchester between the King's men and those who would rise against him. Her father expected war.

So did James Eton. 'Both sides are too stubborn and too certain of their own righteousness,' he said.

'And you, sir?' she asked him. 'You have spoken against the King, would you fight against him?'

He shook his head. 'I hope not to have to decide,' he said. 'I wish only to attend to my affairs here. To farm my land and be left alone, but I doubt I will be so fortunate. I doubt that any of us will be left untouched.'

Chapter Twenty

George frequently worked odd hours, late nights and weekends. Since the death of his wife and then the tragic loss of his daughter Janine, he had found little reason to go home.

Phil worked odd hours for other reasons. Phil was an obsessive who lived as easily in the virtual community of the Net as he did in the outside world. George was never clear which one he preferred.

He had worked with George for close on two years and it was a change for Phil to be, approximately at least, inside the law, though it was more often his approximately outside the law skills that George and his department made most use of.

'Any ideas what these are?' George dumped a list of names and numbers down on Phil's desk.

'Look like PNC references.'

'That's what I thought, but it keeps coming up with "reference not recognized" and throwing me off.'

Phil took another look at the codes and then logged on. The PNC – Police National Computer – was something George had free access to. It was strange for him to find somewhere he couldn't go.

'Maybe they're not PNC refs. Let's take another look anyway, try to get an ident.' He glanced sideways at

George. 'How come you haven't asked the big boss man for access?'

'He's already left for the night.' George smiled. 'OK, so it's a favour for a friend. Might be nothing, but I said I'd check a few names.'

'Anyone I know?'

'Not likely. A body hauled out of the canal. Name of Frank Jones. I pulled his records with no trouble, petty theft, suspected runner for Pierce, though nothing ever stuck. These references were in a file appendix and I got to wondering what they were.'

'OK, we'll give it a go.'

George watched. Phil was methodical. He ran the codes through normal channels first, retracing steps that George had taken already, looking for common input errors, the sort of thing that was often so obvious it could be missed. He got the same results as George had done.

'Obviously not for general consumption,' he said. 'We'll have to find a way back in.' He logged out of the PNC and back onto the Net. 'Might take a little while. First thing is to see who's already cracked it and what route they took. No point in trampling on the grass if someone's already cut a path.'

George nodded. PNC like many government struc-tures was a common target. In the world of information there was no such thing as a secure system. If you were networked, you could be accessed, though many hackers simply tagged a site, added it to their clamed list and then left it alone. There was little point in getting in and then declaring the fact to the world if you might want to go back later. Why force someone to tighten up their system just for the sake of it?

'This might take some time,' Phil told him.

George nodded and prepared to leave him to it. Phil didn't like to be watched, it put him off his stride.

'All right. Let me know if you come up with anything.' But Phil was already engrossed and didn't trouble to reply.

Sarah had taken a couple of days off, which was just as well considering how late they slept.

They made breakfast together, saying little but very much at ease. Then, as Sarah made more tea, Ray commented, 'I dreamed again last night.'

She glanced at him, concerned. 'The same dream?'

'No, this was something new. I think I dreamed about her. About Kitty.'

'Oh?'

'She was riding a horse. Sitting sort of side-on behind a young man.' Ray poured her tea and then his own. 'It was so vivid. I've had a lot of vivid dreams lately, most of them unpleasant, but this one . . . I could smell the air and feel the wind in my face and I knew it had just been raining. There was this overwhelming scent of damp earth and wet grass.' He laughed. 'And gently steaming horse.'

'Very pleasant. I'm not one for horses at the best of times.'

'I've not been close to that many. Never seen the attraction.'

'That was all?'

'Pretty much. Would she have ridden like that?'

'Pillion behind a man? Probably. Not too comfortable or too safe, I would have thought. It wasn't even a proper saddle, just a kind of soft pad. Lord knows how they held it in place, or how they stayed on for that matter. What was she wearing?'

'Wearing? Oh, a long brown skirt. She had it all tucked in around her. And some kind of reddish cloak thing with a cape round the shoulders and a big hood.'

'Sounds about right. A lot of riding cloaks were like that, reddish and caped. Little red riding hood was a West Country Lass.'

'Sorry?'

'The cloth, that's where most of it was made.'

He smiled, suddenly a little embarrassed. 'Getting a bit carried away with this, aren't I?'

'I don't see any harm in it. Did you read something in Jordan's diaries that put this in your mind?'

Ray shook his head. 'Not that I can think. It seems to have come from nowhere. Sarah, I don't believe in all this ghost and past life stuff. I've always been a down-to-earth, difficult to convince bugger. You have to be in my job, no time for all that fancy thinking.'

'But now you're not so sure?'

Ray nodded. 'Now I'm not so sure.'

Phil had news for George when he came into the office the following morning.

'You know that Frank Jones you were looking for? You know he was tied up with the Pierce business?'

'His record said he was suspected of being a runner.'

'Right. Well, those references you gave me, they belong to the Pierce investigation, but they've nothing to do with the locals, this is National Crime Squad.'

George thought about it. 'It was a big bust,' he said. 'No surprise that it had major involvement.'

'Big isn't the word for it. This went international.'

George raised an eyebrow. 'A little out of Frank Jones's league, I would have thought.'

'But the interesting thing is, his isn't the only death associated with the investigation. You remember Michaeljohn?'

George frowned. 'Dealer,' he said. 'Found shot a couple of months back.'

'Informer,' Phil told him. 'They were about to pull him in but it seems they struck a deal.'

'Didn't do much of a job protecting him.'

'No. A troop of boy scouts could have done better. But the thing is, George, Michaeljohn was a key witness. Without him there's nothing that makes Mark Pierce anything more than a middleman and not a very important one at that. The whole thing was in danger of falling apart. On top of that, there's some sort of internal investigation going on. Accusations that someone's been taking backhanders.'

'Any names?'

'Sorry. Officer A and officer B, that's all I've got, but the impression is that it's high level and it spreads a long way. Look, I've done you a printout, but this is bigger than you thought. I don't think you'll be able to cover your tracks. You start poking your nose into this and someone's going to notice.'

George Mahoney nodded thoughtfully. 'Then maybe it's time to declare the interest,' he said. 'See what I stir up.'

Chapter Twenty-One

Ray was reading more of Matthew's journals. On 25 August 1642 Matthew Jordan recorded that the conflict had already come to his home to roost.

A great band of soldiers led by the Prince Rupert did descend upon the town bringing news of the King's intent and calling on all good men to support him in his battle. It is said, among those who saw the King's standard raised in Nottingham three nights ago, that a great storm did rage and lightning hit the earth with such force that ancient trees were blasted not twenty yards from where the King himself was standing. It is in my mind that this whole land will be blasted by as great a lightning before this thing is done.

Prince Rupert's men did first ride to Bradgate with Colonel Hastings at his side and attacked there the house of Lord Stamford, threatening the lives of those within and injuring the furnishings of the great house, before departing with great store of arms and ammunition. He has since set up camp at Queninborough, not above three miles from here. It is supposed the King will find winter quarters soon, perhaps at Oxford, to build strength and plan his strategy. I wish no ill to that town but it will not grieve me if he calls that hothead prince to heel and takes him there.

A few days later, Ray noted, Rupert had been at it again.

> He did send from his camp at Queninborough a letter
> to the mayor and corporation demanding the sum of
> £2,000 sterling, to be submitted by ten of the clock in
> the forenoon. The letter that accompanied this demand
> was read this very day in my hearing. Prince Rupert
> dared to threaten that, should the officials not comply,
> he should 'appear before your town in such a posture
> with horse and foot, and cannon, as shall make you
> know 'tis more safe to obey than to resist His Majesty's
> command'.
>
> The corporation did then send word to the King,
> pleading that they did not possess such funds and asking
> his intervention. They received a message in the King's
> own hand, expressing his displeasure at the Prince's
> action and releasing the town from all such demands.
> Sadly, before this message had arrived, it had been seen
> fit to send certain gentlemen to the Prince, attended by
> six Dragoons, to fetch the sum of £500 to the Prince
> and bring back to the Town Hall receipt of this.
>
> He promises to repay these moneys when this
> conflict shall be over, but I doubt that these funds will
> ever be seen unless the King himself should see fit to
> demand it.

Amused and sympathetic, Ray set the copied notes aside.
He knew Queninborough slightly, though it was no
longer a village in anything but name, being long since
absorbed by the advancing city. Parts of it, he recalled,
were very pretty, though it was years since he had been
there. He had still been with his wife then, accompanying
her reluctantly on one of her antique hunts. He had a

vague memory of timbered buildings and horse shit in the road but that was all.

A folder had arrived from George Mahoney by the second post. It had been delivered just as Ray and Sarah had been leaving for Edgemere and he had not had the time to look at it before. He and Sarah had lunched together then spent the afternoon at Sarah's tiny house on the outskirts of the town. She had a long-standing evening out arranged with her sister and Ray had left her getting ready, arriving back at the cottage in the early evening.

He'd glanced quickly through the file but, now that it was here, felt an odd reluctance to delve further, putting off the inevitable by making a sandwich and a second pot of tea, scanning more of Jordan's diaries before finally giving in and sitting himself down with Mahoney's package.

It contained a picture of Frank Jones, his arrest record printed straight from computer. Photocopies of statements, an assessment made by a prison psychiatrist and another by a doctor. Previous known addresses, aliases, a list of associates – George Mahoney had worked hard on Ray's behalf, and yet, glancing through the small stack of documentation, Ray couldn't place Frank Jones in the frame. It didn't add up. Jones was a petty criminal who'd started thieving from the local shops when he was just a kid and graduated to pinching cars and the odd opportunistic burglary in his mid-teens.

As a career, that had been about as far as he'd got until he was twenty-two. Between time in youth custody and then two years in prison, Frank Jones had found the leisure to get a wife and father a child. At twenty-two, his baby then nine months old, Frank Jones had actually got his first legitimate job, moved his little family into a council flat and for the next five years nothing had been heard of him. He seemed to have turned his life around.

Then it had all gone pear-shaped. The company he worked for had gone bust and Frank had been out on his own once more. Unable to find work and with Christmas just around the corner, it seemed that Frank had gone back to his old ways. He'd been suspected of thieving from cars, radio cassettes and the like. Been pulled in on sus for the odd burglary, but nothing could be made to stick. Then Frank had shifted leagues. In the January he'd found semi-legitimate work as a doorman at one of the local clubs, but the money he'd been bringing home from that didn't add up to the changes in lifestyle that the local police had noticed. He'd bought a car. Nothing expensive, or particularly new, but it was something he'd never managed to do before. And his flat suddenly acquired new furniture, a decent TV and video instead of the ex-rental stuff he'd scraped the cash for previously. It was suspected he was acting as a runner for the local drugs interest, they were known to hold a controlling share in the nightclub Frank worked at, though the three times he was brought in he was always clean.

The drugs link fitted with the theory that Guy Halshaw had been the target and Ray just happened to be in the wrong place at the wrong time. But either way, it was a big step for Frank Jones to take. Car thief to effective hitman. He remembered George Mahoney's comment. If someone had wanted Guy Halshaw out of the way, then why not have him shot? A simple contract might have cost a couple of grand, tops. What had been done to Ray, well, that was much more up close and personal and in a public place in the early afternoon . . . In Ray's eyes, that had never made a lot of sense.

If Frank Jones had been the man responsible, had it been a personal grudge against Guy? Halshaw was an inveterate womanizer, could he have tried it on with someone he shouldn't? Frank's wife, perhaps? He glanced through the notes but could find no record of her having been interviewed, though even George could only be so thorough on such short notice. On the other hand, if you're settling a personal grudge, wouldn't you be able to identify the target? Ray knew that he had never encountered Frank Jones before.

If Frank Jones was settling a personal issue for someone else then that would make more sense, but if so, then what and who and was it Ray himself or Guy Halshaw that was the intended target? And if he was settling someone else's score, then what would it take to make someone like Frank Jones, who from his record tended to go for easy targets – empty houses, unwatched cars – attack a police officer in the open in broad daylight with only his own two feet on which to make the getaway?

Ray picked up the photograph of Frank Jones and looked at it, trying to remember every detail of the man who attacked him that day. He'd seen little. Witnesses said the man had a knitted hat with some kind of logo on it pulled down well over his ears and the lower portion of his face covered by a scarf, though even this slight description was in doubt. There was no agreement even on the colour of the scarf or the design of logo on the hat. It had been a cold day and a man wrapped up against the chill was of little note to most people.

Ray covered the lower part of the picture, just concentrating his attention on the eyes. He had no memory even of seeing the man's eyes, it had all been over so very quickly, but he tried now to superimpose Frank's eyes onto the scene replaying in his mind.

Sighing, Ray put the picture down. There was no way he could be sure. The man who had attacked him could have been Frank Jones, but for all the certainty Ray could put on that judgement it could have been John Rivers or Sarah Gordon.

Angry with himself, Ray put the folder to one side and fetched himself a drink, swallowing single malt with an absence of attention that it did not deserve. He switched the television on and stared at the screen, watching speeding cars chase through improbably empty streets. Outside it had begun to rain and the wind was blowing hard and rain pelted against the window loudly enough to drown the noise of the television. Irritably, Ray increased the volume, then turned it down again. Then killed it altogether. He felt lonely and wished that Sarah could be there. The cottage, and Ray's life, suddenly felt very empty.

He poured another drink and then another, staring at the silent television screen and allowing his mind to wander. His thoughts returned to Sunday and the conversation they'd had with John Rivers and Maggie about the Ouija board. On impulse, Ray crossed to the desk and rummaged for a sheet of paper. With great concentration he tore the paper into rough squares, then wrote the letters of the alphabet and the words yes and no upon them. He spread the torn paper carefully around the edge of one of Mathilda's little tables, then upturned his empty glass at the centre, resting his finger lightly on its base.

Then Ray waited, aware that this impulse owed much more to whisky than to spirits and glad that there was no one there to see. 'Is there anybody there?' he demanded, then laughed self-consciously. 'Dammit, Kitty, if you're a bloody ghost then say something or I'm going to stop believing in you altogether.' He felt more than a little put out. After all, she'd shown herself to Beth. In his somewhat drunken state, Ray couldn't help but feel that reeked of favouritism.

He sighed, turning the glass back the right way up. 'God almighty, how much have I had?'

Carefully, he gathered the slips of paper and threw them into the fire, then poured himself another drink, sipping it with more attention this time as he watched the letters burn.

It was a cool night in August when the rains had come after a hot day and such winds as lifted Kitty's skirts high and threatened to tear her shawl from her hands. She had come home late and was so glad to be back inside out of the storm that for a moment she did not think of what was wrong.

And then she saw it. A fire burned in the grate, though she had been out all day and there had been no one home to set one, and she saw a man, kneeling on the hearth, his hand poised as though he reached for something set beside the grate.

It was the same man that she had glimpsed before, though this time far more solid and more real.

She had begun to speak, meaning to challenge him, though the strange thing was, she felt no fear. But in that instant the man was gone, the fire too, though when she came closer, the embers still glowed and the room, too, was warm despite the fierce wind outside.

Still she felt no fear. Odd as it might seem she felt drawn to this man. He seemed, she fancied, like some friendly spirit, almost an angelic presence, though she knew that should any know those thoughts they would only give more evidence of the devil's influence.

Though, for all that she might wish or feel, she knew him to be just a man, though she knew neither his name nor his origin. He was just a man. The man she had dreamed of. Seen standing in her garden, with much too sweet a scarred and ugly face ever to be an angel.

Chapter Twenty-Two

DI Peterson regarded George Mahoney with more than a little suspicion. He had listened to George's explanation without comment but was clearly far from happy. 'This friend of yours. How much have you told him so far?'

'I gave him access to Frank's arrest record. That's all.'

'All right.'

He could see the disapproval on Peterson's face but was completely unworried by it. Peterson and his ilk had no influence on what George did.

'You should tell your friend to back off.'

'One certain way to make him probe more deeply. Ray doesn't frighten easily.'

'It's no longer his business. He's practically a civilian.'

'He is still a serving officer. Anyway, have you seen his face? He's got to live with that for the rest of his life, that makes it his business.'

Peterson was silent for a moment, then he said, 'Frank Jones was an informant. He was a doorman at the Sphinx. It's just reopened as the Video Wall. Pierce's brother runs it.'

'Did Frank know much?'

'He knew who went in, who Pierce had contact with. Ran the odd errand. And he had access, we'd had him copy some of Pierce's records, give us dates and times of meetings. That sort of thing. He and his wife had been promised protection if he'd testify, but something had scared him and he wanted out.'

'How good was your evidence against Pierce before Michaeljohn was killed?'

Peterson seemed reluctant to answer. Finally, he said, 'It was good. Then that damned fool, Halshaw decided it needed to be better, started planting evidence. He was caught and Pierce's brief got to hear about it. He's been pushing ever since. Frank Jones was our second line.'

'And he ended up dead in the canal. It looks as though he had reason to be scared.'

Peterson scowled but said nothing.

'Why wasn't a watch kept on Frank Jones?' George asked.

Peterson's silence told him all he needed to know.

Chapter Twenty-Three

July and August were months of great change. Matthew wrote to Kitty about the King's visits to Leicester and the changes that had taken place. He came first to Leicester in July and again on his way to Nottingham before he raised his standard in that town. His first visit had been one of great ceremony, he came with Prince Charles and Prince Rupert and had ridden into the city on 22 July, to be met at Frog Island by the mayor and corporation. Three days he had remained within the city, taking his place during the assizes and later addressing a large crowd at the castle. Matthew Jordan had been among them. He wrote:

> To be truthful Katherine, I was surprised to find him such a small man, of so little stature. Though regal enough in his fine clothes and a wig that must have cost more than your father could earn in an entire year of business. I was far back in the crowd and could not catch all his words, but those around me said he spoke of loyalty and the duty of all good men to rally to his cause. With the mayor and corporation of this city so intent on compromise I cannot think that his words will have been well received, despite their smiles and courtesies.

Later he had seen the King more closely and even been presented to him briefly when he had attended service at St Martin's church. The King and his company had walked in slow procession to the church from the town hall and Matthew described it as being a 'fine and moving sight', though Kitty thought she sensed some restraint in his enthusiasm. Some worry that this show of power and wealth would not promise well for the future.

When the King had come again to Leicester there had been no formal greeting and no ceremony marking his presence there. 'He had not even come within the city walls,' Matthew told her. Instead he chose to rest with his ally the Countess of Devon at the Abbey Mansion and this only two days before his standard was raised at Nottingham and all true men called to rally to his cause. It grieved Matthew so much, to think of the strife that would surely come.

She left for her father's house on the day Matthew's letter concerning the King's second visit arrived. She waited only for her father's man to water the horse and then they were on their way. She was worried for her father. He was gravely ill, her brother's message had said and her sister-in-law heavy with child and far from well. He asked would she return to them for a time at least and help with the nursing?

Jack, the manservant, lifted her into the saddle behind him. She did not like riding pillion, it felt awkward to sit sideways with only her grip on the rider's belt to keep her from falling. Then she looked to say the final goodbye's to the friends who had gathered to see her go.

'I will return as soon as I am able,' she told Master Eton.

'You will be missed. Give my good wishes to your father.'

'Thank you. He remembers you always with friendship.'

Mim stood with one of the village women. This woman was as far gone with her child as her sister-in-law and it seemed likely that she would miss this birth. 'You have the herbs I gave you. And you are certain that you know what to do?'

'I have everything, Mistress Hallam, and I've Ellen to read the words you gave me about each one. Her mother makes her practise with her letters every day and will till you come back to us.'

She tried not to feel so worried. Mim had birthed children long before Kitty was even born and had seen her use the herbs that Kitty had left for her many times. Raspberry leaf, to be taken every day in the final months to make the body ready for the birth and to promote the flow of milk. Poppy, a few drops in wine to ease the pain. Lavender to wash the woman both before and after birth to help the wounds heal quickly should she tear and bleed too much. Dandelion for the fever, blended with other herbs that would calm and ease the body. And, though Mim herself could not read, her little grandchild could; Kitty had taught her simple words and checked that she could decipher the instructions she had left behind should Mim forget.

She watched them still as she set off, craning around to wave as the horse walked slowly up the hill and away from the village.

'Hold tight, mistress,' Jack told her, 'the path is not good here and I do not wish to bring you to your father's house with a broken head.'

'You say that my father has been bled twice?'

'Yes, but when the physician came a third time, hoping to cup your father's scalp and to release the humours, he did refuse and commanded that they send for you.'

That was no surprise. Her father had a strong opinion on many of the practices seen as standard. Bleeding he would tolerate to a point, but he had little patience with the theory of humours and the cupping that went with it. Blisters were raised, by heating small cups that were then upended on the patient's body. Sometimes this was supplemented by the use of irritants such as cantharides. The resultant blisters were slit and drained and then kept open to allow the humours release from the body. Kitty's father did not approve. He had said that he observed only weakening of the body from the enemas and the purges and the draining of too many fluids from already sick patients and he had seen too much agony caused by the burning with hot irons and blistering.

He was in the minority though, seen as an oddity by many.

'Why will he not take their help, Mistress Hallam?'

'I do not doubt that his reasons are good. He told me once that in ancient times the physicians used only herbs and gentle measures.'

'He is a good man. Wise too, but we are so concerned for him and if he will not accept the help . . .'

Kitty was anxious enough already. To distract him

she asked, 'Is there more news from Nottingham? I have heard that the King has raised his standard there, but nothing more.'

'The King is still at Nottingham, though there is talk of his heading north within the week. He needs funds and many women have sold their jewels and even the family plate to give him the money that he needs. Prince Rupert seeks action now and has urged the King to force those into line who would prefer neutrality.'

Like the people of Leicester, Kitty thought. Like Matthew Jordan and like her own family, living not a dozen miles away.

Chapter Twenty-Four

On the Wednesday morning Ray drove to Kineton in Warwickshire, the site of the Battle of Edgehill. Even armed with a copy of the battle plan, he found the location confusing, most of it now being farmland under cultivation and with hedges and fences breaking up the contours.

He leaned on a gate, looking towards the clump of trees where the Royalists had made their stand, glancing through the entry that Matthew Jordan had made in his journal and the notes that Sarah had copied for him. Around 30,000 men had met on that day, pikemen and musketeers, cavalry and all the followers and baggage carts that an army on the move needed to carry all its gear.

He knew from what Sarah had told him that people actually came to watch the battle. Local civilians wondering which way the day's luck would fly. He wondered where they would have stood. If they would have watched the entire battle, or gained enough sense partway through to get the hell out of there before the wave of conflict broke, the two armies separating in chaos that left no clear winner.

Prince Rupert had been there. Ray was beginning to see him as something of a liability. He'd led his cavalry on the first charge against the Parliamentary left flank and broken through, scattering their forces. Then, Ray noted, the stupid bugger had given chase across open country, abandoning the field and leaving the infantry without support. Wilmot, on the other Royalist flank, followed Rupert's lead, routing the Parliamentary cavalry though his efforts left the infantry intact and ready to regroup in close formation behind him. Like Rupert, he then gave chase to the scattered cavalry, leaving the Royalists open on two sides with two more regiments in Parliamentary cavalry charging in to attack the confused Royalists before they had the chance to compensate for their loss of horse.

Ray tried to imagine the scene, the Royalist elite guarding their King on the wooded rise. The field left open by Rupert's flight and the Parliamentary forces charging forward, almost reaching the King himself. Sixty of the King's guard were killed in that onslaught and the King himself forced to flee with a handful of his followers, Parliamentary forces snapping at his heels.

Ray felt a vague sympathy for King Charles. So certain of himself and his God-given victory, it must have been the gravest of shocks on that day to be almost defeated before the war had even properly begun.

Rupert had made his way back to the battle when it was all but over. Two regiments of Royalists had managed to establish a new defensive line, but the light was fading and it was too late to carry on with the fight. It was decided to disengage. With the morning the Royalists broke camp and moved off up Edgehill. They were not pursued.

There had been a brief addition to Matthew's diary

for that day. It had clearly been written a few days later when the news reached him because it had been crushed into the margin at the bottom of the page. It recorded only that Kitty's niece had been born and that they had called her Elizabeth Ann.

'May God be praised,' the Reverend Jordan wrote. 'And may He have mercy on this little soul, born into such troubled times.

Sarah had come over to Ray's for the evening. She had arrived early and interrupted him while he was looking again through the folder that George Mahoney had sent. The scattered pages were lying on the kitchen table.

'What's that?' she asked him, direct as ever.

'I suppose it's work.'

'Suppose? I thought you were on the sick.'

Ray grinned at her and then turned to fill the kettle, wondering if he should tell her about Frank Jones. It would be good to talk to someone, to Sarah particularly, and her insight might be useful.

She had picked up the clipping when he turned back and was reading it. 'Who is he then, this Frank Jones?'

'That's what I'm trying to find out.'

'Are you supposed to have this stuff? It looks kind of official.'

'Let's just say it came from a friend.'

She eyed him thoughtfully, then sat down at the table pulling the rest of the material towards her. 'So, tell,' she said.

Ray sat down opposite. 'A few days ago this clipping

arrived through the post. No name, no message, just the date scribbled on the bottom. It's the date I was attacked.'

'Ah. This is the guy that did it to you?'

'I don't know, but it looks like someone wants me to think that.'

'You know this Frank Jones, do you?'

'Never met him and I can't make any connection to anything I was working on.'

Sarah narrowed her eyes. 'The newspaper articles at the time, they suggested you might have been mistaken for someone else.'

'I thought you said you only read the headlines.'

'I lied.' She smiled at him. 'Actually, I went to the archive and looked it up.'

'Oh? Spying on me now?'

'I want to know who I'm sleeping with, that's all.'

'Well, I think I'm flattered. And did it tell you who I might have been mistaken for?'

'An Inspector Guy Halshaw. He was involved in some big drugs case. I didn't look that bit up, I ran out of lunch hour. So what do you think, was this Guy Halshaw the target or was it you?'

Ray laughed. 'That's the crux of the whole thing, Sarah. I wish I knew. The next step is to find out if there's any direct connection between Halshaw and Jones. And to find that, I need more information than I've been able to get hold of so far.'

'And can this . . . friend . . . get it for you?'

'I don't know. He thinks I should stay out of things, wait for whoever sent me the clipping to make the next move and see what the story is.'

'Sounds like wise advice, but I don't suppose you'll take it.'

'I don't like feeling useless, or helpless. If someone killed Frank Jones, if he didn't just fall into the canal and hit his head, I want to know.'

'Equally,' Sarah pointed out, 'if he did just fall, why is someone so keen for you to think it was something other than an accident?'

Ray got up to make the tea and Sarah skimmed through the rest of the notes.

'From petty thief to GBH seems an odd step,' she commented.

'I said you should have been a copper.'

'But we never decided if I'd be a good cop or bad cop. Does he look like the man who attacked you?'

'I couldn't say. It all happened so fast, officer, I didn't get time to see his face. It could have been anyone and I've not gone through almost twenty years in the job and not made enemies. I don't know of anyone who could claim that. Different times I've had my car smashed up, tyres slashed and had shit posted to me in a Jiffy bag. It happens. I could almost have accepted being knifed one night in a dark alley, but this was just bizarre and I can't account for it. It's too . . . personal.'

'And a knife in the back wouldn't be? You have an odd way of thinking about these things, Ray.' She paused, sipping her tea. 'And this friend of yours, what does he think?'

Ray hesitated, habitual caution making him reluctant to say too much about George, then reasoning that he had trusted Sarah so far and that she was likely to meet George Mahoney soon enough anyway.

'You remember I told you about a friend wanting me to go into partnership?'

'Yes, of course. It's the same man?'

'Yes. George Mahoney. I've known him six – almost seven – years.'

'Another copper, you said.'

'Actually he's a bit higher up than that. George is ex-army and now DPG.'

'What's that?'

'Oh, Diplomatic Protection Group. He's a co-ordinator.'

'That's, like, protection for VIPs?'

'That sort of thing, but he's had enough and wants to set up on his own. Corporate security, he reckons. Seems to think there's money in telling big business how leaky their security is.'

'You fancy that? It doesn't sound much like you.' She smiled. 'Did you work with him before?'

'No, no I didn't. I met him after his daughter died. Drugs overdose. Officially it went down as accidental, but there were complications and George was always convinced that there was more to it. There was nothing to suggest she was into anything harder than smoking a little gear. One of her friends said she'd once tried coke and been sick for days. She didn't inject, there were no track marks anywhere on her body, no needle marks at all apart from the one that killed her.'

'Could be she tried it once and got it wrong?'

'Could be and chances are we'll never know.'

'It must be unbearable for him,' Sarah commented quietly.

'I think if he gives himself time to think about it, then it is. I guess, maybe, George wants the chance to open things up again.'

'Is he able to do that?'

'If he goes into business for himself there's nothing to stop him.'

'Hang on a second. I thought you were talking about corporate security, not setting up in the private eye business?'

'Disapproval, Sarah?'

'No. Not exactly.' She laughed. 'I don't see you tracking down divorce cases, that's all.'

'No, neither do I. And the security business is still on. George wants to take on other stuff at the same time. Cold cases, like his daughter's. I don't know, it's all up in the air at the moment.'

'But the idea excites you. You like getting your hands dirty.'

Ray nodded. 'Put like that it sounds kind of unsavoury,' he said. 'But yes, I do and it does.'

Chapter Twenty-Five

By the end of November Kitty had returned home. She had been absent for almost three months but the changes she noted in the village made it feel as though it had been much longer.

Children played mock battles on the village green and the Reverend Randall preached politics from the pulpit. Much of the village was instinctively loyal to the King, he represented the tradition and the order they had all grown up with, however much they might disagree with the details. Randall was Parliament's man and in his view the King was a sinner about to be punished by God, and Randall made certain that the village knew that they were next in line for God's wrath if they did not change their ways.

Kitty had no doubt about the man's sincerity. He believed in the need to create a better world. One that had justice in it and in which the elite was not corrupt and driven by the passions of the flesh. The problem was that he saw sin everywhere. Where he loved most was where he most imposed his discipline. He cared deeply for his wife and clearly cherished his children, but his need to keep the things he cared for pure and unsullied made him a strict master and a hard man to love.

Martha Randall found solace in good works and making her worth known all over the village, interfering and organizing. The children often found their way to Kitty's house. She was mildly surprised to find that only the boy, Samuel, could read and write. Little Hope could barely recognize her letters. They were curious about her simples and her medicines, about her books and the notes she made concerning the sickness she attended. Informally at first, then with more design, she began to teach them. An hour every day and more on Saturdays when they joined the other village children in her little class.

Samuel tried hard but struggled and sometimes Kitty had to fight to keep his interest, but Hope was genuinely bright. She absorbed knowledge and craved learning as though it were a drug. Even Edward Randall was impressed. He told Kitty so one Sunday after service. Hope had tried to figure one of the psalms and had most of the words.

'We have neglected her learning, I fear, Mistress Hallam,' he said. 'I think that we should give it more attention. It is right and proper that the child should read the Holy Book.'

'There are many things that she could usefully study,' Kitty suggested. 'Both of your children are eager to learn.'

'Perhaps so,' Randall said. He looked distractedly over her shoulder and frowned. There seemed a little too much haste in his next words. 'But I fear there may be such a thing as too much learning, mistress. From that may come the sin of pride.'

He turned to speak to someone else leaving her surprised at the sharpness in his voice. She turned and looked behind her. Martha Randall stood there, her face like thunder.

Chapter Twenty-Six

In early December, Ray read in Jordan's diaries, Matthew's nephew had just returned from London.

> The King's men tried to enter there on the last day of November, marching into the city through Brentford at the west of London and, Thomas tells me, they got no further. The Earl of Essex brought the trained bands to block the way. They did outnumber the King's men by two to one and rather than confront them in the streets the King drew his men back and they now reside at Oxford where it is supposed that they will spend the winter.

'What are "trained bands", Sarah?'

'What?' She glanced at the reference. 'Oh, sort of part-time soldiers. A lot of them were just apprentice boys, pretty much untrained really.'

'But they drove the Royalist army back at Brentford.'

'Sheer weight of numbers,' Sarah commented. 'And it's going to be hard to march straight through any town when its inhabitants don't want you there and every man jack of them is prepared to fight. Charles probably figured it wasn't worth the trouble.'

Ray nodded, then he gathered up his things and reached for his jacket, which was hanging on the back of the chair.

'And where are you off to?'

'I'm going to see an old colleague. I've been thinking about it all morning, now I'm going to do it.'

'I thought George Mahoney told you to hold off?'

'I'm going to see an old colleague, that's all.'

Sarah's look told him she believed none of it.

'OK, OK, so I can't leave well alone. I always was an impatient sod.'

'You must be getting better,' Sarah commented. 'Look, drop by my place later and we'll have dinner together.'

'Sounds good.' He kissed her, much to the amusement of the records office staff, then took off before he could change his mind.

The colleague he wanted to see was his superintendent, a man Ray had worked under for the past nine years. The welcome he got was warm, but when Ray told him about the clipping, Superintendent Walters was not forthcoming.

'I've no idea who would have sent you this or why they think Frank Jones might be the man who assaulted you. In fact I can't tell you much more. They fished this stiff out of the canal, took a couple of days to figure out who he was and as far as I know the jury's still out on whether he fell or was pushed.'

'Which way are the odds going?'

'On it being a straightforward fall. He'd been drinking, the towpath's muddy. Slips, in he goes and clouts his head on the way down.'

'Is the inquiry . . .?'

'Ongoing. You know the score. If anything else comes up then it'll warrant more attention. Meantime, the man slipped and fell and now he's dead. It happens.'

Ray nodded, his mind working overtime. 'Why did it take so long to identify him?' he asked.

'I understand he didn't have much on him. Keys, loose change.'

'No wallet?'

'To be honest, Ray, I don't recall. We didn't deal with it here at Central. It was over by the marina, that's West Desk, not us. You know that.'

'And there was no suggestion of a connection, either to me or Guy Halshaw?'

'Not that I know. You'd have to ask Halshaw.'

'He still here? I thought he was on the move. Promotion.'

Superintendent Walters nodded. 'Few months back. He's a DCI now, surprised you haven't heard from him.'

Ray shrugged and got up, ready to go.

'You've got another medical review in about a month, I understand.'

'Surprised you remember,' Ray said.

'I do keep in touch with events. Have you made any decision yet?'

Ray shook his head, not wanting to talk about Mahoney and the possibilities that were emerging. 'Have to see what the doc says. Take it from there, but I doubt I'll be back.'

Walters nodded. 'Probably for the best,' he said. 'You know we'll do all we can for you retirement-wise. Put a decent package together.'

'Good of you. Anyway, I'll be in touch.' He noted with mild amusement that Walters glanced uncomfortably at his scars and didn't even offer to shake his hand.

When Ray arrived at Sarah's she was busy cooking and looked surprisingly in control.

'I thought you were a disaster in the kitchen.'

'Oh, I am, but even I can manage pasta if I buy the sauce and any fool can defrost dessert.'

Ray laughed and gave her the wine he had bought. 'Will it go with what you're cooking?'

'Of course it will.' She smiled. 'Actually, there's beer in the fridge if you'd rather.'

He took two bottles from the fridge and found the opener, drank his straight from the bottle but sorted through the cupboards for a glass for Sarah.

'So, how did it go, this visit to an old colleague?'

'I can't say it got me very far. The official line is that Frank Jones probably fell. Apparently he'd been drinking and it's perfectly possible that he slipped.'

'So why is someone trying to make you think otherwise?' She laughed. 'I think we keep asking that one.'

'I'm sure we do. I don't know, Sarah, but I got the distinct feeling that I was being sidelined. Told it was no longer any of my business. My own fault, I suppose. I had enough visits when I was first in hospital, people wishing me well, but I suppose I didn't make the effort to keep the contacts going.'

'And why do you think that was?'

He shook his head. 'I think I'd just had enough,' he

said. 'It suddenly occurred to me that there was no one I was really close to. Oh, I mean, there were people I'd worked with for years. Would trust absolutely in a tight corner. Some of them I drank with off duty, but no one I was really close to.'

'Except George Mahoney?'

Ray looked surprised. 'George? God no, we can go months and never even talk on the phone.'

'That might be so,' Sarah argued. 'But when you do talk there may as well have been no gap in between. I always think that's a good test of friendship. And you must trust him, he's the only one of your colleagues you'd dream of telling about Kitty.'

Ray nearly choked on his beer with laughing. 'God,' he said, 'you can just think what my old super'd say if he knew I was chasing ghosts.'

Chapter Twenty-Seven

Kitty closed her eyes and allowed the pages to fall between her hands. Then let her finger trail over the open page, until she was certain that the answer would be there. Then she opened her eyes and read the verse her finger rested upon.

'He that dwelleth in the secret place of the most High shall abide under the shadow of the Almighty.'

Kitty sighed. Comforting, she thought, but, as always, so obscure. She would have to think about the message the verse held for her.

'What are you doing?'

Kitty jumped. She had been so absorbed that she had not heard Hope enter by the kitchen door.

'Hope! What on earth are you doing here? Do you not know how late it is?'

Hope shrugged. 'I know,' she said. 'But no one will notice I am gone. They think I'm sleeping.'

'And so you should be.' Kitty looked closely at the girl's pinched face. Her eyes were red as though she had been crying. 'What is it, sweetheart? What is wrong?'

Hope flopped down into one of Kitty's chairs. 'They're arguing again,' she said. 'They've been arguing all day and Samuel and I can do nothing to please them.'

Kitty knelt by the chair and gathered the child into her arms. 'I doubt they are angry with you,' she said.

'Sometimes, when adults are angry, they can find nothing right with anyone.'

For a few minutes, Hope allowed herself to be comforted. Then she pulled away and looked over at Kitty's Bible. 'What were you doing when I came in?' she asked.

Kitty sighed. 'A foolish thing, I suppose. Sometimes, when I need comfort or advice, I close my eyes and let the Bible fall open where it may. Then I look to see what inspiration it has to offer.'

Hope looked thoughtful. 'Do you think my father could do that when he is worried or in need?' she asked. 'Sometimes, I think he needs advice.'

Kitty shook her head. 'I doubt your father would approve,' she said. 'But I have always felt that if the Bible is the word of God, then it is only God's word that I am reading and God's voice helping and advising me.'

'Could I try it?' Hope asked her.

'I don't know, sweetheart. I am certain that your father would not like you to do it. Your mother either.'

Hope scowled. 'They like of nothing,' she said.

'Hope, that isn't fair. Your parents want only what is best for you.'

Hope looked at her in open disbelief and Kitty knew in her heart that her words sounded hollow.

'Come,' she said. 'We must get you home before someone notices that you are gone and has the entire village out searching.'

Reluctantly, the girl got to her feet and waited for Kitty to fetch her cloak.

'Can I come tomorrow?' she asked.

'Tomorrow, yes. But in the day, and if your mother has nothing she needs you to do. And promise me, sweetheart, no more creeping out at night.'

Hope mumbled something that might have been a promise and Kitty felt that she could push no further. The Randalls' arguments had become famous in a village where nothing passed without every inhabitant knowing of it. Martha Randall had little interest in her children, village gossip said. She shouted at the servants even when nothing wrong could be found to berate them for. She preached more piety even than her husband and believed in such strictness in the holy law, and in all other things that no one knew how to fulfil her wishes.

Martha Randall, everyone agreed, was a scold who should be put more firmly in her place, though Randall himself got little sympathy. It was the children that Kitty's heart went out to. Caught in the middle of exacting parents – though Kitty knew that Randall loved them deeply, for all that he was so strict – with no escape from the daily disapproval, Kitty doubted it would be the last of Hope's nocturnal visits to her home.

Christmas was a few weeks past and Kitty had received a letter from the Reverend Jordan telling of the latest events in Leicester. He was still living with his family at Belgrave, but there was talk of demolishing the houses on the outskirts of the city and withdrawing the entire population within the city walls. Matthew was far from happy with the prospect.

*It seems that we have moved into the midst of trouble,
the town being of strategic importance to both sides.
At this time the Parliamentary forces occupy the town
and the mayor has felt obliged to write to the high
sheriff, Sir Henry Hastings, to assure him that the
town and corporation have done nothing to encourage
this. The King's men are garrisoned still at Ashby and
at Belvoir. I cannot think that he will allow the town
to remain long in other hands.*

Kitty worried so much about Matthew Jordan and his
family and wished him back in the village where she felt
that he would be safe. The truth was she missed him too.
His gentleness and concern and his friendship.

'Is it grave news, Mistress Hallam?'

Edward Randall's children were sitting at her kitchen
table copying a text she had prepared for them.

'It is from a friend, Samuel,' she told him. 'He is
concerned about the war.'

'Our father says it is a righteous conflict,' Samuel
said. 'Do you think so, mistress?'

'I don't know,' she told him. 'I find it hard to believe
that anything that can split families and kill young men
can be a good thing.'

Hope was frowning over her copying. 'Our mother
has our father read her letters to her,' she said. 'She finds
it easier. She can reckon and write the household ledgers
but she does not like to read.'

'And when she does the accounts our father says he
cannot read them and has them all to do again,' Samuel
added.

Hope giggled and Kitty reproved them both for such

disrespect. 'Many women cannot read at all, Samuel, and many men cannot do it well. There is nothing to be shamed in that. I was lucky, my father taught me more than adequately. Your mother was perhaps not so fortunate.'

They were in the kitchen and had not heard Martha enter by the front door. 'I am glad you think me worthy of your pity, mistress, though I think it will be you who craves pity when God judges your pride.'

'Mistress Randall! Believe me, I meant no offence.'

But Martha Randall had heard enough and brushed Kitty's attempted protest aside. 'I will not hear you, mistress. I had come to thank you for your work with my children but to tell you that you need do no more. It seems I have chosen my moment well. Their father will hear what you say of me behind my back.'

'Believe me, no offence was meant.' Then, realizing what else Martha Randall had said, 'I don't understand. You say that I have done enough? Am I to understand—'

'That my children will come for no more lessons. Their father considers that Hope knows plenty already. Too much it seems, since she seeks to correct her elders. And Samuel will be leaving a week from now to share a tutor with his cousins.'

'I see,' Kitty managed to say. 'Of course, I will abide by your wishes, but truly I meant no offence.' She looked at the woman's stony face and her heart sank but she knew that she must try again. 'Hope is learning so fast,' Kitty said. 'It is wonderful that Samuel goes to share a tutor, he speaks often of his cousins and I know he will take pleasure in being with them.'

'I am relieved to know that you approve my plans. For my own children.'

'But Hope,' Kitty said, determined to plough on, though she knew the situation was already ruined, 'Hope has such a quick grasp of all things. It seems wasteful to end her lessons so soon.'

'Wasteful, Mistress Hallam?'

Kitty knew that she had made a mess of things. She searched desperately to find the right words. 'My father believed that such talent as a quick mind and skill at learning were God-given and should be nurtured.'

The woman flinched. 'And your father presumes to know what God should wish for? Is he a minister, Miss Hallam?'

'You know that he is not.'

'Then what you claim comes near to blasphemy. Hope knows enough learning for any woman to take to her husband and already she has far too much will. And I assure you,' she warned again, 'their father will hear from my own lips, and from theirs, how you speak of their mother when you think there is no one to hear. How you encourage them to speak of me.'

'I've done no wrong,' she tried again, but the woman was hustling the children out of the door. She's jealous, Kitty thought suddenly. Oh Lord, she thinks I seek to take her place.

After they were gone, Kitty crossed the room and barred the door, wanting no more interruptions. Suddenly she felt so very tired. She went upstairs and lay down upon her bed, staring out through the window at the grey sky and the church spire and the woods beyond and knew that if she were honest the woman's accusations, in part at least, were true. How often had she wished the children were her own? Allowed herself in idle moments to imagine what it would be like to have a husband and a family and a proper place in this society that only tolerated her because she was useful, but in which she had no authority or status.

She thought of her own childhood. Her mother had died when she was very small, but her father had been a loving and indulgent man. She had known what it was to be cherished, and from her earliest teens, even before she had fully understood, had known what it was to be desired. There had been games that she had played with her friends, trying to guess whom their husbands might be. Songs and chants to be said as they pulled the petals from daisies in the fields. She got up and crossed to the mirror, wiping away the tears. Her cap had come loose as she lay on the bed and she pulled it off, freed her hair and combed it through ready to pin it back again.

Kitty and her friends, they would pick flowers and pull the petals one by one chanting possibilities.

> Tinker, tailor, soldier sailor,
> Rich man, poor man,
> Beggarman, thief . . .

Over and over again until the petals were gone.

Chapter Twenty-Eight

Beth was dreaming. She was walking in a field of flowers with the sun warm on her head and shoulders and birds singing in a blue sky. She felt content, at peace with the world and, in her dream, she knew that she was on her way to meet a friend. In her hands she carried a garland of flowers. The scent of them was so strong it seemed to surround her and engulf her senses. Perfume of rose and lavender and the honeysuckle her mother grew in the garden and others that she could not name.

The heat of the day was making her sleepy and the scent of flowers dulled her thoughts so that the man was standing right in front of her before she even realized that he was there.

She could feel his anger. It surrounded her as the scent of flowers had surrounded her only moments before. It reached out and filled her thoughts and she breathed it in like sour perfume. And then Beth saw another figure. A woman in long skirts, running across the fields and shouting at the man to get away.

Beth was more afraid than she could ever remember being in her life. The man's anger flooded her thoughts, though when she looked at him his mouth moved but she could not make out the words. She thought she knew him, was certain that she knew him, but her mind refused to tell her who he was. He was only a tall figure, dressed in black with a touch of white fabric tied at the throat. And then, as she looked closer, she realized with shock that she did know this man. He was reaching out for her, his hand raised as though he meant to strike her down, and as she fell to her knees amongst the field of flowers, terrified of what this man would do, Beth looked up and recognized her father's face.

Ray had spent the night at Sarah's and didn't get home until the Friday morning. There was a message from Mahoney on his answerphone suggesting they meet for lunch again the following day.

'Call me if you can't make it,' George said. 'Otherwise I'll assume same time and place as last week.'

Ray was still standing beside the phone when it rang. It was Maggie.

'I've been trying to get you since yesterday,' she said, an edge of anxiety in her voice. 'I'd have left a message but I didn't know what to say.'

'What's wrong? Are the kids all right? Is John?'

'Oh Lord, I'm making a right mess of this. Yes, we're all fine, Ray. I'm sorry to impose but is there any chance of you calling round today, say around lunch time?'

'Of course, but—'

'Look, Ray, I've got to rush, there's someone at the door. I'm about to have a coffee morning.'

'Lovely,' Ray sympathized. 'I'll be round about half one, two o'clock.'

'Great,' Maggie said. In the background Ray could hear the door bell ring again.

He was tired. He wandered upstairs and lay down on top of the bed intending to rest for half an hour. Instead, it was nearly twelve when he awoke and he wasn't certain then what it was that had disturbed him.

And then he saw her. The woman sitting on a stool he knew he didn't have, looking into the mirror above the washstand and combing long brown hair into a neat tail before pinning it back at the nape of her neck.

Ray stared. He was oddly unafraid, but he was aware that the room had grown uncomfortably cold. She was singing to herself, he realized, singing or chanting something to a simple tune.

'Kitty?' Ray said.

The singing stopped and the woman half turned towards him before vanishing from his sight.

Part III

Chapter Twenty-Nine

'I don't quite know how to put this,' Maggie said. 'But did you talk to the kids about Kitty?'

'Why?' he asked. He'd not mentioned his conversation with Beth to anyone, not knowing what to make of it.

'Well, Beth brought a note home from her teacher yesterday. They were told to draw a picture of something they did with their family at the weekend and Beth drew this.'

She pulled a drawing from her bag and handed it to Ray.

'Oh my God,' he whispered, staring at the picture Beth had drawn. A gallows from which four corpses hung. A fire was lit beneath their feet and they were labelled in a careful, childish hand. Mummy, Daddy, Gareth and Beth. At the side of the picture looking up at the hanging figures stood a woman dressed in black and there were lines on her face, criss-crossing like scars.

'We met the kids out of school,' Ray told Sarah, 'and I went in and talked to Beth's teacher. It's quite possible Beth overheard us talking and that it played on her mind. She's only a little kid. I told her teacher what she said to me and she understands why I didn't mention it to Maggie and John, though I think Maggie's really pissed off at me for not telling her. The teacher said the best thing to do is not make any more fuss. See if Beth lets it drop too, she said that sometimes kids hear things but don't realize what they're hearing until later when something reminds them and they try to make sense of it.'

'Sounds like a lot of psychological hooey to me.'

Ray smiled at her. 'But I really didn't think about talking to Maggie about what Beth said last Sunday. I assumed she'd just been listening and, well, you know what an imagination kids have. I wish I'd said something though, but she ran off happily enough to play with her dad and I thought making a big thing of it was not the right way.'

'I think I'd have felt the same way,' Sarah agreed. 'It's a very odd thing for a child to draw though, isn't it? I really don't know what to think, Ray, but I like Maggie and John and I'd hate to think this got in the way of us being friends.'

Ray nodded. He hoped he'd made peace with Maggie but it still worried him.

'I saw her today, Sarah.'

'Who?'

'Kitty, at least, I think it was her, she had her back to me.'

'You, seeing ghosts? No. That is something. What was she doing?'

'Combing her hair. Sitting in my bedroom, looking into the mirror and combing her hair.'

'A vain ghost.'

'You believe me, don't you?'

'I believe you saw something. Hey, I thought you were the born-again sceptic.'

'So did I. That's not all, she was saying something, or chanting. A nursery rhyme or little song, something like that.'

'Maybe she *was* a witch.'

'You think it might have been a spell?' Ray laughed. 'Who knows. I wasn't scared. The room was dead cold, but there was nothing frightening about her. It was just strange, I'm not used to being invaded, especially by ghosts who want to comb their hair in my bedroom.'

Ray met George Mahoney for lunch on Saturday. 'I went to see Walters,' he told Mahoney. 'Asked him about the clipping.'

'Any joy?'

Ray grinned. 'You're not surprised?'

'I know you.'

'No joy, he knew little and cared less. Not his problem. Halshaw's moved though, do you know where?'

'Up to Manchester, but right now he's in the same boat as you're about to be. Retirement due to ill health.'

'Ill health? Halshaw? I never knew a fitter bugger.'

'Stress,' George Mahoney said, savouring the word.

Ray was incredulous. 'Stress? Halshaw? My God, the man thrived on it. He never went after a woman unless she was married to someone twice his size. Never went after a perp unless the odds were way off. Halshaw loved all that glory stuff.'

'The doctors said stress,' George reiterated. He smiled. 'You didn't like him much, did you?'

'Guy Halshaw? I didn't dislike him. We were just of a different type. I thought him a good enough copper and he had the nerve to stick to his guns over that drugs business. Liking didn't come into it.' He frowned, calculating the time since the attack and Halshaw's retirement. 'Bit sudden, wasn't it?'

'There are rumours that he didn't go quiet into that good night. That he was allowed to retire rather than face disciplinary proceedings.'

Ray frowned. 'No, I can't believe that. He was a lot of things, but he wasn't corrupt.'

'The suggestion was that he was overzealous. That maybe the evidence wasn't always there before Halshaw made an arrest. You said yourself he played a wide field when it came to running someone down.'

'I didn't mean that way, George. Look, Halshaw was like most of us. If he was certain someone was guilty he didn't let a lack of evidence stand in his way. He kept on pushing till he had it.'

'Or planted it if it couldn't be found. I'm not making accusations, Ray, I'm just reporting what's being said in the rumour market. And there's another thing, I've asked a lot of questions this week, most of them the quiet sort of questions that no one notices but it turns out we aren't the only ones with an interest.'

'Oh?'

'Not a lot I can tell you yet, Ray, and I'm sorry about that. But there's an internal investigation going on.'

'Into what?'

'It's more of into whom. Rumour says that someone was taking backhanders from Pierce. Halshaw was involved but it's not clear how. And he wasn't the only one.'

'And I suppose that's all you can tell me?'

'I don't know a lot more. Yet.'

Ray frowned, far from satisfied with George's responses. 'So, what's the bottom line?'

'You're treading on toes, Ray,' he said. 'There are those who think you should butt out and retire quietly.'

Chapter Thirty

In the spring of 1643 Matthew wrote that he and his family had been forced to move within the city walls. Most of the property in the outlying area was demolished and the building of new defences had begun. Kitty had urged them to come to her, or to go to Edgemere where she had heard of a house to rent belonging to a friend of her father's.

Emotions had begun to polarize and tales of atrocities had begun to filter back to the village. After Edgehill, there had been talk of a Royalist massacre of civilian women, who had been waiting by the baggage carts. Camp followers or soldiers' wives, no one was certain. In his latest letter to her Jordan had spoken with horror of the battle of Hepdon Heath on 19 March, a week or so before. The King's men had lost the battle, but not content with just a victory, Sir John Gell, the governor of Derby, had paraded the naked corpse of the Earl of Northampton around the city walls, demanding that all should come and see how God's enemies perished.

These were lonely times for Kitty. The ease and regard with which she had once been accepted by the village was no longer there. An atmosphere of dread and sadness pervaded the place. Randall's preaching had become more and more political and there seemed to her to be so little joy in his form of worship. He had even forbidden his congregation to sing the psalms.

To make it worse, Randall's wife complained constantly of her. She corrupted the children, Martha Randall said. Taught them to think too highly of themselves and not respect their elders. And more forcefully now, she objected to Kitty's presence at the birthing of infants and the sickbeds of men. Calling her corrupt and immodest. Many of those who had previously come openly to her for help now came in secret and by night.

She thought about returning to her father's house.

The worst time so far came one cold March Sunday as she left the church. Edward Randall, his face stern, crossed the churchyard towards her, calling her name.

'Mistress Hallam, I would speak with you.'

'Of course, sir.'

'I have heard grave news of you. Accusations that I would have answered.'

Oh what now?, she thought. What was she supposed to have done?

'The dolly. That idol I ordered from the church. I am told that you kept this thing. That you took it to your house and have it there still, though I ordered it destroyed.'

She nodded her head in acknowledgement, somewhat surprised that it had taken him this long to find out. 'I have it, yes.'

'Then you will give it to me now. God will not be mocked like this.'

You or God? she thought, but deemed it wisest to keep such thoughts to herself.

Randall walked with her to the cottage and pushed inside the door ahead, looking around as though he expected to see the straw dolly hanging there. 'Well, mistress?'

'Be patient, sir, I will fetch the thing.'

He watched her come back down the stairs carrying the woven straw in her hands then he snatched it from her and carried it out into the street. Most of the village had heard the exchange in the churchyard and, it seemed, most had followed to see how the argument turned out. They stood in silence as Randall came outside. They made no sound as he lifted the dolly into the air, displaying it like a trophy won in battle. And then he tore it between his hands, ripping and shredding the little idol until only wisps of straw remained, blowing in the chill March wind.

Chapter Thirty-One

Sunday and Ray was restless. Even Sarah's presence couldn't ease his mood. He was thinking of the previous Sunday, which they had spent with John and Maggie, and worrying in case this business with Beth had spoiled the chance of their friendship deepening. A man with no great history of relationships, Ray was beginning to realize that he liked having them and didn't want this embryonic association to slip away.

'Oh for goodness sake,' Sarah exploded finally. 'Get in the car and we'll go over there. I'll drive.'

'What, uninvited?'

'They're friends. You're allowed to call in and see friends.'

'I suppose.'

Sarah drove, taking her little Fiat rather than Ray's tank of a Volvo. Ray sat uncomfortably beside her. He was a bad passenger at the best of times and hated small cars, especially when driven by a female Stirling Moss. He knew better than to say so.

'So,' Sarah said. 'George Mahoney thinks you're stepping on toes?'

'Looks that way. I'm going to talk to Jones's widow.'

Sarah glanced at him, then gave her concentration back to taking a thirty-mile-an-hour bend at sixty-five. Ray flinched and closed his eyes.

'Do you think she'll see you?' Sarah was asking.

'I don't see why not.' If I survive that long Ray thought. 'I'll make out he was an informant of mine. Come to give condolences now I've heard.' Jesus woman! Who taught you to drive?

'Think she'll buy that?'

'Won't know unless I try. You ever thought of taking up rallying?'

They arrived at John and Maggie's about ten minutes earlier than if Ray had been driving. The children were playing in the front garden and greeted them with shouts before running in to tell their parents.

'I couldn't rest,' Ray told Maggie. 'Not knowing if you were still speaking to me.'

'Oh, don't be so soft,' Maggie told him. 'I'm not mad with you, Ray. I'm just a bit put out by it all.'

'Is Beth OK now?'

'Well . . .' Maggie shook her head. 'She seems fine, but she's having these awful dreams. It's not like her to have nightmares.'

'What are they about?' Sarah asked.

'She dreams the house is burning and she can't get out,' John told her. 'Then her hair catches fire and is burning her face. She woke up the other night screaming the place down and tearing at her hair trying to put out the flames.'

'Do you think she heard us talking about the fire?'

'I don't remember that we did,' John said. 'Anyway, let's be reasonable about this, she's seen stuff on TV far worse than talking about a house fire. We watch the news. Talk about things that happen, no, it's not that.'

Ray hesitated, then said, 'She spoke to me about Kitty, you know that. Do you think it would help if I had a chat with her now? I'm not good with kids, but . . .'

John and Maggie looked at one another. 'I don't see that it would do any harm,' John said. 'And it does seem to be something that you and Beth share. She likes you,' he added. 'And I can't say that about many adults.'

Maggie nodded. 'OK, do what you can. I'm really not mad at you, Ray, I'd just like to know what's going on here.'

Beth was in the garden when Ray found her. He'd waited until Gareth had gone inside, lured by some favourite programme on satellite. Beth was playing on the swing.

'Want me to push you?'

'No, thanks. I'm feeling a bit sick actually. I've been swinging for ages.'

'Ah.' He found a place to sit down on what might be a rockery once the weeds were pulled out. 'Your mum says you're having nightmares,' he said, feeling that coming straight to the point might be the best way.

Beth regarded him thoughtfully. 'Do you get nightmares?'

He touched his face. 'Yes, I do. And I'll tell you something, they scare you just as much when you're grown up as when you're a kid.'

She looked doubtful as though not certain whether to believe him. 'Can I touch it?' She pointed to his face.

'Touch . . .? Oh, sure. Why not?'

Beth slipped from the swing and touched his cheek

lightly with her fingertips. She giggled. 'It's all smooth,' she said, 'and your whiskers are all clumpy.'

Ray nodded. 'I have the devil's own job shaving.'

Beth giggled again.

'Sorry, maybe not the best way of putting it. I'm not used to children.'

'You don't have any?'

'No. I don't have any.'

Beth took herself back to the swing. 'Do you believe in ghosts?' she asked.

'I'm not certain, Beth. I'm not even sure I know what a ghost is.' He paused, dredging a half-remembered theory from somewhere in the back of his mind. 'There are some people believe that what we call ghosts are sort of recordings. That buildings and wood and oh, all sorts of things, can record stuff that happened in that place a long time ago. A bit like recording your voice on tape.'

'How?' Beth asked.

'I don't know really. But it's like, whenever you go somewhere you kind of change that place for ever. You leave an impression of yourself, like an invisible fingerprint. If you think that we're all made of atoms,' he was flying blind now and hoping he could land, 'if you think that everything is vibrating, all the time, then maybe if two vibrations get interlocked . . .' He was losing her, losing himself for that matter. 'It's just a theory,' he said.

Beth nodded, looked thoughtful. 'So, why am I seeing her?' she asked. 'You live in the place she lived so you can play the recording. Why can I?'

'I don't know,' Ray confessed. 'Maybe, when one

person starts to look. Starts to play the tape, then it's similar to switching on a television or a radio. It only takes one person to switch it on but a lot of people can share it. Maybe the more people who look at it the stronger the signal gets. I don't know.'

'Are you going to help her? Daddy says that people believe that ghosts are souls that can't rest, but that's not the same as you've told me.'

'There are lots of different ideas, and sometimes even grown-ups don't know which one's right. Several might be, all at the same time.'

Beth absorbed this. 'Are you afraid of her?'

'Of Kitty? No, not at all. I feel sad for her.'

'So do I,' Beth said. 'It's not Kitty that's giving me bad dreams, you know. It's that man.'

'Man? Which man, sweetheart?'

'The man that hated her. He told her that she was going to burn in hell and he was going to send her there.'

'I told her that I didn't believe in hell,' Ray told the others later. 'And that I didn't think you did either.'

'I don't,' John told him. 'I believe in punishment for evil but that's a very different thing. I don't have anything that tells me that Kitty was evil any more than I believe that she was a witch.'

'And if she was, would that have made her evil?'

John sighed. 'There are certain doctrines I abide by, Ray. Evil, no, not in my book. But a lost soul, certainly.'

*

Ray and Sarah returned to the cottage late in the evening. Ray was clearly still troubled and Sarah tried to help.

'We should try to find out why she's suddenly become so intrusive,' she said. 'Maybe the old stories are true and someone's disturbed her grave.'

'If that were true, we'd have packs of wild ghosts roaming the streets whenever they build a new road or tidy up an old cemetery. No one would be able to move without falling over pissed-off spirits. Anyway, we've no idea where she was buried so how would we know if she'd been disturbed?' He sighed. 'Maybe George was right. I should be focusing on the here and now, not something so long gone.'

Sarah was frowning. 'There must be a record somewhere of her execution and where she was interred.'

'And if she wasn't executed? What if she proved herself innocent or escaped somehow?'

'We know she was found guilty. That *is* in the records. Though, if by some miracle she had escaped, she couldn't have chosen a better time to disappear. The whole country was in turmoil. People must have been on the move all over the place.'

'What I don't get,' he said, 'is what she wants. I don't see how we could reopen the case at this late stage.' He laughed suddenly. 'God, listen to me. I'm really losing it, talking like this about a bloody ghost.'

'A couple of weeks ago you would have bet everything on there being no such animal.'

'I know, and I still don't believe she's a restless spirit. It's like I told Beth, we stumbled on the switch somehow and started the playback. I don't know how, but that's what it is.'

Sarah just smiled. 'Well, Einstein,' she said, 'I wish someone would hurry up and find the bloody off button.'

Chapter Thirty-Two

There would be no May Day celebrations that year. Edward Randall would not countenance such pagan worship, the whole village knew that and it was an idea not even forwarded.

Kitty felt sad for that. She knew full well that there was nothing Christian in the festival, but to see the children dancing, dressed in their best clothes and garlanded with ribbons and flowers was something that gave her great pleasure. Like many of the festivals that the village had traditionally kept, it was more an affirmation of solidarity and friendship than of worship and Kitty felt that this was being further undermined.

As a child, she had gone with her father and brother and her friends to gather flowers with which to make garlands. Her father loved to celebrate and any excuse for music or sugar cake or any kind of enjoyment was enough for him. Kitty realized now that hers had been an idyllic childhood in so many ways and that security had helped her cope with her injuries when it would have been so easy, particularly in the early days, just to curl up and die. Life with Matthew Jordan had simply been an extension of her childhood. For all the responsibilities that there had been, there was also contentment and the knowledge that she was valued. It was a hard lesson to learn that she now meant nothing.

Early on the May Day morning, Kitty and Mim walked away from the village and into the woods. It seemed so sad not to acknowledge the festival in some way that they had decided, the two of them, to steal an hour or two away. The sun was low enough for dew still to be on the ground, soaking the hems of their skirts as they crossed the meadow.

'Kitty, Mistress Hallam, wait for me.'

Kitty turned around. 'Hope!'

Breathless, the girl caught up with them. The linen ties of her skirts were only half fastened and her bonnet had been pulled onto uncombed hair.

'Hope, child. Just look at you. If your mother should see you like this.'

Kitty knelt and began to set the girl to rights, fastening the ties on her skirt and trying to ease the tangled hair into some kind of order.

'I saw you from the window,' Hope told them. 'The morning was so bright, I could not bear to be inside.'

Kitty exchanged a glance with Mim. 'Well, you may come with us,' she said. 'But only for a little while. You know your mother does not wish that you should speak to me.'

Hope pulled a face.

'I'll take her back in through the kitchen,' Mim said. 'Then if she's missed I can say she ran some errand for me.'

'We shouldn't encourage the child to lie.'

'Many things shouldn't be encouraged,' Mim said comfortably, 'but it seems to me they are. What harm can there be in the child being here?'

191

Kitty sighed and held out her hand. Hope clasped it quickly, dancing beside her as they walked on.

'Where are you going, Mistress Hallam? My father says that it is May Day. That in pagan times people danced to please their gods and committed acts that should not be spoken of. He's going to preach about them on the Sabbath.'

'Even though they should not be spoken of?' Kitty laughed. 'We had a maypole here, in this village, every year until this one. I don't think it encouraged so many unspeakable acts.'

'Really. The Reverend Jordan allowed such things? I wish I could have seen it.'

Hope's eyes were round and her expression caught between horror and excitement. 'Wasn't he afraid that he might go to hell?'

'For permitting children to dance on the green? No, I don't believe he feared judgement for that.'

They turned into the cool avenue between the trees and then took the narrow path deeper into the woods until they came to a clearing circled with oak and birch.

'I've never been this far,' Hope said. 'It's beautiful, Kitty.'

'I think it is my favourite place,' Kitty told her. 'The trees are so old. Master Jordan told me that people used to worship in places like this before they had churches built.' Then she laughed, seeing Hope's expression. The child looked at her as though she had gone completely mad.

They sat in the sunny clearing on grass dotted with early daisies and talked of the years past and Hope made a chain of the white flowers, which she hung proudly around Kitty's neck.

'How do you make garlands, Mistress Hallam? Would you teach me how?'

Kitty looked around her. 'Really, we should use willow,' she said. 'The withies are more flexible and easy to work. Ah, that will do instead.'

Honeysuckle wove around the trees. It was not yet in flower but last year's vines, brown but still flexible, clung to the branches. Kitty pulled some free, twisting one vine into a ring and then weaving the others around it until she had a framework strong enough to circle the girl's head. She took twigs of birch and newly opened oak leaves, still bright spring green, wood anemones from beneath the trees, late bluebells and the chain of daisies Hope had made, binding them tight with split and twisted honeysuckle vine. Then she took off the girl's bonnet and placed the garland on Hope's tangled hair.

'You look like a princess,' she said and watched with pleasure as the child danced about the clearing, bowing to imaginary courtiers, the flower crown bouncing upon her soft brown curls.

Chapter Thirty-Three

On the Monday morning Ray drove to see Frank Jones's wife. Her address had been in the file that Mahoney had provided him with.

Helen Jones still lived in the council flat that Frank had moved to six years before. Their child was almost seven and Ray arrived when his mother was still not home from the school run.

Ray waited, parking his car in front of the block of flats and watching the procession of young mothers, many with pushchairs, make the morning trek home. He had only the slighest of ideas as to what Helen Jones would look like. Blonde, someone had told him, and Ray tried not to stare at every blonde woman that passed him by. He needn't have worried, she stood out a mile when he finally saw her, a young woman walking alone, dressed in faded blue jeans and a tight black top. It was her face that gave her away, the strain that shadowed the eyes and put lines where no woman that age should have them. He waited until she had gone into the block and then followed, aware of the stares he got from the mothers still chatting on the street. Their interest had little to do with his scars, it was pure recognition and he had faced it a thousand times. The 'he's a copper' look, and the buzz of interest as to what he was doing there. Ray had long since learned to live with it, but it seemed strange after so long a break to have slipped back into the invisible uniform. But then, George Mahoney had been retired from the army for almost a decade and, if you looked at the way he moved you'd never have known.

He didn't bother with the lift. Hated them, anyway, Helen Jones only lived on the third floor. Even so he was panting by the time he'd reached the top of the stairs. Got to get back in shape, he told himself, pausing to catch his breath before knocking at Mrs Jones's door.

'Helen Jones?'

'Yes?' She studied him for a moment. 'You're police,' she said.

'DI Ray Flowers.' He still had his ID card, it was out of date but he waved it at her anyway.

'You'd better come on in.'

She stepped back, waiting for him to close the door, then led the way through to the living room. It was clean and tidy and, he guessed, not long decorated in pale blue paper with a flower border at dado height. The suite was covered in worn blue velour but the TV and video were new. Ray remembered the report in the file about Frank Jones's spending.

Helen gestured to a place on the sofa, but she didn't sit down. Instead, she stood across the room, staring out of the picture window at the street below. She was far too thin, Ray noticed, and far too pale, the bright lipstick she wore only accentuating the whiteness of her skin.

'Well?' she said. 'I've already told the other lot I don't know nothing.'

'I came to say I was sorry, about Frank,' Ray told

her, though something inside him despised the deceit. 'Frank was, shall we say, *helpful* to me once or twice.'

She looked sharply at him and for a moment he wondered if she would ask him for money, say Frank was owed and he should be paying. Instead, she picked a half-empty pack of cigarettes off the window sill and lit one with nervous fingers, before shaking her head at him. 'I don't know what you're trying to pull, mister, but Frank was no one's grass. He was going straight. Had been for years. All this,' she gestured vaguely at the flat, 'all this and me and the boy, we meant too much for him to play the fool.'

All this, Ray thought. She'd said it with such pride. He got up, joined her by the window. 'My mum's place was like this,' he said. 'Looking at the block from the outside, it might have been the same building. You think the councils have a countrywide master plan. This is how you build social housing.'

He glanced sideways at her but she hadn't moved. 'His record says they could pin nothing on him, not that he was going straight. That nightclub he worked for, you know who runs that place?'

'He worked as a doorman. And before you ask, the stuff he bought for the flat, he won the money. Your lot already checked that.'

'Horses, was it?'

'Lottery.' She almost spat the word. 'He won the bloody lottery. Five numbers. It got us eighteen hundred quid. Or didn't your lot tell you that?' She stubbed the half-smoked cigarette, screwing the butt into the ashtray.

'I've been on the sick,' Ray told her. 'Like I say, I came to offer sympathy, not to accuse him.'

'Oh sure. Well, you've done that so you can go now.'

She looked at him again, staring as though making a connection. 'You're that pig they attacked,' she said. 'The one they burned.'

'Unless there's another poor bastard looks like me, though I was never what you'd call handsome anyway.' It almost raised a smile.

'Not exactly well named, are you? Flowers, I mean.'

Her voice had softened, the abusive tone had never sat easily anyway. He guessed she had just grown used to being hurt lately and preferred to attack first. He decided to try telling her the truth.

He touched the scarring on his face. 'Someone's trying to tell me that your Frank did this.'

'Frank!' Her outrage, he felt, was genuine. 'Now look here, mister, my Frank wouldn't hurt a fucking fly. You ask anyone round here, they'll tell you the same. Even at that frigging nightclub, it was Frank who used to talk the punters down, when the others just wanted to kick shit out of anyone making trouble, and he was going legit in the new year, enrolled in that doorman's course the council runs and everything. You think my Frank would do something like that . . .'

She broke down and began to cry.

'I don't believe it,' Ray told her quietly. 'But someone wants me to and I need to know why.'

He found a box of tissues beside the sofa and put them close to her, then went and found the kitchen and set about making them both some tea. She made no objection and when he came back with the tray she took the mug he handed to her.

'You don't believe it?' she said.

'No. I've looked over Frank's record and it doesn't fit. I've tried to fit Frank's face onto the face of the man who attacked me and that doesn't fit either.'

'I don't understand.'

'Neither do I. Tell me, Helen, did you know a detective called Guy Halshaw?'

'Halshaw. That bastard. Came here once looking for drugs. I told him, anyone brings drugs into my house and they'd be out that fucking window. We've got a kid to take care of.'

Ray wasn't sure he saw the logic, but he let it pass.

'Frank'd warned me about him too. I let the others look where they liked but I never left Halshaw alone. Not for a minute. Frank said he planted stuff. So I watched him. I never let his hands out of my sight once. And do you know what that bastard said, just when they were leaving?'

Ray was beginning to think that he could guess.

'He told me that if Frank went down I'd never have to worry about being lonely. He'd make sure of that.'

'Did you report it?' Ray asked her.

'Bloody right I did. They said they'd be looking into it. Sure. Police-speak for fuck off and mind your own business.'

Ray sipped his tea, thinking deeply. Twice in a few days he'd heard the same things about Halshaw. He'd worked with the man for years, but never closely. Halshaw had taken a fast track into vice and Ray had always been CID. A general-purpose copper and quite happy with that.

'Helen, did he try to contact you again after that?'

She shook her head. 'No, but they wouldn't leave Frankie alone. Every week it was after that, at least once a week they'd pick him up on some excuse or other. Frank joked about it. Said now he knew what it was like to be black.' She stared down into the mug. 'Nice tea,' she said. 'Mine's never that good.'

'It's all in how you warm the pot.'

'I never use the pot now. Not just for one. The lad, Ian, he doesn't like tea.' She sniffed, blinking to clear away the tears. 'He misses his dad,' she said.

Chapter Thirty-Four

Hope had been unable to sleep. At church that Sunday her father had preached the wrongness and evil of pagan practices and Hope had felt that somehow he was speaking most directly to her.

'Hellfire and damnation await those who turn aside from God's will. Hellfire and damnation both in this world and the next. Not even death will bring respite from the wrath of God.'

His words had echoed around her dreams and she had awoken in the early hours with them still in her thoughts.

Kitty didn't seem to reckon much as being evil. She was patient and accepting of difference and, Hope thought, she was the wisest and most comforting person that she knew.

But what if Kitty was wrong? What if, even by just making garlands on May Day and talking about the festivities they had attended in earlier times, they were condemning themselves?

Hope's father said that the thought was like to the deed and Hope knew that she had thought wistfully about the things Kitty had described. That she had wanted to wear her garland home for everyone to see and not have to creep inside the house with Mim's collusion and hide it swiftly, wrapped in an old shawl and pushed to the furthest corner of her bedroom cupboard.

Hope was afraid. She wasn't certain if she feared her parents' displeasure more than that of God, in fact she had trouble sometimes distinguishing the two, but she knew that she was afraid and badly in need of comfort.

She thought of creeping from the house and going to find Kitty, but at this hour of the night everyone would be in bed and Kitty would be sleeping.

Had Samuel still been home she might have confided in him. But Samuel was far away with their cousins in Devon and Hope had no idea of when she might see him again. She missed him terribly. Without Samuel in the house she felt so utterly alone.

Silently, Hope crept from her bed and cast a shawl around her shoulders. The house was in darkness and there were no sounds except for the slight creaking of settling timbers and the light wind outside.

She felt her way down the stairs and into her father's study. On a table beside the window stood the large, leather bound Bible that Edward Randall read to his family twice each day and used most often to preach to his flock on the Sunday. It was a King James translation, written in the common tongue, something Edward Randall heartily approved. He kept a Latin copy on the book shelf near to his desk and often pored over both, comparing the translation, making certain that he should not be found wanting when he delivered God's word.

Hope had great respect for her father's faith. It would be so much simpler, she thought, if she could have a fuller share in it.

A candle stood beside the Bible and Hope lit it with the tinder box and flint, then she closed her eyes and opened the book, allowing her finger to run down the page as Kitty had done until she felt it right to stop.

'As thou knowest not what *is* the way of the spirit, *nor* how the bones *do grow* in the womb of her that is with child: even so thou knowest not the works of God who maketh all.'

'What are you doing?'

Hope turned guiltily to face her father. 'I couldn't sleep,' she said. 'I thought, if I came down and read awhile . . .'

He crossed the room to where she stood and looked down at the page she had been reading. 'I heard you come down,' he said. 'I, too, found it hard to rest tonight.'

'I should go back to bed now, I suppose.'

'In a moment.' He sat down in the chair behind his desk and motioned his hand towards her. 'Read it,' he said. 'The passage you were studying.'

Her heart pounding, Hope began to sound the words. She was still not fluent, though most of them now came easily enough. She was reading Ecclesiastes, she realized, by chance, or God's will, one of her father's favourite books. He listened with closed eyes to her halting rendition, then held up his hand for her to cease.

'Cast thy bread upon the waters,' he said softly. 'I often wonder what bread we really cast and what will return to us after the many days.'

'Father?'

He shook his head. 'Do not trouble yourself. Sometimes, in the early hours of the morning my thoughts wander most unprofitably. Did you find comfort in the holy words?'

Hope nodded. 'Yes, Father,' she told him, glad to be able to do so honestly and grateful of whatever chance had brought her to read from that page.

'The voice of God can always be relied upon to comfort. Go to bed now and try to sleep.'

She curtsied and took her leave, grateful that at least there were some things upon which her father and Kitty seemed to agree.

Chapter Thirty-Five

When Ray arrived home that evening Sarah was already there, having let herself in with the spare key he'd given her. She had some information for him. It had been faxed through from the Leicester records office.

'Excavations,' she said. 'I thought about what we were saying and wondered if there'd been anything dug up that might be relevant.'

'And is there?'

'Just maybe. This is from a local history magazine. A couple of the groups put them out.' She pointed out one of the articles. 'It was what's called rescue archaeology,' she said. 'There's a car park there now and shops, but a group went in and dug what they could before the developers took over.'

Ray read the article. An outline of a building had been found and fragments of seventeenth-century grenades. From the little written evidence they had and the objects found it was speculated that the building had been some kind of overspill prison and that the prisoners had been employed in the making of grenades.

'No bones though?' Ray felt vaguely disappointed.

'Well, no, but they've been able to match the building to documentary evidence. It's possible Kitty might have been held there.' She frowned. 'Isn't there a bit in Jordan's diaries about her being taken to court in a wagon?'

'Um, yes, I think so.'

'That would fit. If she'd been held at the castle, where the assizes would have taken place, then she wouldn't have needed transporting. The cells are underground there.'

'OK, so Kitty was imprisoned at this place. There's no evidence that she died there.'

'Well, no,' Sarah admitted. 'But it's the best bit of evidence we've got so far.'

'You've a lot to learn about evidence. I'd call it conclusion jumping.'

'Well, whatever. Lord, don't you nit-pick? Read the bit over the page. There was a prison breakout, two men and a woman escaped after one of the grenades went up and blew a bit of the wall down. Apparently, they even found powder marks on some of the bricks.'

Ray scanned the report, but was less than convinced. 'I'd love to think that the woman was Kitty,' he said. 'But it's not enough, Sarah. And I don't see that excavating the site of somewhere she might possibly have been imprisoned could have started these appearances. Even if it had, wouldn't she be more likely to haunt this bloody car park rather than come all the way back to the cottage?'

Sarah shrugged. 'Given the choice I know where I'd rather be,' she said. 'And the timing fits. I asked for reports from about three years ago. I don't know, maybe they unearthed something personal to her, I could try to get a list of finds from the site.'

'Do that if it's not too much trouble. Where would she have been executed anyway?'

'Could have been one of two places. Maybe outside the castle, close to St Mary de Castro church, but more likely on what's now Gallowtree gate, close to the Angel Gateway.'

'Angel what?'

Sarah laughed. 'It's a rather scruffy little alleyway running from Gallowtree gate through to the market-place. The name always intrigued me. When I was a kid someone told me that the gallows stood in front of the Angel Gateway and if the hangman got it wrong and executed an innocent person, God's angel waited at the entrance to take their soul to heaven. It was the kind of stuff I loved when I was a little kid.'

Ray grinned. 'A kind of divine insurance policy?'

'I guess so. It's a nice story though, don't you think?' She swept the faxes aside and sat down at the table. 'Anyway,' she said, 'how was your day out in the real world?'

He told her about his visit to Helen Jones and what she had said about Halshaw.

'And you never suspected Halshaw of anything underhand?' Sarah asked.

'I didn't work that closely with him as a rule. There were rumours, but there were always rumours about a successful officer and Guy did nothing to quash them. I think he liked the image, you know, being a bit of a fly boy. To be honest, Sarah, most of the time I got on with my job and let the rest wash over me. I saw a lot of people mangled by the rumour machine. Saw a lot more who lived for the work and couldn't see life outside of it. For them every little titbit was precious. Not that I had much of a social life either.' He laughed. 'I used to go home and listen to my music or watch bad cop shows on TV.'

'Were you . . . are you a good policeman?'

'Right the first time. I was, I got results, and I jumped through the promotion hoops because it's what Anne always wanted.'

'Anne?'

'My ex-wife. It's daft, I know, but Anne was ambitious for me. Take your sergeant's exam, she said, and I took it to keep the peace. Put in for a transfer to CID, she said, and I did it. Actually, it was a good move for me. She wanted to be married to a DCI at the very least.' He grinned. 'I almost made it.'

'But I thought you parted years ago?'

'We did, ten, no, closer to twelve, but the habit was ingrained by then. I went through the motions because it seemed easier. You could almost say I was a copper by default, I couldn't think what else to do with my life.'

Sarah snorted rudely. 'I don't believe that,' she said.

'Believe it, there's a lot of truth in it. Oh, I cared about the job, cared about the people. You get to meet someone like Helen Jones and you remind yourself why you took the job on in the first place. But I wasn't like Halshaw. I might not have had much of a life outside of work but work wasn't my life. It was for Halshaw. It defined who he was and, stress or no stress, I'm sure what George said was right, I can't see him retired willingly.'

They went to bed early, leaving the lights out and the curtains open to let in the blanched gleam of a fat full moon. Their love making was gentle, a little clumsy, neither being quite back in practice. After all this time of being alone, Ray couldn't believe how lucky his life had become. It scared him.

Kitty often did not sleep well. This night she had drifted into a restless doze and finally into dreams. In her dream, the man she had seen in her room knelt on the bed beside her. He lay down, pulling her to him and holding her tightly, his hands stroking the length of her body and his voice soft as he spoke words she could only half understand but which were full of his love for her.

Kitty turned onto her back and looked up into his face. He bent to kiss her, his mouth gentle on hers and so familiar, though no one had ever kissed her that way. She wanted the dream to go on and on and when his hand moved to touch her breast she reached out for him wanting to be held so tightly it would be as if he could never let her go.

No man had ever touched her as this man did and no man had ever seen her naked, but she was naked now. Her nightdress gone and the covers on the bed pulled back. And Kitty wanted him. Wanted him so badly that it hurt. Wanted the hands that touched her so intimately, caressing her breasts, moving across her belly, resting so lightly between her legs to go on touching and caressing. For him to go on loving her and wipe away all of the loneliness and pain.

In his dreams, Ray touched the woman he was growing to love. He tangled his fingers in the thick red hair and held her face while he kissed her mouth with a passion that made him clumsy and unsure. He felt her arms around him, the length of her body, cool and smooth against his own and the warm scent of her skin. Ray felt that he could never be close enough to her. Even inside her it still wasn't enough. The need to possess, to become a part of this woman, was just so strong it frightened him even while it filled him with elation.

It hurt when he made love to her, she was so tense and scared though she could not have born it if he'd sensed her fear and stopped. And then it didn't hurt any more. He held her, telling her how beautiful she was and how perfect and all the words that she had dreamed a man might say to her and that could be real only in a dream and then, suddenly, he was gone. All taken away so abruptly that the emptiness he left behind was worse than any pain that she had ever known.

Kitty awoke, her body soaked with sweat and her heart racing. Her nightdress lay on the floor and the covers on the bed were pulled back and, although it was far from her time of the month, her thighs were smeared with her own blood.

Ray dozed and woke in the early hours of the morning. A strange scent filled the room, like garden flowers and cool damp air. It clung to the woman who lay, breathing softly beside him.

And it was all wrong.

Ray propped himself up on one elbow and leaned over to look at Sarah's face but it was Kitty who lay beside him, the unmarked side of her face pale in the moonlight and her dark hair loose around her.

Ray cried out in shock. Was out of bed and backed against the wall when Sarah herself appeared at the bedroom door.

'Ray? What's wrong?'

He was now more outraged than scared. He pointed at the place where Kitty had lain. 'She was here,' he told Sarah. 'In my bloody bed.'

Sarah switched on the light and pulled back the covers. The scent of roses and lavender rose up to meet her.

Part IV

Chapter Thirty-Six

Tuesday morning found Ray decidedly unsettled. They had finally slept again, making up the bed in the guest room. Neither prepared to go back to sleep in Kitty's room.

At breakfast Ray was quiet and disturbed and Sarah uncertain as to how to approach the subject of Kitty's appearance at so private a moment.

'You all right?' she asked finally when the silence had become as close to uncomfortable as their relationship had ever got.

Ray sighed. 'I'm sorry,' he apologized. 'But I don't know what to think. It was so damn vivid. I could touch her, her skin was warm and . . .' He gave up, not willing to admit to Sarah just how real the dream or whatever it was had been. His feelings for Sarah were so strong and so certain, or had been until he had held Kitty in his arms. Suddenly, his emotional world was in turmoil.

Sarah reached across the table and took his hand. 'I don't know what to say,' she told him. 'I didn't see what you saw, or feel whatever it was you felt, but I know it was . . . well . . . real, what happened. Her perfume, if that's what it was . . . and did you feel how cold the room got?' She broke off. 'Look, I have to go. I need to change before I turn up for work. Sure you'll be all right?'

'I'll be fine. I might give George a call, see how things are going on his end.'

'Do that.' She grinned. 'At least we know what we're dealing with on that front.'

Sarah left and Ray mooched about unsure what to do with himself. He had planned to go to the records office later but wanted to speak to George Mahoney first. It was ten before he could catch him.

'I've got Halshaw's address for you,' George said.

He dictated slowly while Ray wrote it down. His hands were stiff this morning and the pen felt awkward in his fingers.

'I've been talking to some people,' George said. 'They say we should leave well alone.'

'Who?' Ray wanted to know.

'You know better than that. Look, the bottom line is that Halshaw got himself in too deep. A deal was struck, high level, it resulted in a major drugs ring being smashed and some of the main dealers put inside. Others turned informant and their families have been given protection, new identities.'

'Very FBI.'

'It happens here, you know that as well as I do. Look, we're talking international, not some local bust, however impressive. Halshaw seems to have landed himself right in it. Planted evidence. The ironic thing is, he didn't need to, it was already there, but he was seen and the case against one of the main dealers almost collapsed because of it. Three years of planning nearly went down the toilet because of one overzealous copper. Halshaw's lucky he kept his retirement package.'

Ray absorbed the news. 'But what does that have to do with us?' he asked. 'It explains Halshaw, but it gets us no nearer what I want to know – who attacked me and why. Was Guy Halshaw implicated in that and what the hell had Frank Jones to do with any of it? We may have been warned off one way, George, but someone else wants me involved or they wouldn't have sent me that clipping.'

'And that worries me. You were happy to leave well alone before. You'd have slipped into early retirement and not left a ripple. Now you're all set to make waves.'

'George, I know that tone, you want to get to the bottom of this as much as I do. I want to know who sent it and what they want from me.'

Thoughtfully, Ray replaced the receiver and stood at the foot of the stairs looking up towards the door at the top. He climbed the stairs reluctantly and went into Kitty's room. His room now, he reminded himself sternly. Ray stood for a moment in the doorway before sitting down on the edge of the bed.

Bending towards the pillow he could still catch the faint scent of lavender and roses. Kitty's perfume. And, if he closed his eyes, he could still see in every detail the face of the woman who had lain beside him. Could taste her skin and feel the warmth of her body. Could feel it so strongly that his own body began to respond.

Angrily, Ray snapped his eyes open and pushed himself off the bed, promising himself that he would sleep only in the spare room from now on.

There was something else he had not told Sarah. Had no intention of telling her. He had pulled on a bathrobe while they had been making the bed in the spare room and it was only afterwards, when he had gone to the bathroom, that Ray had realized he had drying blood smeared on his own skin.

Chapter Thirty-Seven

Ray had always found motorway driving tedious but it was the quickest way to get to see Guy Halshaw. He had thought of phoning ahead, if Halshaw was away the whole exercise could be a tiresome wild goose chase. In the end he had decided to risk it without giving him notice, feeling he'd rather Halshaw be unprepared.

He had spent the previous night at Sarah's house, hoping to be away from hauntings for once and forcing himself to put the events of the night before firmly out of his mind. Even so, he had awoken with Kitty's scent in his nostrils and suffered from a moment of panic before realizing that it was only the perfumed oil that Sarah had put into her bath, the smell drifting in when she opened the bedroom door. The feelings he had experienced for Kitty still took some getting used to. He kept reminding himself that Kitty was someone who had been part of another world. Sarah was here and now and he was profoundly grateful for that.

Sarah had become so very special to him and he found that he was now eager to move on, to put his old life behind him – and that included this business with Halshaw. This hook-up George planned was fast becoming more and more exciting and he hoped fervently that Sarah would also be a big part of his future, though he was having a hard time getting used to the idea that someone like Sarah could possibly want someone like him.

He stopped at the motorway services for a late breakfast. Being midweek most of the people in the restaurant were on their own, reps and business people travelling to the next job. The woman at the counter stared at his hands when she served him and asked if he needed any help to carry his tray. Clearly, she meant it kindly and Ray managed to thank her, but he was taken aback. It suddenly occurred to him just how accepting the newest people in his life had been of him and how little of an issue the sight of his injuries was to them.

He sat down at a table close to one of the few family groups in the restaurant. A little boy stared at him, his eyes wide and his mouth falling open. Ray smiled automatically at him and was unprepared for the look of shock on the child's face.

His mother bent towards him, telling him, very obviously, not to stare and she smiled at Ray, that kind of embarrassed gesture people make when they don't know what else to do. Ray did his best to ignore them, turning towards the window and concentrating on his food, sugaring his tea and slipping the extra packs into the pocket of his jacket.

He'd met this kind of reaction before, but just lately had almost forgotten about the way he looked, his focus being so much on other things. It was only stupid incidents like this that reminded him. He caught sight of his reflection in the window. He'd seen it every day for months but suddenly he viewed his appearance as a stranger might see it and, despite himself, he felt shocked.

He thought of Kitty and how it must have been this way for her. Acceptance from those who knew her until her otherness had faded and almost gone, then the shock of strangeness when the new people came and they looked again only at the outside.

Suddenly, Ray felt hurt by it all and wished that he had never come. That he'd not strayed from the shelter that in these last few weeks he'd built around himself and to which he had so quickly become accustomed.

He wanted to talk to Sarah. The need so great that he groped in his pocket for his mobile phone and called her, knowing that she would be at work and maybe unable to speak to him.

'What is it?' she wanted to know. 'Is everything all right?'

'I'm OK,' he told her, amazed at how true that was when he heard her voice. 'Just missing you. It's cold out here in the real world.'

'Daft bugger,' she told him. 'Come back soon, OK, but don't push yourself too hard. I'll talk to you tonight.'

He felt better and was smiling when he switched off the phone. Once more he caught sight of himself in the window. His was a clown's smile now, big and clumsy and mostly on one side of his too-fat face. But suddenly he didn't care.

Make the most of it, he told himself, enjoying the euphoria. The bubble's bound to burst.

He had problems finding Halshaw's place. It was on a new development on the outskirts of Manchester, too new for his *A–Z*. Finally he asked at a garage and they gave him approximate directions. A local woman walking a mardy Pekinese filled in the rest. Halshaw's place was a very ordinary modern semi at the back of the estate. It had a FOR SALE sign outside, planted in the small patch of lawn. The remnants of a dying hanging basket hung by the front door and Halshaw's car was parked outside. The same car that Ray had been standing next to the day he was attacked.

He had not been prepared for that. He'd not been prepared either for the sudden panic it evoked in him or the flash of memory, sharp enough to bring pain, which made him want to call the whole thing off and run away.

Slowly, Ray calmed his breathing. It's just a car, he told himself. It's just a bloody car. Even so, he walked to Halshaw's front door across the patch of grass and not along the path beside the car.

Halshaw's face when he opened the door was an absolute picture.

'Ray, oh my God, Ray? How the hell are you? Come inside. Come in.' He stood back and allowed Ray to pass. 'That room there, go in. I'll get the kettle on unless you'd rather have a beer?'

Ray was tired already, beer would, he felt, just about finish him off. He shook his head. 'Tea, coffee, whatever, will be just fine.'

'Right, well, make yourself at home.'

Ray sat down and looked around. By odd coincidence, the Halshaws had chosen the same wallpaper as Helen Jones. Only theirs was pink instead of blue and they had no border. In fact the whole room was very pink. The two sofas in dark pink linen, the curtains in an almost matching fabric. The carpet, fortunately, Ray thought, was a biscuity-beige and there were pale green cushions scattered across the furniture, mostly piled at the end of one of the settees as though someone had wanted to get them out of the way.

No one had dusted in quite some time.

Halshaw didn't fit with this pink room, Ray thought, though Halshaw himself had changed greatly since the last time Ray had seen him. He was thinner, older looking, and Ray could never before remember Halshaw unshaven at two in the afternoon.

'How's Gaynor?' Ray asked when Halshaw came back in.

Guy put their coffee on the table. 'Left me,' he said. 'I mean, look at the place, you probably guessed that. She was always the tidy one, was Gaynor.'

'I'm sorry,' Ray said.

'She took the kids. It was about two months ago. She just upped and left one day.'

'I didn't know. It must be hard for you.'

'We're selling the house. You saw the sign?'

Ray nodded.

'Not had much interest. A couple of people came to look, but that's all.'

Ray wondered if he should suggest Guy dusted, tided himself up. He decided not to bother. 'I was surprised,' he said, 'when I heard you'd left the force. What are you going to do?'

Halshaw shrugged. 'Haven't thought about it yet.' He grinned, there was a touch of the old Halshaw about his smile. 'Wait to see how much she stings me for first, I suppose, then decide. There'll be alimony and money for the kids and she'll want her share of this place. Not that it'll be much, we've only been here five minutes.'

'There's no chance of making up then?'

Halshaw's smile faded. He shook his head. 'No,' he said. 'No chance of that. Not that I'd want to now, you understand, we'd not been getting on, not for a long while.'

Ray couldn't help but wonder how much of Guy's inveterate womanizing Gaynor had known about. Which particular blonde had been one too far? He decided not to ask, instead he said, 'I heard you were part of a big bust. That the Pierce job was just the start of it?'

Halshaw seemed to brighten, then he looked suspiciously at Ray as though trying to decide just what he knew. He nodded. 'I guess that's what did it for me in the end,' he said. 'Doctors said it was stress.'

'That's too bad, Guy. It's taking out a lot of good officers these days.'

'Yeah, dead right it is.' Halshaw smiled again and again Ray caught a glimpse of the man as he had been. 'I'll tell you, Ray, we hit the big time with that one. FBI, Interpol, they were all in on it. Three fucking continents, we smashed the chain right back to the source.' He paused, frowned and reached for his coffee mug. His hands shook a little and Ray caught the whiff of brandy as he lifted the mug from the table.

'It must have felt good,' Ray said, trying to be enthusiastic, thinking of what George had said about Guy's stupid mistakes.

'Damn right it did. But it finished me.'

Guy swallowed half his coffee and peered thoughtfully into the mug. 'Look, I'll just go and get a top up. You all right?'

Ray nodded that he was and watched Guy as he left the room, wondering if he ought to tell him just to bring the bottle in. It was a revelation seeing Guy Halshaw like this. So close to breaking and with so little left in his life. Silently, Ray blessed everything that he had so recently gained. Then he blessed it again, just to be sure.

When Halshaw came back Ray said, 'I saw someone the other day that you might remember. She's one reason I've come to see you.'

'Oh? Who?'

'Helen Jones. Widow of Frank. They pulled him out of the river.'

Halshaw gulped more of his coffee. 'That bitch,' he said. He made no comment on Frank. 'She nearly landed me in the shit, that one.'

Ray looked interested. 'Oh?'

'Sexual harassment. So she said. It never stuck.'

'Someone sent me a newspaper clipping about Frank, with a note that inferred he did this to me. I thought it might have been you?'

'Me, why the hell should I do that?'

'I don't know, hoped you'd tell me.'

Halshaw shook his head and drained his coffee mug. 'So, Frank Jones falls in the canal. Good riddance to him, that's all I can say. He was filth. Just like the rest and we'd have proved it in time.'

By planting evidence? Ray wondered. Interesting, he had deliberately said that Frank had drowned in the river, Halshaw had unthinkingly said canal.

'She's a nice-looking woman,' Ray commented. 'No one could have blamed you for having a go.'

Halshaw grinned. He was playing with his coffee mug, clearly wondering about getting another refill. 'Yeah,' he admitted. 'She was something. Too good for Frank though, everyone said so.'

'She seems to have loved him.'

'Loved!' Halshaw was amused. 'Love didn't come into it. Just out for what she could get. Just like all of them.' Then he seemed to brighten. 'On her own now though, isn't she? Might be glad of a little company next time I'm down that way.'

Ray made no comment. This was a parody of the Halshaw he'd known, an exaggeration of the worst traits. He was depressed by it, but certain now that Halshaw had sent the clipping. He doubted though, whether he was about to find out why. 'Did you send me that clipping, Guy? What did you want? I'm not bloody psychic, you want me to know something then include a letter, a bit of a clue.'

Guy Halshaw was silent, he played with his coffee mug, turning it restlessly in his hands before finally setting it down on the table.

'Look, Guy, I've come all the way up here. If there's something you want me to know you may as well spill it.'

'I didn't ask you to come.'

'If you sent me that clipping, and I think you did, then you as good as asked. Guy, I've heard there was trouble in the Pierce investigation. Accusations that you were a little overzealous when it came to the evidence.'

'Who the fuck told you that?'

In the brief flare of anger Ray saw again the Halshaw of old. So certain of himself. He pressed on. 'I heard you weren't the only one up for it. That it went right to the top. That someone was on the take and you took the rap for it.'

This last bit of speculation was thrown in on impulse but Halshaw stiffened. 'Someone's got a big mouth,' he said.

'True, is it? So why'd you send me the clipping, Guy?'

Slowly, Guy Halshaw shook his head. 'I'm out of all that, now,' he said. 'And bloody glad I am. Nothing more to say, is there.' He got to his feet. 'Look, I don't mean to be rude but I've things to do and I really ought to be getting on.'

'Sure,' Ray told him, getting to his feet. He searched his pockets for a scrap of paper, found a sachet of sugar and a pen. 'Look, this is my number. Just in case there's anything you want to say. If I'm not there, leave a message on the machine and I'll get right back to you.'

Halshaw made no move to take it so he put the crumpled pack of sugar on the table. 'Nice to see you again, Guy. I mean that. Hope things start to work out for you.'

'Yeah, thanks,' Guy Halshaw said.

Ray had been gone for only a few minutes when Halshaw's doorbell rang again. He opened it cautiously.

'Oh, it's you. You'd better come in.'

The visitor glanced at his watch.

'Still wearing that thing?' Halshaw said.

'Yeah, well, it's a souvenir, isn't it.'

Halshaw made no comment.

'What did Ray Flowers want?'

'Nothing. What could he want? He heard I retired, came to look me up.'

'It's a long drive to make, considering he hardly knew you. What's wrong with the telephone?'

'How the hell should I know?'

The man pushed Halshaw backwards, trapping him against the wall. 'What's your game, Halshaw? Conscience getting to you, is it? Remember, your wife and kids might have left you, but we still know where they are. You're in this up to your neck.'

He released Halshaw and let himself out, slamming the front door behind him. For a moment, Halshaw stayed where he was as though still held by the other man, then he dived for the phone and dialled his wife's number.

There was no one home.

Guy Halshaw took a deep breath, forcing himself to relax. They wouldn't do anything, not really. They might threaten but . . . He shook his head, wondering who he was kidding. Then went through to the kitchen and poured himself another drink.

Ray had driven away from the house feeling very depressed. He was tired from the journey, even more tired from his encounter with Halshaw and his hands were hurting him. He didn't think he could face the drive back today.

He found a Travelodge and booked a room. It was still too early to call Sarah at home and he didn't want to interrupt her at work again. He lay on the bed and tried to watch the television, channel-surfing until he found a *Columbo* rerun. It was a programme he'd always had a perverse liking for. It must be nice, he thought, to be able to be that certain all of the time.

Though he felt pretty sure that Halshaw had sent him the clipping he was still puzzled by the fact that the letter had a Middleton postmark. Guy had told him that he'd not been there in months. The clipping had been redirected from Ray's old address but Ray had no memory of Guy ever having been there. Of course, it wouldn't have been so difficult to get Ray's address, a phone call or two would have managed that, but it still didn't explain the postmark. If Guy had genuinely not been there then someone must have forwarded it for him. Someone who had Ray's old address. The people who had his new one could be numbered on the fingers of one hand. Even the hospital didn't have his new address until more than a week after he had left.

Now, who would Guy ask to forward a letter for him? It had to be either an ex-colleague or the hospital and Ray felt he would bet on the second. Guy had visited him there, would be likely to remember what ward he was on.

OK, next step, talk to the hospital and ask if they'd passed on a message to him, see if he could definitely track it back to Halshaw.

Satisfied with that small step and that Columbo was close to solving his case, Ray closed his eyes and fell asleep.

Chapter Thirty-Eight

The earth was baked hard. The month was June and it had been unusually hot for weeks now. The dust from the path wormed itself into her shoes and ground between her toes. More tired than she cared to think, Kitty turned gratefully off the main path and into Soutbby wood.

The wood was cool and green and the light soft, filtered through the trees. Halfway between the path and the village, just off the track, was a deep pool fed by springs. Kitty promised herself that she would rest awhile there before returning to the cottage.

The birth she had attended was a difficult one. The woman had been in labour three days before her husband finally came for Kitty. Before Randall came to the village there would have been no hesitation. Kitty would have been asked for as soon as the first contractions came. But the Randalls' continuing disapproval had made things hard for Kitty, Martha's hatred of her growing despite Kitty's attempts at reconciliation.

The child had presented wrongly and it had taken all of her skill to birth it safely. The woman had lost a great deal of blood, but by the time Kitty had finally left, the bleeding had slowed and the woman and baby slept peacefully. She would have liked to stay a little longer, Kitty reflected, but a messenger had arrived to give notice that Martha Randall would be attending on them later to see how the mother fared. It was something Martha had taken upon herself to do frequently of late, seeking to undermine Kitty's position even further. Kitty had decided it was best to leave. She thought of the child she had helped to birth and she smiled, remembering the red and grumpy face and the relief and pride of the parents. It was worth all the time and worry.

She reached the pool and sat down. The water was always clear and cold and green, reflecting the canopy of trees. It was late on the Sunday morning and, knowing that the entire village would be in church by now and that no one would be surprised at her absence because of the birth, she could not resist the impulse. She took off her clothes and stepped naked into the water, breaking the mirrored green and splashing silver towards the sun.

Martha was not in church either but was, as promised, on her way to see the new child and its mother. Her path led through the churchyard and into the woods. It was a relief to be out of the hot sun for a time and Martha did not hurry herself. In her mind she was rehearsing what she would say to the new parents. How she would welcome the baby and make arrangements for the churching of its mother as soon as she was fit enough to rise. Martha had been slowly discouraging the villagers from calling on the Hallam woman in time of need and Martha was pleased that, more often now, her advice was asked for. It grieved her though that she did not have Kitty's skills to call upon and could not more completely take on her role.

It would take time, Martha told herself, but eventually the Hallam woman's role would become untenable in the village and she would be forced to move away. On that day Martha would go down on her knees and give thanks to God.

She paused, her thoughts broken by the sound of splashing water. Curious, Martha stepped from the path.

Kitty turned on her back, her face and breasts towards the light, her hair twining coldly about her arms. Sometimes the scars still burned. There were places on her scalp where the hair had never regrown and the scars became sore and itchy with the heat. She twisted and turned her body in the chill water until the cold grew too much to bear, then reluctantly she pulled herself back onto the bank.

She felt in no great hurry to dress. Kitty wrung the water from her hair and stroked it from her body. The sun was very hot and the chill on her skin slowly displaced by its warmth gave her pleasure. The pool had grown almost mirror still again and she could see her reflection in its surface. Now in her middle twenties her body was more rounded than when, at seventeen, the young men – and the not so young – had pursued her. It all seemed like a lifetime ago, not just a few years.

Water from her hair trickled down her body and between her thighs. She watched it, absently, tracked it with her fingers, aware of the pleasure that her own touch gave her. She caught her own reflection again in the pool.

The angle at which she sat showed for an instant only that part of her face that had not been scarred. Briefly, she saw the image of the woman that she might have been. It might, had things been different, have been her child born that day. Or her husband's hand that touched her and not her own and she remembered her dream, the man who had come to her, lay beside her in her bed and made love with a passion and a tenderness that Kitty had never known in her waking life and probably never would.

Suddenly the years of despair, kept at bay by years of not giving herself time to despair spilled over. Kitty began to cry, softly at first, then with more intensity. She lay down on the grass, pressing her body against it, fingers digging deep into the soft ground at the water's edge, her body writhing as she wept her pain and loneliness back into the earth.

The bells began to toll, marking the end of the morning worship and above the more distant sound Martha, already horrified by what she had seen, heard Kitty cry out, 'Why didn't you take me? Why didn't you just let me die?'

It was as if the words had broken the spell that had kept Martha frozen to the spot. The nakedness, the touching, the mad cries as this woman writhed upon the earth. She had been right all along. Kitty Hallam was an unholy woman. She must get away. If Kitty should see her there, bewitch her as she had convinced herself Kitty had tried to bewitch the children . . . Martha began to run, back towards the village, pursued by her own demons.

Hands of thorn and bracken tore at her feet and pulled at her hair. Catching at her skirts as though they meant to slow her down. Something ripped at her hair, pulling her cap free and dragging out the pins so that she ran like some wild, unkempt thing. Like Kitty Hallam herself, shameless and unrestrained. Martha ran, faster than she had ever run since childhood, back to the village, back to the church and to her husband wishing his flock a good morning outside the door. The crowd parted for her and she stumbled, falling at Randall's feet.

Her voice cracked and strained with emotion, Martha cried out to him with what was left of her breath, 'Husband. I have seen great evil in the Southby wood. I swear to you, the devil is at work there and he has Kitty Hallam for his whore.'

She was still naked when they came for her. She lay on the grass, half sleeping, exhausted by her own anger and the drowsing heat of the noonday sun.

It was their silence that frightened her most. She struggled into her clothes, pulling her cap over wet hair that she bundled under it with no hope of order.

'What have I done? Why do you all look at me like that?'

But they said nothing, men she had known for years crowding around her, not wanting to meet her eyes.

They didn't touch her. Randall had ordered her

bound, but no one moved to carry out his orders and no one laid hands on her. It was their silent momentum that forced her back along the path and into the churchyard. She reached out a hand to Thomas Myan, whose wife she had nursed through fever, whose children had played in her garden. But he just drew away. 'Thomas, what do they say I have done?' But he would not answer her.

Terrified and bewildered, Kitty had no choice but to match their pace. She felt the blood drain from her face. Light-headed already with the sun and lack of sleep, she felt now as though she walked through some horrific dream.

They emerged from the wood and forced her through the gate that led into the churchyard. Women and children gathered by the church door, Martha with them, her hair still loose and tangled around her face. On seeing Kitty she let out a piercing scream and fell heavily onto the path, her hands clutching at the air and her body twitching as though in a fit.

'She's bewitched.' Who first voiced the thought, Kitty did not catch but once said it was carried through the crowd.

'You say I am a witch?' Kitty couldn't believe it. Of all the things she had thought she could be accused of this was one that had not occurred to her.

'On what evidence?' she demanded. 'Who has spoken out against me?' Then with sudden concern, 'Someone should attend to Martha. Take her out of the hot sun, she is clearly ill.'

No one moved, all eyes were now on Randall who stepped forward to face Kitty. Martha remained, untended and prostrate on the ground. Kitty felt her own rising panic. It took her breath and caught at her words. 'You can't just leave her there. For pity's sake . . .'

'Silence, woman!' Randall thundered. 'You.' He pointed to one of the women. 'Attend to my wife. You.' His finger pointed accusingly at Kitty's escort. 'I ordered her gagged and bound. Tie her hands. Would you wish her to curse us with some sign, or give the chance to pronounce some devil's spell?'

There were vague moves amongst the crowd, but none came forward to obey. Kitty realized for the first time that they were afraid of her. Their silence, her own shame and confusion had muddled her perception and she had not recognized their fear. The absurdity of it. The sheer hopelessness and stupidity of her situation struck her with an almost physical force. She couldn't help it. Hysteria rising, she began to laugh. Her laughter echoed around the closeness of the churchyard, was carried in the heat of the day until it seemed the only sound. The men retreated. Women gathered their children to them. Only Randall stepped forward. He struck Kitty hard across her open mouth. The laughter stopped, replaced by broken choking as Kitty fought to regain control. Something was found to bind her hands, a kerchief taken from a woman's dress to cover her mouth. Randall's fury was a tangible thing.

'You dare to laugh in the face of God,' he said. 'You will burn in hell, Kitty Hallam, burn until you cry for mercy and know that none will be offered to you. Not for all eternity. It grieves me that we do not burn witches here in England, that I cannot put you to the torch myself.'

Kitty stood totally still, the full horror of her situation now dawning on her. Randall touched the scars on her face with fingers that almost caressed. 'And you of all people should know the heat of hellfire.'

Chapter Thirty-Nine

Ray had breakfasted and was on the road by eight. He drove back without a break, his route taking him to the Middleton hospital. He hoped he remembered the schedule right and that the ward sister he wanted was on duty. She'd just come on and was very surprised to see him.

'You look great,' she said. 'Now, if you could just lose some of that weight . . .'

She made him coffee in her tiny office and he asked her about messages she might have received for him after he had left.

'Oh yes,' she said. 'Someone claimed he was an ex-colleague, thought you were still in hospital. He said he'd moved and wanted you to have his new address but that he'd lost yours in the move.'

'What did he sound like?' Ray asked her.

'Oh, I'd say about your age,' she said thoughtfully. 'Local accent, but educated so it wasn't really strong. He sounded kind of nervous or upset. I thought at one point he might have been drinking, then I wasn't so sure.'

'So, what did you tell him?'

She laughed. 'Am I being interrrogated?'

'Yes.'

'That's all right then. I was afraid it was some new chat-up line. He said could I give him your address and of course I told him no. We don't give that kind of information out. I suggested that if he was an ex-colleague then you might have a mutual friend who could help him out, but he didn't seem too keen. Said you worked in different departments or something. Anyway, finally, to get rid of him really, I said that if he sent a note here, with covering postage, then I'd redirect it, but I warned him that we weren't a postal service. Did I do right?'

'Yes, of course you did. Was there a covering letter?'

'And did I keep it? No. I don't think I did, but I'll have a rummage through my desk later if you like. There was a brief note that said something like "With reference to our phone call of the 20th, could you pass this on to Ray Flowers", then DI in brackets.'

'You remembered that well,' Ray commented. 'It was really as formal as that?'

'Yes, that's why I remembered. It seemed odd, like a business letter, but it was just a brief note, no address, no name.'

'Right,' Ray said. Halshaw, definitely Halshaw.

She smiled at him. 'So what's this mystery about? Can you tell me?'

'I'd rather not. But I will tell you something else. I've met someone and I feel like a kid again.'

'At your age,' she said.

'At my age,' Ray agreed.

Once home he'd phoned Maggie and asked about Beth. She was much better, Maggie told him, the dreams hadn't come for two nights now, but she had become very curious about the man who hated Kitty.

'Tell her his name was Edward Randall,' Ray told her, 'and that he was a nasty piece of work that deserved a good kicking. No, maybe you shouldn't tell her that.'

Maggie laughed. 'What did happen to him?' she asked.

'I don't know. I've Matthew Jordan to thank for what I do know and he doesn't say.'

'Maybe Kitty told Mathilda,' Maggie joked.

Ray fell silent, the obvious suddenly hitting him.

'OK, what have I said?'

'That I'm a stupid fool.'

'Funny, I'm sure I would have remembered saying that. Why, are you?'

'Maggie, it all started with Mathilda's diaries and I got so wrapped up with Matthew Jordan that I'd almost forgotten that.'

'You mean you haven't read them all?'

'I've skimmed most of them, but not properly, no. Maggie, I hate to speak ill of a woman I really liked but to be honest reading about shopping trips and tea parties puts me to sleep.'

'Need a hand?' Maggie asked him. 'I mean, I feel we're sort of involved anyway now.'

'You wouldn't mind?'

'Of course not. It'll make a change from endless coffee mornings and parish meetings. Look, I'll tell you what. Bring Sarah and the books and come to dinner on Monday. We'll pack the kids off to bed and have a nice adult supper and a bit of a snoop.'

Ray laughed. 'A nosy vicar's wife.'

'The best kind. Is it a date?'

Ray agreed that it was, reflecting that a couple of weeks before he would have been horrified at sharing Mathilda's thoughts like that. Now though, it seemed that Kitty had made the journals a legitimate archive, well in the public domain.

Chapter Forty

That first night they kept her confined in one of the cellars of Master Eton's house. He was still absent, business to do with the war keeping him in London for much of the time. Randall had demanded that the servants let him in and give him use of the house.

The cellar, used for storing wine, was cold and dark. She was imprisoned in a tiny room at the very end of it and given neither light nor food or drink. They had left her bound, but her hands had not been tied behind and she could at least remove the cloth around her mouth. For a time she hammered on the door, cried to be let loose, begged that some message be sent to Master Eton, but no one answered her. No one came near. Later, when her bladder grew too full she was forced to relieve herself in one corner of the room.

She tried to think what would happen to her now, but, despite having heard of witches being tried, she knew few of the details and those she did know she tried not to think of. Her best hope, she thought, was to call on those few friends who might have influence and who might still believe in her. To pray that they might speak out in her favour before the courts.

If she could get messages to them.

Finally, she slept fitfully, curled on sacking in the

corner furthest from the door, waking cold and stiff when Randall came at dawn.

They loaded her onto a cart, binding her more tightly this time. Without her hands to support her, she could not sit up. She lay on the floor of the cart, thrown about by its rocking, her body bruised and sore before they had been travelling more than a few miles. No one spoke to her or told her where she was being taken. It was only later in the journey when the men asked where they should find lodgings for the night that she realized she was being taken to the Leicester assizes. It was the first glimmer of hope so far. The town was in Parliamentary hands, but Matthew was there and Matthew she was certain would never let her down.

Hope was utterly distraught. At the church events had occurred too rapidly and too unbelievably for her to really take it in but by the time they had returned home, the full implications of what had happened had begun to sink in.

Her father had departed to oversee Kitty's incarceration and her mother had been carried upstairs to bed. Mim was left to deal with the hysterical child alone.

'She isn't evil. I don't believe what they said about her. My father should know, Kitty is not the devil's servant.'

'Hush, my lamb. It is a mistake. It must be. Your mother had been too long in the sun. Trust God, my little love, it will all be well.'

But Hope could hear the uncertainty in her words

and would not be calm. She wept and cried out and shouted her protests until finally exhaustion won and she allowed Mim to hold her while she cried.

She slept awhile, clinging to Mim, waking only when her father returned. They heard him in the hall, calling for his wife.

'We put her to bed, sir. She was overcome.'

'Have her brought down. I want the household gathered in my study. We must pray together that God will protect and guide us.'

Hope and Mim went out into the hall. Randall noted the girl's reddened eyes and came over to her. 'Don't weep. Pray.' He hugged her and then tidied her cap and wiped away the fresh tears that threatened. 'I know that you were fond of Mistress Hallam,' he said gently, 'and the fault is mine for allowing you to be so close. But you must put her from your mind now, and let God's will be done here.'

Hope swallowed hard, trying to be brave. There was so much she wanted to ask, but she didn't have the chance.

Randall looked up and frowned. 'Your mother,' he said. 'Mim, take Hope into my room and wait there. We will join you presently.'

The other servants had begun to drift inside. They did not dare speak, but the glances they exchanged told of all the fear and uncertainty, all the gossip that had changed hands in that afternoon. They could hear Randall and his wife out in the hall. Randall's voice quiet and controlled. Martha, still verging on hysteria, though she was silent as she allowed her husband to escort her into his room.

'Let us all pray,' Randall said quietly. 'Let us ask God to see into our hearts and to cleanse them of all misdeeds. Let us ask that he speak to the heart of Mistress Hallam and teach her to confess her faults and her wrongdoing that she may be purified. Let us pray for those who will have the task of judging her, that they may be righteous in the sight of God and that God may see fit to protect us from the evil that is come into our midst.'

Hope choked back a sob. It hurt so much to know that her father believed in Kitty's guilt and that she could do nothing. Hurt even more to know that Hope herself had sometimes doubted that Kitty might be right when her teaching had been so different from all Hope knew. Hurt worst of all that she doubted now.

Her mother had begun to weep again, her cries getting louder until they threatened to drown out Randall's words. He had opened the book of psalms and begun to read the ninety-first, asking the protection of his God.

'He that dwelleth in the secret place of the most High shall abide under the shadow of the Almighty.

'I will say . . .'

Martha had begun to moan, her body swaying back and forth as though she were in great pain. Randall ignored her, raising his voice to be heard over the noise his wife was making.

'. . . I will say of the Lord, *He is* my refuge and my fortress . . .'

Martha had begun to grind her teeth. She shook as though she had fever. She cried out, but the sounds she made had no words in them. Finally she raised her hand and pointed at her daughter.

'She has spirits in her. They torment me. They drive me mad and try to force me to defile the name of God. Oh husband, help me. I cannot bear the spirits. Drive them out of her. Drive them out.'

Terrified, Hope stared at her mother. Her father had ceased to read. His face was stern. 'Martha, sit down. Quiet now.'

'No, no, I won't sit down and I will not be silent. That woman has transferred her evil to the child. I can feel it. I can feel that whore's evil pouring from her.' She moaned again, tearing at her hair. 'Cast it out. You must cast it out.'

Hope's nerve broke. She was only eight years old and had seen her dearest friend accused of witchcraft and now her own mother was accusing her too.

'She isn't evil. Kitty isn't evil! And I hate you. I hate you. I hate you.'

She flew at her mother, biting and scratching, screaming hysterically as Martha tried to fight her off. The child clung to her, tearing at her mother's face and screaming Kitty's name and by the time they finally pulled her away, Martha's face ran with blood, nail marks down both cheeks as though clawed by some giant cat.

'Take my wife to her room and tend to her face,' Randall ordered. Then he turned to his daughter, looking helplessly at her tearstained face and the bloody fingers. Finally, he reached out his hand and took hers.

'We will go to the church,' he said quietly, 'and we will pray together, all night if need be, until you ask God to forgive you and I will ask Him to remember that you are just a child.'

Chapter Forty-One

That afternoon Ray went back to see Helen Jones.

'You again,' she said when Ray appeared on her doorstep, but she let him in and led the way into the kitchen. 'Ian's watching TV in there,' she said, indicating the living room. 'I don't want him upset. You want tea? I'll make it in the pot.'

'Would you like me to do it?' The comment earned him a half smile. He was beginning to value Helen's smiles.

'I went to see Halshaw,' he told her as he filled the kettle.

'That creep. I suppose he was slagging us off.'

'Not really. In fact he said you were an attractive woman.'

'Coming from him, that's an insult.'

Ray plugged the kettle in and leaned against the counter, watching her as she turned fish fingers on the grill.

'Helen, I have to ask you this, did Guy Halshaw ever come back after that day they did the search? I don't mean officially, I mean, did he come back?'

Her shoulders stiffened.

'Why?'

'Because I think he did and I think he was making a nuisance of himself. That Frank objected.'

She nodded slowly. 'I've never seen Frank so mad. That bastard Halshaw, he was spreading rumours, saying I was giving it to him when Frank was away.'

'Did Frank believe him?'

'First off, then he saw sense. We'd neither of us ever even looked at anyone else since we got together. I know that might be hard to believe, but Frank was a good man.'

She turned to face Ray, 'He was all I ever needed and I know he wasn't perfect. He'd got a past and so had I but we'd made a clean start with one another.' She paused, turned back to her cooking but her shoulders were shaking now and Ray could see she was close to tears. 'Then that bastard came on the scene with his "you know that you want me" line and he had power. That was the thing that scared me. He kept saying what he could do to Frank if I wasn't good to him. He harassed Frank every chance he got.'

'Helen, I'm sorry, I really am. What did you do? Did you make a complaint . . .?'

'Complaint! I tried that before, remember? When did any of your lot listen to complaints about one of your own?'

'I'm listening now.'

She fell silent. The kettle had boiled and Ray made tea for them both, warming the pot first and keeping his back to Helen while she recovered.

'I'm pretty certain that Halshaw sent me that clipping,' Ray said.

'Figures, still trying to rubbish Frank even now he's gone.'

Ray shook his head. 'There's more to it than that.'

'Like what?'

'I don't know. But I was quite happy to leave well alone until that clipping arrived. Now, I've got to get to the bottom of it.'

She looked thoughtful. 'Would he know that?' she said. 'I mean, would he be certain you'd look into it?'

'We didn't know each other that well, but I suppose it's a question of reputation. Guy was always a go-getter. If everyone else said there was nothing to investigate, he'd find something.'

'Even if it meant planting the evidence?'

'Even that apparently. Me, I was always a slow starter. Bit of a lazy bugger, but once I'd sunk my teeth in I didn't let go.'

'So he wanted you to look at Frank. Do you think Frank was murdered?'

'I'm beginning to wonder,' he said.

Ray took two mugs from the drainer and she passed him the milk. It occurred to him that Helen would probably never have thought she could have this kind of conversation with a policeman; he was touched by the trust she was beginning to show in him.

'The way I read it at first was that someone had turned vigilante,' he said. 'That Frank was in the frame for the attack on me and someone decided to take the law into their own hands. So I asked around but no one was connecting Frank to me. The official line is that he was a petty criminal who fell off the towpath because he was drunk and even the rumour mill tells me the same thing.' He sighed, his mind working, nagging at the problem. 'Helen, I want you to do something for me.'

'What's that?'

'Make me a list of Frank's contacts. Past and present. Anyone he talked about.'

'I told you, Frank was clean, he'd been straight for years.'

'I know what you told me, but look. You still move in the same circles, live in the same place. The only difference is that Frank learned some sense. I want to know about those that didn't learn. People he worked with maybe at the nightclub. Any little thing he might have said that you didn't connect at the time.'

'Why do you want to know this? You're not even a copper any more. Not a proper one anyway.'

He laughed. 'I'm not quite finished yet. Helen, I happen to know that my erstwhile colleagues aren't going to follow this up. I want to know who did this to me and who killed Frank.'

He glanced around the tiny kitchen, the cheap furnishings and the laminated chipboard counters and the woman who could be pretty if she had not been so scarred inside. 'I've no proof,' he said. 'And I might be wrong but my instincts are telling me I'm not. All of this.' He gestured as she had done three days before. 'You, the boy. It meant everything. I didn't know him but I'm willing to believe that. Frank was scared of something, wasn't he? He probably tried to keep it from you but almost certainly he let something slip.'

She stared at him, this big ugly man, standing with her teapot cradled in his hands and she nodded because her throat had tightened and at first she couldn't speak.

'He was scared,' she managed finally. 'Wanted us to

248

move but I wouldn't unless he told me why. I didn't want
to pull up roots, not when we finally seemed to be getting
somewhere. Ian's old enough for me to get a bit of a job.
Frank's mam was going to have him in the holidays and
Frank was going on that course, the doorman's training
thing, you know, and suddenly all he wanted to do was
up and leave.'

'The night he died?'

'We'd had a row about it. We didn't row, not Frank
and me, but this time he'd gone storming off. Said he was
going for a drink. I thought he'd cool down and when he
got back we'd talk. But he never came back. I thought
he'd only gone to the local pub, not all the way to bloody
Middleton, it never entered my head to go looking for
him there. I went to the police station just down the road
and I reported him missing next day but it was three days
– three fucking days – before they told me his body had
been found.'

She sat down at the table, her head in her hands.
'I'll make that list for you,' she said. 'I'll tell you everything Frank ever told me, but please, find out what
happened to him. Whatever it was and whatever he did,
I want to know.'

Chapter Forty-Two

James Eton returned home the day after Kitty's arrest. The village could speak of nothing else, but at first, Eton could not believe what he was hearing.

'A witch?' he asked Mim. 'They are saying that Mistress Hallam is a witch?'

'Mistress Randall has accused her, sir. She spent all night railing and shouting until finally Master Randall ordered her given an infusion of poppy. She slept, finally, just before dawn, when Master Randall brought Hope back from the church. The poor lamb has been up all night, though her father says she should be allowed to rest today.'

Eton was confused. 'Hope?' he asked. 'What has the child to do with this?'

'The mistress accused her too. Afterwards, when we all gathered to pray together. The master took her to the church to pray God would cleanse her soul.'

Eton shook his head. 'And is her father satisfied that God has done so? Or will she, too, be bound hand and foot and dragged off to the courts?'

Tears filled Mim's eyes. 'Don't say that, sir. Please, don't even think it.'

Eton patted her on the shoulder. 'Don't fret, Mim. I'll follow on to Leicester, see what can be done. You take care of the child, I doubt any other will if her own mother could accuse her.'

He stayed long enough to eat and have a fresh horse saddled for him, then James Eton left in pursuit of Kitty and Randall. The cart had left at dawn, but Eton on horseback would be faster and he calculated that he would be no more than an hour or two behind by the time they reached the town. He would find Matthew Jordan, go to the assizes and see what went on, and if an end could be put to this nonsense.

Even as he made plans, James Eton's heart sank. He remembered that day when Kitty had told him of her dreams and shuddered as he thought of what might happen if she were tricked or forced to confess such thoughts to others.

He had heard of many accused of working for the devil. He had never heard of any being released or found innocent when matters had progressed this far.

Chapter Forty-Three

Early on the Friday morning, Ray went back to talk to Superintendent Walters. Walters was surprised to see him, but made him welcome. 'Have you thought any more about this retirement deal?' he asked.

'I've been thinking about it, yes. I don't think I'll be coming back, there are other things I'd like to do with my life and I'm not getting any younger.'

Walters smiled broadly and Ray knew that he had given him the right answer. 'I'll set things in motion,' Walters told him. 'I think you'll find it's for the best, Ray.'

Ray nodded. 'I'm sure I will,' he said. 'But that's only part of what I came for. I went up to see Halshaw, asked him about that clipping?'

'Oh?' There was a wary note in Walters' voice. 'What did he say?'

'He didn't admit to anything.'

'Then presumably it wasn't him. It's hardly something you'd go to lengths to hide. It was only a news clipping after all.'

'So why deny it if he did? And I'm sure he did. I've done some checking. The letter was forwarded to me from the hospital. Halshaw sent it care of them.'

Walters frowned. 'Ray, I don't mean to be rude, but I thought you were retiring from all this. I don't see what's got you so fired up.'

'Halshaw sent me that clipping because he knew I'd respond. He had dealings with Frank Jones.'

'From what I heard he had more dealings with Frank Jones's wife. Look, Ray, Jones fell in the canal and drowned. He'd drunk too much. End of story. It's tragic, but it happens. And as for Halshaw, well, we know that things weren't exactly friendly between them. Halshaw was after the man's wife. Maybe he was just trying to stir things up.'

'And why would he do that?'

Walters sighed. 'If you've seen him recently then you don't need to ask. He's lost it, Ray, completely unbalanced and drinking like a fish. He's been that way since before he retired, took a lot of covering up, but he'd been a fine officer in his time and it seemed better for everyone just to let him slip off quietly. Kinder all round than making an issue.'

Ray considered that and how it fitted, or not, with what George had told him. 'Was there anything to connect Frank Jones to what happened to me?' he asked.

Walters shook his head. 'You think he might have been looking for Guy Halshaw?'

'That's always been the assumption. I grant you, different reasons, but it's not a new idea.'

'I can't tell you anything more than you already know. The investigation will go on until we've found who did this to you. But there's never been any reason to suspect Frank Jones.'

'Helen Jones thinks he was pushed,' Ray told him.

'On what evidence?'

'None that would stand up in court. She says that

Frank was being harassed by our lot. Not just Halshaw, he'd long gone by then, but others after Halshaw left. She thinks that Frank went to meet someone the night he died. Why trek all the way over to Middleton when his local was just down the road?'

Walters' face was expressionless and Ray wondered what buttons he'd pushed. He hoped Helen would forgive him for putting his theories out as hers.

'Helen Jones is a troublemaker,' Walters said. 'If she had a complaint – a legitimate complaint – then she should have made it when her husband was still alive, not go mouthing off when it's too late.'

'She did make complaints, about Halshaw. They were never followed up.'

'Is that what she told you? Fuck's sake, Ray, you believe a little cow like that? OK, I know Halshaw's reputation, but she encouraged him. And I suppose, who can blame her? Compare Halshaw to a loser like Frank Jones. But I don't like this kind of talk, Ray. I think you're forgetting which side your bread is buttered.'

Ray looked thoughtfully at his erstwhile superior and then got up to leave. 'I don't think I ever forget that,' he said.

Chapter Forty-Four

'I cannot allow you to visit her. I'm truly sorry, Master Eton, sirs, but until their lordships have considered her case she is to receive no visitors.'

'Sir, I have known this woman these last eight years. Never have I known anything but good to come from that association. I cannot believe now that any should see evil in it. And though I may almost, almost mind, understand that you must keep us out, this gentleman is her brother. Surely you cannot deny access to her kin.'

'I follow orders, sir. Nothing more, and until those orders are modified, no one can be allowed to see the prisoner.'

Beside the wall in the governors' chambers stood a wooden bench and Matthew sat down upon it. He had not been well and the shock of this news had been very grave. Kitty's brother turned to him in concern.

'Are you all right? Is there something can be brought for you?'

'Jonathan, I thank you, but I will be well enough. It is Katherine that concerns me, the rest is nothing.'

Eton was still arguing with the governor, but to no avail. Until Kitty's case had been heard, there could be no contact. Finally, they had to be content to hand over the food and wine and extra blankets they had brought for her and leave, hoping that their gifts might be delivered.

'Have a mind, sir,' Eton said. 'Sir Henry Hastings is a friend of long standing and I will be appealing direct to him.'

'And I will be glad to hear his words. If the high sherrif decrees that you might see the woman then so be it. Until then, gentlemen.'

'What now?' Jonathan Hallam wanted to know as they stood outside the courthouse.

Eton shook his head. 'I do as I have said I will and make my appeal.'

'I can't believe it,' Jonathan said. 'Katherine, accused like this.' He looked at Master Eton. 'Sir, I have to ask this. I can stay here only a short time. Our father is ill and there is the business to run, my family to care for. While I am gone . . .'

'Matthew and I will do all we can.' He took the young man's arm, half angry at the unspoken reasons Jonathan was so eager to depart, but respectful of them all the same.

'I understand,' he told him gently. 'Matthew and I have no family to taint with this business and I have friends powerful enough to keep me safe from harm. Kitty will understand that you must protect your own. Your wife and child and father and you may be assured, we will do everything we can.'

Randall had already departed. He had changed his horse at the inn and then ridden back, arriving close to evening. His wife, he was told, was still confined to her chamber, but she had consented to eat some of the broth that Mim had prepared for her.

'And Hope?' Randall asked.

'She slept for a time, sir, then insisted on getting up. The rest of the day she has spent with Mim, helping in the kitchens. The child seemed happier with company and with something to occupy her mind.'

Randall nodded his approval. Hope should not be left alone to brood. He was tired and hungry and his bones ached from the long ride, but there was still much to be done. He glanced outside. It was already dusk, but Randall felt that one more thing had to be completed before he could allow himself to rest.

'I want everyone gathered on the green, an hour from now, and I want a fire built. Have my wife told that she must be there. Hope too. I would see this business finished.'

An hour later it was almost completely dark and the wind had grown chill after a warm day.

The village watched as Randall had everything Kitty owned dragged from her house. Clothing, bedding, the brightly woven rugs. Even her books and the little stock of medicines she had begun to prepare, ready for the winter.

The fire was burning well. Randall began to pile her belongings onto it, the flames roaring as he fed them. He tore the clothing and bedding into strips between his hands, as he had torn the Lammas dolly, casting them into the inferno as though he cast the evil back to the fires of hell, and, watching him, Hope knew that it was Kitty that he burned. Kitty that he imagined curling and twisting in the heat, devoured by the flames. She could hardly bear to look, but the memory of her mother's accusations and her father's genuine fear as they had spent that last night in prayer proved enough to keep her eyes fixed on the burning and on the shadow of her father, cast upon the wall of Kitty's house as the flames seemed to dance around him.

Martha stood close by. She said nothing, her gaze fixed upon the fire and her hands clasped fervently at her breast. Sometimes, Hope noticed, her lips seemed to move as though she prayed, but there was no sound. Hope stayed close to Mim, out of her mother's line of sight, fearful of the accusations and her mother's searing hate for a woman she scarcely knew.

Then her father was calling to her. Holding out his hand and beckoning forward. Hope did not want to go. Some part of her was terrified that he would throw her into the fire. Tear her apart like so many useless rags ready to be consumed. But Randall took her hands and closed them around one of Kitty's treasured books. 'Cast them into the flames,' he told her.

'Cast them . . . Her books? Even her books?'

'Most especially her books. Do it, child, do it now that we may all witness that you cast this evil away from you and have the Lord's forgiveness.'

For a moment, Hope stared at him, her eyes filling with tears. The horror that he made her a part of Kitty's punishment overwhelming her.

'But, when she comes back. When she sees what we have done?'

Randall shook his head, deliberately choosing to mis-understand Hope's words. 'She won't be coming back, child,' he said. 'There is nothing to fear from her now. Cast the evil aside.'

Trembling so much that she could hardly walk, Hope moved reluctantly towards the fire. Tears blurred her eyes so much that it seemed she saw many fires burning so brightly she was almost blinded. She threw the book away from her, blinking the tears back and watching the pages burn. Then her father handed her another and a third. Latin words and Greek and complex images of plants and animals, of strange places Kitty could never have thought to see but which the books made as real to her as her own village, Hope stood and watched them burn. Watched as her father cast what remained of Kitty's treasures onto the fire. Her glass jars of medicines. Her shawl, her letters and a small wooden box that had stood on the mantle above the kitchen fire. Even the candles and the rush tapers she used to light her house. Everything she had ever touched, Randall seemed intent on destroying.

He had lifted the final book and held it between his hands.

'Her Bible,' Hope whispered. 'You cannot burn that?'

'No. I cannot burn this.' He tucked it under one arm and then circled Hope with the other, drawing her close to him and stroking her hair. 'We will take it to the church, you and I. Give it back to God and let Him make it pure and whole again. And then, I think perhaps that you should take it to your chamber. And you may bring it and read a little to me each day. Some good must be forced out of this.'

Chapter Forty-Five

Ray sat outside the flats waiting for Helen Jones. He had copies of one of Matthew's journals in the glove compartment of his car and he took them out now, looking for a particular passage. It was dated 2 July, three days after Kitty had been arrested.

> *I went to her, and they let me have five minutes with her in her cell, but the warder stood beside the door and would let her say nothing of consequence. I have never seen her so unkempt or so distraught. I had brought her food and wine, but the warder took my pack from me and searched it, then laid it aside. I do not know if Kitty will receive any of it. It is thanks to Thomas Stone, my niece's good husband, that I had been able to visit even for so short a time. His coin that bribed the porter and his influence that kept my visit from being reported to the courts. I promised her that I would speak for her. Be witness to her character, but my poor young friend, my heart tells me that there is little I can do. It is rare for such charges to be dropped or found for the defendant. And it grieves my heart to think that in living memory, in the King's father's time, nine were hanged on such flimsy evidence as Kitty finds herself charged . . .*

A tap on the window brought Ray back to the present. It was Helen and her son.

'You'll get me a reputation,' she said. 'Come on up.'

He stuffed the notes back into the glove compartment and got out of the car.

'What's that?' Helen asked him. 'Another case?'

'I suppose it is in a way.' He smiled at the young boy who looked curiously at him.

'Can I go and play now, Mum?'

'Sure, but home by five.'

'OK.' He dashed off to join another mother and her waiting child.

'Neighbours,' Helen said. 'His best friend.'

He followed her up to her flat and made the tea. It seemed to have become an accepted thing.

'I've started that list,' she said. 'God, you wouldn't think you knew so many people until you start to write them down. I've done what you said. Tried to think of anyone he'd talked about, even if it was only the once. I don't know all their full names. Sometimes I don't even know their names. It's like, he'd talk about a bloke comes into work who drives a BMW or something. He was into cars.'

She paused and looked helplessly at Ray. 'Most of it's probably just useless,' she said. 'But once I'd started it was hard to stop. It was like claiming a little bit of Frank's life back for myself. Is that stupid?'

'No, it's not,' Ray told her. 'Of course it's not.'

He thought about what Walters had said about this woman earlier that day. Of course it was possible that Helen Jones had him fooled, but he didn't think so. It was Walters who was wrong.

She pulled the list out of the kitchen drawer telling

Ray that it was still incomplete. Already it ran to a dozen pages. Ray flicked through them. Helen was right, she had been thorough. Names and connections and fragments of conversation overheard on the phone, all with approximate dates and anything else she thought might help.

Ray knew that 90 odd per cent of this would be irrelevant, but the fraction that was left might give the answers.

'Is it all right?' she asked him.

'It's great, love, really good. You missed your calling.'

She laughed. The first time she had and it pleased him to hear it.

She poured the tea while he continued to flick through. One name leapt out at him and he froze. The coincidence was just too much.

'Helen, who's this?'

She looked. 'All I know about him is what's there. He called Frank a couple of times. Frank said he might be able to put work his way when he'd got his certificate. Security stuff, you know.'

Ray nodded but his mind was working overtime.

'Does it mean something?'

'I'm not sure. There's someone else I'd have to talk to, but it might. It might well do.'

They chatted for a few minutes more while he drank his tea but he was eager to be off and Helen, feeling his change in mood, did not try to delay him.

'You're onto something, aren't you?' she asked again as he was leaving.

He hesitated, then nodded. 'I think I am. I'll be in

touch, soon as I've anything to tell. Meantime, finish the list for me.'

She nodded and Ray saw the eagerness in her eyes. He hoped he wouldn't have to let her down.

Chapter Forty-Six

Randall stayed only for a day at home, long enough to reassure himself that his wife had calmed and his daughter was as little disturbed as could be expected after such an experience. Reluctantly, he left her in Mim's care, knowing that, for the time at least, Martha was incapable of caring. Though he left word that the two should not be left alone, mindful that Mim had been close to Kitty Hallam.

He was deeply affected by the whole affair. Never would he have countenanced such an accusation against Kitty Hallam, a woman he had seen as having sound morals for all that her judgement could be based too much on emotion. And, after all, women were creatures of emotion and could not be blamed for the state in which God moulded them.

No. If it had not been for the sight of Martha, fallen in such a fit and the statement of the men who had found Kitty, naked and dishevelled, her appearance fitting so clearly with Martha's description, if not for these things then he could not have believed it.

And then there had been the business of the Lammas dolly. That the woman had kept it might have been passed off, as he had indeed dismissed it, as a case of misguided loyalty to the villagers. Now, it seemed far more sinister and complex. It made Randall wonder what sort of teaching the Reverend Jordan, Kitty's protector, had propounded to his flock and just how deeply the evil ran.

But worst of all, as far as Randall was concerned, was the revelation that had come unwittingly from his own child and which, in his mind, sealed Kitty's fate beyond hope of redemption. On the night when he had burned all of the witch's goods and then taken Hope with him to the church she had spoken of Kitty and how much the Bible had meant to her. He had encouraged her to talk, knowing that his child needed reassurance from him.

'She read from it often?' Randall asked, eager that Hope should confide in him.

Hope nodded. 'She said that in time of trouble, God's word gave her answers.'

'She said that? Then perhaps a priest might be found to read to her in prison. It would be good for her soul should she accept such ministry. It would encourage the judge to leniency, perhaps.'

'You think so?' Hope asked shyly.

'We will see what can be done. Did she have a favourite passage? Something that gave most comfort to her?'

Hope shook her head. 'I do not think so, Father. No, Kitty said that when her heart was troubled, she would let the book open at whatever page it might, then close her eyes and run her finger along the passage until she felt it right to stop. Then she would read the words.'

She sensed her father's sudden tension, but not under-standing the reason she pressed on. 'That night, when you found me in your study, I had remembered what she said—'

'And you did this thing?' Randall's voice was tight with rage. 'You committed this blasphemy? Lord God, child, do you not realize how close you've come to damning your own soul?'

Hope stared at him. 'I meant nothing wrong. You told me that you went to the Bible to ask for help. You told me when you came down that night that you did the same thing.'

'That I . . .' Randall's voice failed him. He gazed at Hope with a mix of disgust and wonderment not knowing what he could possibly say to this misguided child. She backed away from him, her eyes wide with panic. He could see her small body trembling and knew that she was terrified of him and what he might say or do to her. Knew also, just how easily she could have mistaken what he had said to her that night.

He felt tears begin in his own eyes and he dropped down onto his knees, reaching out for his child. Reluctantly, she came to him, allowed him to wrap his arms around her and hold her tightly.

'I'm afraid, Father.'

'And so am I, Hope. So am I, my sweetheart.'

Randall was not, by nature, a demonstrative man and his use of such endearments did not come easily. He held her close, stroking her hair, not caring that her cap had come loose and fallen to the floor. He kissed her face as he had not done since she was a tiny baby. He stroked her and wept over her and prayed to God that He should spare the soul of this child who had done no conscious wrong and Randall wrestled with the teachings of his church, burned so deeply into his mind, that thought was deed and deed once committed was up to God to forgive and that man could do nothing to put it right. And, most of all, he cursed the woman who had done this to him. Done this to his child.

'Will I go to hell?'

'No, my sweet. No, you will not go to hell. God is my witness, I will find a means to right this thing. You will not go to hell.'

But he could tell that she did not believe him.

'I loved her, Father,' Hope whispered. 'I loved her so much.'

'I know you did. I know. And do you still?' he asked, fearful of the answer.

Hope shook her head. 'I don't know,' she whispered. 'I just don't know.'

And that, he thought, as he turned his horse once more away from home, that was the most fearful thing of all. That the witch still had influence on his daughter's mind and there was nothing he could do to make it not so.

Chapter Forty-Seven

Ray had found a payphone and called George, not wanting to trust his mobile to such an important question. It was late in the day but George Mahoney promised to do what he could and try to get back to him later. Ray thought that would be it for the weekend so was astonished to find Mahoney on his doorstep at nine o'clock that same evening.

'George!'

'Hello, Ray, hope you don't mind me dropping by.' He glanced around the living room, his look approving. 'This is nice. I much prefer older places.' He smiled at the woman seated on the shabby old sofa. 'You must be Sarah. I'm George Mahoney.'

He shook her hand and Sarah got up. 'Would you like a drink?' she said. 'I can see to that and keep out of the way if you've business to discuss.'

'I'd love some coffee if you've got it. It's been a long day, but unless Ray objects, please stay. I'm sure Ray's brought you up to date.'

'More or less.'

George settled himself in one of the armchairs and looked approvingly at the glowing fire, stretching out his feet towards the blaze. 'It's getting cold outside,' he commented. 'I think we might even get a frost.'

'This early in the year?'

'It feels chilly enough. Right, the information you asked for.'

Sarah stood in the doorway waiting for the kettle to boil. Ray leaned forward to take the photocopies George had passed to him.

'An investigation,' he said. 'Into Walters?'

George nodded. 'It was dropped after the drugs bust,' he said. 'Walters and co were riding high on success and by then no one seemed to care how they'd come by it.'

'And he offered Frank work,' Ray mused. 'An informant. I'll bet Frank was his informant. He worked at the nightclub and we know that was a key in the distribution network. A lot of information must have passed through there, some of it relating to the sources.'

'It sounds plausible,' George agreed.

'The money,' Ray went on. 'Some lottery win.'

'Do you think Helen knew he was lying to her?' Sarah asked.

'I don't know. But if she did, she couldn't have guessed the source.'

He fell silent, thinking things through and Sarah went to make the coffee. When she returned Ray was asking George how he had come by the information so quickly.

'Once you'd set things in motion two weeks ago I pushed for anything I could get before the doors closed on me. I've not made myself popular.'

'Will it mean trouble for you?'

'No. One of the advantages of my position. I can quote national security at people and get away with most things. Unfortunately, in this case it's my lot that want this hushed up. And I suppose, from their point of view, you can see

269

why. Biggest drugs bust in years coming, fortuitously enough, when confidence in the police force is at a low ebb. The last thing anyone wants is another corruption charge laid at their door. This was amongst the information I'd already gathered. When you mentioned the name, I thought I recalled seeing it in one of the files, so I put a little pressure on a few people and this is what I came up with.' He paused. 'There's more,' he said. 'Frank Jones was under surveillance on the night he died.'

'What! You mean someone saw it happen?'

'Unfortunately, no. Where Frank Jones went into the water was a blind spot. One team lost sight, by the time the second got there it was too late. But he was observed meeting someone and there's a possibility a second was waiting for them further upstream, towards the Weir Head. Anyway, they think they can ID the man he met.'

'Walters,' Ray guessed.

George nodded. 'Problem is, neither observer is 100 per cent and no one wants to push Walters until they have more proof. The Pierce case is shaky enough as it is and there are worries, higher up, that any more evidence of police corruption will just about finish it off.'

'I'm going to see him again,' Ray said. 'Confront the bastard.'

'I wouldn't advise it, officially.'

'I trusted him,' Ray protested. 'Years I worked with him and I find out he's as corrupt as hell.'

'I'm missing something here,' Sarah said. 'If Walters was using Frank Jones as an informer, well, I can see that might be morally reprehensible in some ways but isn't that how the police function?'

'You haven't seen the report,' George explained. 'Walters used Frank to get the information he wanted then used it to pressure this end of the drugs cartel.'

'He was on the take,' Ray said. 'My bloody superintendent. And I'll bet Halshaw was in it with him.'

When George left about an hour later Ray found he couldn't settle. He guessed that it would be all but impossible to track Walters down on a weekend. The superintendent had never been an overtime man. He was anxious about what to tell Helen. She had said she wanted to know the truth about Frank, but truth, he knew, was a funny thing. Sometimes people liked the idea far more than the reality.

He nagged at the problem for the next couple of hours until Sarah grew quite tired of it. She took his hand.

'Come to bed, Ray, and for goodness sake put this out of your mind for tonight. It's bad enough having Kitty share our bed without inviting Frank Jones too.'

Ray winced at the reference to Kitty. They had not slept in her room since that night. 'You're right,' he said. 'I'm sorry.'

She pulled on his hand, urging him to his feet. 'Come and show me how sorry,' she said.

Chapter Forty-Eight

Kitty's brother had been allowed to see her thanks to Master Eton's intervention. Judge Henry Hastings had allowed him a few moments with her, but warned that they could not be left alone.

The jailer stood by the door, doing his best to listen to the conversation between prisoner and visitor while Eton kept him involved in conversation as it would have been disrespectful to ignore him.

'I am so sorry,' Jonathan whispered. 'Oh my poor sister. What will become of this?'

'Only the Lord knows that. I am innocent, Jonathan, you do believe that, don't you? I could not bear it if you thought me guilty.'

He shook his head, vehemently. 'Never, Kitty. Never will I believe that. And you still have friends. Good and powerful friends who will stand with you no matter what.'

Kitty shook her head. 'I will not risk a single one,' she said. 'Neither will I risk you, Jon. When you leave here, you must go home. And you must promise me that you will not return.'

'Kitty . . . I—'

'No, no excuses. And I know this must have been in your mind too, for all that you would not say it to me. I know the risk to family of those accused. How my reputation will tarnish yours and I will not have that, Jonathan. I will not countenance it.'

'And if I am seen to turn my back on you. That will give ammunition to your accusers. How can I do that?'

'You know full well how you can do that. And I know full well that these thoughts have been in your mind. No. No, I hold no malice towards you. It is sound common sense. My father needs you and your wife and child. They most of all. None of this can or should be laid at your door, so go now. I am grateful to have been able to say goodbye. Tell our father that I love him and, please, Jonathan, assure him of my innocence.'

'He needs no such assurance, Kitty, you know that.'

'Now go and, Jonathan, please promise me that you will keep away. One of our family brought before the courts is enough.'

On his arrival in Leicester, Randall went directly to Judge Henry Hastings.

'I have allowed her brother to speak with her,' Randall was told. 'It seemed compassionate.'

'Compassion! That woman is beyond all such deserving.'

'The case against her is not yet proved, Master Randall. I must deal with her as my conscience sees fit.'

Randall sighed and took the wine that Henry Hastings offered. The judge's chambers overlooked the castle green. Through the mullioned windows Randall could see Saint Mary's church and, close by, the executioner's block. 'The woman is guilty,' he said. 'Guilty and deserving of death. She has bewitched my wife and corrupted my daughter's innocent mind. That, neither I nor God can forgive.'

'You presume to know God's will in this?'

'I presume to know what is right and what is wrong and what she did to my child is wrong beyond all doubting.'

Henry Hastings listened as Randall told him of Hope's words. Of what Kitty had taught her to do and of the night of fear that had followed the revelation.

'She is afraid that she will go to hell,' Randall said. 'Oh, it's true enough, I preach judgement and hellfire from the pulpit, yes, and I believe my words. But Hope is just a child. A child whose only real guilt is that she trusted too readily and listened too well.'

Henry Hastings sighed and poured more wine, offering to refill Randall's glass. 'It seems to me,' he said, 'that the times are bound to the corruption of innocence, and, truly, I feel for your pain. But this business reminds me heavily of past mistakes. Nine women died, following accusations made by a child.'

'I know that, sir, but matters are different here. Hope made no accusation. In fact, she sought to defend Mistress Hallam. Something to my mind even more disturbing than if she had accused, if she had tried to proclaim her own innocence in this by accusing that woman of coercion.'

'It distresses you that she did not? In truth, man, I would be glad that your child understands loyalty and honesty. There's little of either present in these times.'

Randall shook his head. 'I know that you mean to comfort me,' he said. 'But I can take none. No, I would see no one unjustly accused, but truly I believe that any investigation into this would bring only further proof.'

Henry Hastings nodded. 'This thing must be properly dealt with,' he said. 'I will not follow the mistakes of the past and I have given much thought to this. There is a man called Prescott, you may have heard word of him. A man of God trained in the law and an expert on the way of heretics and witches. I think we should send for this man. Have him test the woman.'

Randall got to his feet and placed the wine glass back on the sideboard. Tired already, the wine had begun to tell on him.

'It sounds like good reasoning,' he said. 'I will go with your decision. Let the man be sent for.'

Chapter Forty-Nine

The Monday morning after George's visit, Ray went to see Walters.

'I've come up with something that might interest you,' he said.

'What about? You're not still chasing Frank Jones? I thought you could make better use of your time.'

Ray smiled, noticing that Walters winced at the clown mask the expression made on Ray's face. 'There was a witness,' he said. 'Someone saw him die.'

Walters' expression was impossible to read but Ray could feel that he'd hit home.

'I've heard nothing about this,' Walters stated irritably. 'Someone's stringing you a line.'

'Maybe,' Ray pressed on. 'But you'll just love what else's coming out of the rumour mill. Word is, you did for Frank Jones. That he'd got too expensive and you decided it was time to cut costs.'

Walters' face had flushed red. He rounded angrily on Ray. 'More rubbish from that little bitch, I suppose.'

'If you mean Helen Jones, then no. It's not from her.'

'If I thought for one minute you gave credence to this nonsense, Ray . . .'

Ray smiled at him again, knowing just how much it

upset his one-time superior. 'Just passing on the word,' he said. 'I like to keep folk amused.'

DS Enright was coming in as Ray left.

'What did he want this time?'

'Reckons the word puts me in the frame for Frank's murder.'

Enright glanced at his wristwatch. 'Got a meeting,' he said. 'You think Halshaw's been stirring? Or is it Helen Jones?'

Walters shook his head. 'He says it's not the Jones woman.'

'Well, I suppose we ought to find out. If it's Halshaw, he could do with another reminder. If it's the woman, I don't believe she knows anything. Pure speculation.'

'Well, you'd better make sure,' Walters told him.

Ray met Sarah for lunch and told her what he had said to Walters.

'What do you think he'll do?' she asked.

'I don't know, we'll have to wait and see. If we're wrong about the connection then he won't do anything. If I'm right, then hopefully he'll be provoked.'

'And then what?'

Ray shrugged. 'I haven't thought that far,' he said.

They gave their order to the waitress. There was a basket on the table with sugar in one side and packets of sauce and salt in the other. Ray played absently with them, extracting a couple of each and slipping them into his pocket, rearranging the rest as though to hide the gaps.

Sarah shook her head at him.

'My guess is that it happened like this,' Ray said. 'Frank Jones attacked me thinking I was Halshaw. I still don't know what pushed him over the edge, but I'm pretty certain it was him. Halshaw put two and two together and realized it should have been him in hospital. Maybe he even saw Frank running away. Maybe Frank had threatened him, I don't know that part. He went to Walters, who was looking for a way in. Told him that Frank could get him what he needed but that he wanted Frank keeping off his back. Maybe Halshaw didn't know what Walters intended to do with Frank's information. I don't know that either. Anyway, Walters pulled Frank in, told him Halshaw had recognized him and made a deal.'

'You think you'll prove it?'

'Not with what I've got now. You heard what George said on Friday night. The investigation was dropped and it will stay dropped unless I can pull something spectacular out of the bag.'

'Supposing you're right,' Sarah said, 'what must Frank have felt like when he realized he'd got the wrong man? Are you going to tell his wife?'

Ray nodded. 'If this gets to court it'll come out anyway. I'd rather tell her myself. She deserves that.'

'Do you think Halshaw was transferred because Walters knew he should have been the victim?'

'I think that's why Halshaw wanted to go. He didn't trust Frank not to try again and didn't trust Walters to control him. At heart Frank wanted to go straight, I'm sure of that.'

'Do you hate him for what he did to you?'

Slowly, Ray shook his head. 'I thought I would, but I don't. Couple of months ago what had happened to me was my entire life. It was everything I thought about. Now it's not. And Frank's dead. I'm still here.'

'From what you told me Helen said Frank was harassed even after Halshaw went away.'

'Walters keeping his man above suspicion, I'd guess. Then, from what George tells us the unit in charge of the Pierce inquiry got to him and wanted him to replace the informant they'd lost. Maybe Frank let this slip to Walters and he panicked. Maybe he threatened to give evidence that would prove Walters' involvement. To my mind that seems more likely. Maybe he was trying a little blackmail. Any way you look at it, he wound up dead.'

Chapter Fifty

Prescott, the expert in the ways of witches, arrived in mid-July to a town preparing itself for war. The ancient ramparts along the Rawdykes were being renovated and reinforced and of the houses outside of the town's defences many had been demolished to prevent them providing cover for the enemy. As Prescott rode through the Magazine Gateway and into the castle yard he was confronted by a crowd of former residents come to argue their case for compensation. He rode through them, a black-clothed figure on a bay horse, thrusting them aside as though he barely noticed their presence in the yard.

He was brought before Judge Hale to present his credentials. Randall had arrived before him and stood waiting in the outer chamber. The two men, alike in dress, their hair cropped short and both believing themselves to be servants of God, entered Judge Hale's chambers together.

'I had thought to see Sir Henry Hastings,' Prescott said as introductions were made.

'Colonel Hastings, he is now. He has joined the King's men. You will deal with me in his absence.'

'So be it.' Prescott nodded. 'I am asked to present my credentials to the court.'

'I am sure they are impeccable.' Judge Hale had little patience with this business. A war was already under way that could tear the country apart. He felt obliged to respect his predecessor's wishes, even though their loyalties forced them into separate camps, but he thought this whole business much waste of time and public money when both could be better spent.

A little put out by his reception, Prescott tried again. 'I have studied widely in Europe, sir. There is not an element of witch law or a classification of heresy that I have not scrutinized. The writings of Sprenger and Kramer are—'

'I am sure that you are more than qualified for the task in hand,' Hale interrupted. 'Master Prescott, I will tell you now that I have no liking for such trials as these. The assizes in this town are no strangers to witches, or at least, to those accused.'

'I have heard this, sir.'

'Then you will have heard, also, that those women were innocent. Nine women hanged, Prescott, on the flimsiest of evidence—'

'The boy showed every sign of bewitchment, sir, the court judged rightly.'

'And the boy then recanted his statement. Admitted that he lied. Nine souls accused and nine lives taken. I want no repetition of that.'

'That the boy recanted does not mean that he was any less bewitched,' Prescott said steadily. 'The power of those women died with them, the boy could no longer remember what had been done to him.'

Hale regarded the man with open distaste. 'Do what you want, sir,' he said, 'but be certain, I will have no repetition of those earlier crimes.'

Jane Adams

'The bewitchment has already taken place. That need not be proved.'

'I refer to the hangings, sir. Those women died needlessly.'

'Your pardon, sir, but their innocence was far from certain.' Prescott paused. 'And you should consider, sir, that the line is narrow between witchcraft and heresy. If you would give me leave to establish such a charge—'

'The woman is accused of witchcraft. Let it stand.'

Prescott bowed slightly. 'As you will,' he said.

Kitty was grateful to be outside even though the task to which she had been assigned was a distasteful one. She had been taken with a dozen others, all under close guard, to a building close to the town walls and there set to the business of making grenades ready to be stockpiled in the magazine. Kitty knew nothing about such work, but they had been instructed briefly as to the composition of the explosive powder and they were closely watched to ensure that such instructions were followed. Cannon powder, pitch, brimstone and linseed oil. Each proportioned and mixed and packed into ceramic fire pots.

The prisoners were not allowed to speak. They worked in silence around a central table on which the makings of the explosive pots were laid. Twice, Kitty risked lifting her head from the task and looking around. Twice she was cuffed around the ear and told to attend to her work. There were eight men, as far as she could count, and three other women, their hair and faces caked with dirt, clothes hanging in rags with the filth and stench of prison clinging to them.

The overseer held a silver pomander to his nose whenever he came close to check the quality of their work. She caught the scent of it, an orange vinaigrette mixed with cloves and nutmeg. We must all stink, she thought. No water, no change of clothing, locked up with the same foul bedding to sleep on and an overflowing pot in the corner of the cell that was emptied so rarely that Kitty marked the times as ones of celebration.

She dared not raise her head to see the sky but she could feel the sun on her back and at least breathe fresher air. For a brief moment, Kitty allowed herself to hope.

Chapter Fifty-One

Frank had read to Ian almost every night and, now that Frank was gone, it had become important to Helen and to Ian that the little ritual be continued.

Helen had left school with nothing in the way of exams and little real ambition, but her hopes for Ian were so much higher and the boy loved his books. Frank had always liked to read. His choice of books ran to the lurid. Horror, mostly, but with the odd thriller to balance things out. His mother had taken him to the library since he was a little kid and he had taken Ian, every Saturday, chosen four books for himself and let Ian choose his four. Nowadays, there was Ian's school reading book as well. It came home every night in its red plastic wallet and Helen took terrific pride in how often the book was changed and how well her son could read.

It was seven thirty when the door bell rang. Helen frowned. Visitors at that time of night were rare and she resented this special time with her son being interrupted. She opened the door on the chain and peered anxiously at the man outside. Behind him were four more in uniform, three men and the token woman.

'What the hell's going on?' Helen demanded.

The CID man glanced at his watch. 'Open up please, Mrs Jones. I've a warrant here to search your flat. I'm sure you'd like me to do it quietly before the entire block comes to watch.'

Helen stared. Behind the police officers, landing doors were opening, curtains twitching. She looked at the warrant the man held in his hand and then reluctantly slipped the chain and opened the door.

'Yeah, yeah, I've heard it all before,' she said as the man cautioned her before leading her into the living room, 'what's the frigging charge?'

'Suspicion of supplying controlled substances, Mrs Jones. Not the first time, is it?'

Helen turned furiously to confront this intruder. 'Not the first time you lot've got it bloody wrong either. Well, fucking well get on with it, then get out of my home.'

Ian was scared. 'Mum?'

'It's all right, love. It'll all be fine.'

She crossed the room and picked up the phone but the CID officer was there before her, clamping his hand down on the receiver. He nodded to his colleagues. 'Get on with it.' Then to Helen, 'I'm afraid I can't let you do that.'

'I've not been charged, I'm allowed to use my own frigging phone.'

'Language,' he said. 'And in front of the child, too.'

Helen glared at him. 'What's your name?'

'Detective Sergeant Enwright to you, love. Now sit down.'

Fuming, Helen did as she was told. She didn't understand what was going on or why this was happening unless it was just part of the persecution that had so upset Frank. Though she sensed something different in this, something more personal and Helen's first thought was that this was to do with Ray Flowers and what he'd been poking around in.

Ian came and perched on the arm of her chair, eyeing this stranger warily. Helen was determined she would face him down. She picked Ian's book from the floor and shifted over on the sofa to leave room for her son, then opened the book at the page they had been reading.

'You don't mind if we carry on?' she said. 'I'm sure you don't need my help to act like a fascist.'

'Oh, big words,' Enwright mocked.

Determinedly, Helen ignored him and began to read.

Prescott had insisted on being taken straight to see Kitty and Randall had accompanied him. Kitty had been sleeping. Their entry startled her awake, the lights they carried momentarily blinding her as she struggled to sit up and see who had come into her cell.

Randall ordered her to stand and Kitty got to her feet, gazing suspiciously at the newcomer. Randall was a known threat. This other one who stood aloof, regarding her with eyes so cold that they made her shiver in spite of the stuffy heat, he was clearly something new.

'This is Master Prescott,' Randall told her. 'An expert in the study of your kind.'

'And what would that be?' Kitty asked him. 'Am I no longer of human kind?'

Randall began to answer, but the other stopped him, raising a hand and gesturing for silence.

'Let the woman rile you at your peril, sir. The devil will guide her words and confuse your thoughts.' He set his candle on the floor and began to circle Kitty, looking her up and down with the same expression she had seen on those inspecting livestock with a view to buy.

'You wish to inspect my teeth?' she asked him. 'Perhaps you can tell my age that way. Or lift my feet and see if they are rotten.'

'Or cloven, like your master's,' Prescott said.

'Cloven! . . . What?'

But Prescott raised his hand again and Kitty, more from confusion than solid fear, fell silent.

Prescott paused when he had completed his circuit and looked her in the eye. 'I will inspect your teeth, woman, though I doubt if your age could be told that way. And I will inspect your feet and your eyes and any other section of your person that I see fit to inspect. I will search for the marks and workings of your master wherever he has hidden them upon your body and I will not cease until I have the evidence that the court requires.'

'And if it isn't there?' Kitty questioned. 'In truth, man, I have done no wrong. I am no servant of the devil. I fear God and worship him as best I might.'

'You fear God,' Prescott repeated. 'I'm glad of that, Mistress Hallam, glad of that indeed, for it makes my work easier. Though let me tell you, if you did not already fear the Lord a brief time in my presence would convince you of the rightness of such thoughts.'

He stepped closer to her. So close that she could feel his breath on her cheek. Over his shoulder she could see Randall with a pomander raised to his nostrils and, even in the dim light, see how pale he had become from the heat of the tiny cell. Prescott seemed immune. His voice was soft, almost gentle as he said, 'I could have you tried for heresy, you know that, don't you? I could bring charges of heresy and then nothing could protect you. I could put you to the rack. I could burn you with irons and tear your body limb from limb and there would be none to prevent me. You know this, don't you?'

For a moment she was too taken aback to speak and she could only stare at him. Then she recovered herself a little. 'I am neither witch nor heretic,' she told him. 'The charges they have brought against me none but a fool would believe.'

'And none but a fool would deny. I ask you, woman, would you rather confess your sins and be tried and hanged as a simple witch, or be tortured and burned for heresy as the law permits?'

'I have spoken no heresy.'

'You have spoken against your minister. Disobeyed him when he ordered that idol burned. Sought to corrupt his children and denied his teachings. You are as much heretic as any Cathar or Bogomil. I tell you woman, I could have you burned for what we have proof that you have done, never mind what you might be persuaded to confess.'

'You might accuse me, but that does not make me guilty.' She turned to Edward Randall. 'Have you listened to this man? Your wife tells you that I have sinned and I understand that you must believe your wife, that you yourself believe that I have done wrong, but this man would increase my so-called crimes. In all conscience, can you allow that?'

Randall turned away and said nothing but she could see the anxiety written on his face.

'Master Randall will not speak for you,' Prescott told her. 'He would not wish to risk his soul.'

After a time Helen's nerve failed her. She stumbled over words and found it impossible to keep the story in her head. Ian wasn't listening anyway. He continued to stare at Enwright, his eyes round with fear and his body jerking with shock at every noise and crash from the other rooms as the officers searched. From time to time, Enwright wandered over to the doorway and watched, giving instruction to the searchers. The rest of the time he sat looking over at Helen with a quiet smile, head slightly to one side as though listening to the story.

'Oh, don't stop on my account, ' he said, when finally her voice cracked and she could go no further. 'I was enjoying that. Weren't you enjoying that . . . Ian, isn't it?'

'Don't you talk to him!' Helen pulled her son closer. 'Don't you even look at him. You hear me? You hear me?'

Enwright just smiled at her. 'A cat can look at a king,' he said. 'And I don't think he's any king.'

An officer appeared in the doorway with a piece of paper tucked into an evidence bag. Enwright went over and took it from him. He frowned as he read the list of names, the remainder of the list that Helen had been preparing for Ray.

'What's this?' he asked her.

'It's a piece of paper.'

'Funny. It's obviously a list. What are they? Contacts? Buyers? What?'

Helen hid in half-truths. 'It's just a list of people

Frank knew,' she said. 'I was getting a list together of people that phoned me and stuff, you know, to say they were sorry he was dead.'

Enwright scanned down the list. 'That's a good few names,' he said. 'I can't believe that many were sorry when Frank snuffed it.'

Reflexively, Helen hugged her son, lifting a hand to his head as though trying to stop him from hearing.

'Frank was a good man,' she said. 'There were a lot more people than that sorry when he died. What's up, pig? Scared no one's going to care when someone does for you?'

The faint smile on Enwright's face faded. He shoved the list back at the uniformed officer. 'Anything?' he demanded.

'The place is clean, sir.'

Helen followed him as he left the room. She followed him from room to room as he pulled drawers from cabinets and emptied them on the floor. Dragged Helen's clothes from the wardrobe. Marched into Ian's room and tipped his books and toys from the shelves.

'Sir!' The uniformed officer holding onto the list watched in disbelief.

'Call this a search?'

'But, sir, the place is clean. I told you. There's nothing here.'

Helen said nothing, she was past words. Ian had begun to cry. The uniformed officers seemed unable to figure out what they should do.

'There's only one sort of language scum like her understand,' he told them. 'Remember that.'

He turned back to Helen as they left. 'They found nothing, this time,' he said. 'But you should watch yourself. Who knows what might turn up if you can't keep your nose out of other people's business. You might not get so lucky, next time.'

Helen slammed the door and locked it, feeding the chain into the latch. Then she dragged the hall table across the threshold and stood still, leaning on it and trying hard not to cry. Ian was sobbing. The mess and the threats she could put aside. They didn't matter. What cut her to the quick was that they had scared her son. She reached out and grabbed him, kneeling on the floor and cuddling him close. 'It's all right,' she soothed. 'It's going to be all right.' Then she struggled to her feet, still keeping a tight hold on her son and pulled him through to the living room. For a moment she hesitated, angry that it was really all Ray's fault. Then she found the piece of paper he had given her and dialled his number.

Halshaw had been drinking steadily all day and becoming more and more depressed. The truth was he could no longer see any way forward and could not even bear to look back. The sugar pack that Ray had given him still lay on the table and he picked it up, turning it between his hands and studying the creases as though they might map out the answers.

Then, in a sudden energy of decision he reached for the telephone and dialled. The engaged tone purred back at him. Halshaw closed his eyes and lowered the receiver.

Chapter Fifty-Two

They had her listen to the charges brought against her. They were couched in such absurd terms that she might have laughed had she not been so afraid. She could not see herself in the portrait that they painted, that these righteous men went to such pains to depict. But she listened, knowing that there would be no counsel to defend her and perhaps no witnesses willing to speak in her favour and, as she listened, her heart sank and she knew there could be no hope of reprieve.

Item: That said Katherine Hallam did consort with Satan in Southby wood on the Lord's own day, committing with him sinful and unholy intercourse.

Item: That she did bewitch the children of Master Edward Randall, being minister of that parish, so that they did disobey and disregard the order and discipline of their parents' house and their father's teaching. That they did obey only the words and directives of said Katherine Hallam against the word of God.

Item: Further that said daughter of Master Randall did, under bewitchment by said Mistress Hallam, take shape of a cat and attack and claw at her mother's face and hands when informed of the accused's arrest.

Item: That when Mistress Randall sought to tell her husband of Katherine Hallam's sinfulness that said

Katherine Hallam did bewitch her and cause her to fall to the floor in a violent fit.

Item: That Katherine Hallam did seek to use the Holy Book for purposes of divination and other mischief, against the law of God.

Item: That the accused did keep within her bedchamber a certain idol that she claimed contained spirits for use in the infernal rites of Satan.

Item: . . . .

Matthew had come again to the prison, but he was not allowed to see Kitty. Each day for the past five he had come to her only to be turned away and he was desperate to let her know that he had not abandoned her.

Matthew Jordan, one-time priest of God, now just a man afraid for the life of his dearest friend, stood in the courtyard and gazed at the blank walls. 'Katherine,' he whispered. 'Katherine, can you guess that I am here?' Then more loudly, so that the guard on the gate stared at him, 'Katherine. Katherine, do you know that I am here?'

And then he shouted, 'Katherine, I've come to see you but they won't let me inside. Can you hear me, Katherine?'

The guard at the gate moved towards him now. 'Come, sir, please. Get yourself home or you'll be inside this place as well.'

'I know that she is innocent. They have it wrong, she could never do harm. Never.'

'Then if she's innocent, sir, the court will find her so and she'll be home.'

'I want to see her, let me see her, please.' The old man trembled, close to tears, but the guardsman was quite unable to help.

'Go home, sir,' he said. 'Please go home, you can do nothing here.'

Chapter Fifty-Three

At Maggie's suggestion Ray and Sarah had spent the evening with her and John reading through Mathilda's diaries. It had been a relief in the end to share the task with others, somehow it felt less like prying and more like research.

Mathilda had known about Kitty for years. It was a conclusion they reached slowly but once reached it was obvious.

I had my visitor again today.

Many times Mathilda had repeated the same phrase and Ray had thought nothing more than it being Mathilda's strange way of annotating events.

Once they had taken this reference to mean Kitty the rest fell into place. 'She'd been seeing Kitty for years,' Ray concluded. 'Every few days for all the time she'd lived there.'

'It certainly looks that way,' Sarah confirmed.

'How the hell did she put up with it? I mean, how can you plan anything in your life when this ghost might turn up unannounced any time?'

'She obviously coped. Maybe it stopped her being lonely.'

'Did you ever ask Mathilda's cleaning lady about Kitty?' Maggie asked.

'Yes, when I found the first entry, but the name meant nothing to her.'

'I never heard Evie mention a ghost,' John commented. 'Mind you, knowing Evie, if she did see one she'd probably dust it and tell it to mind out while she did the hoovering. And I certainly never saw her.' He laughed briefly. 'I feel quite left out.'

John always slept in the spare bedroom, Ray thought wryly.

'Have you any idea what this anniversary is?' Sarah asked. 'Mathilda mentions Kitty returning on the anniversary, as though it had special significance. Seeing as how she was used to Kitty being around it seems odd she should note her coming in a particular way like that.'

'Her death?' Maggie speculated. 'Actually, that's a point – why doesn't Matthew Jordan mention how she died?'

'Because he passed away in the August,' Ray told her. 'He'd not been well for a long time. He complains of having a fever in his final entries and on, I think, the 26th, someone else has written that he died in the night. It must have hit Kitty really hard.'

'If she knew about it. Do you think they told her, or just let her think he no longer cared?'

'I've no idea. But I hope his family got the news to her somehow. Matthew visited the prison every day, but they only allowed him to see her twice. He sent food and clean water, but he never knew if she received it. He records in his journals that he used to stand in the courtyard and shout, just so that she would know he still cared and still came to try to see her. It nearly got him arrested as well. I think only the fact that he'd been a priest protected him. That and his nephew's money. The twice he got in was only because his nephew had managed to bribe the guard.'

'He should have forgotten they were cousins and married her,' Maggie said. 'What a sad waste.'

Chapter Fifty-Four

Apart from the day of her arrest she had been naked before no man until now. They stripped her and put a blindfold over her eyes while the man called Prescott touched her and Randall watched.

And Prescott talked, explaining what he did and the importance of it all. 'The devil leaves his marks,' Prescott said. 'At his infernal sabbaths where he makes their soul his own he marks them where his fingers touch.'

'She is badly scarred,' she heard Randall say. 'How can you be certain of what you find?'

'Trust me, sir. I have had much practice.'

She tried hard to control herself but she knew her body shook as the man's hands moved across her skin. His touch sickened her, its intimacy so threatening and invasive. He held some metal device in his hand and every few moments pricked her skin, sometimes so lightly that she could hardly perceive it, sometimes plunging it so deeply into her flesh that she cried out in pain.

'How long will it take?' Randall questioned. His voice told her that he had no taste for this.

'How long does God's work take?' Prescott asked.

She lost count of time. It might have taken hours for Prescott to complete his task or it might have taken days. Finally, they left her, throwing her clothing to the floor and leaving her to scrabble in the dark as she tried to find it.

Her body hurt, but it was her heart that pained her more. There were points upon her body where she had been unable to perceive his touch and each time he came to one and it was clear that she felt nothing, the man cried out in exultation.

'You see,' he told Randall. 'Now you see. The devil touched her here and here. There is no perception. His fingers burn so coldly that all sensation is for ever destroyed.'

And after so long a time of this, after so much hurt and so much tension as she waited each time for the pain to come – or even worse, the absence of it – she began to doubt her own knowledge. What if she was truly guilty? What if she did not know of her own guilt? If the devil, as Prescott said, had so confused her mind that she no longer knew that she had sinned?

The thought terrified her above all other thoughts. Or almost all. As Prescott left her he had told her what form his questions might take when he returned. He would give her time to reflect, he said, on which other persons shared her guilt. Which of those she counted friends had joined her in her sin.

And then Kitty knew real fear. The thought that Mim or Hope or any of those she had loved could be condemned. Could be put through what she had been through, be locked alone in some dark cell and have their souls stripped bare by such a man as this.

She wept until sleep finally overtook her but even her dreams would not give her peace. In her dreams her friends came to her. Begged her to set them free from the enslavement she had cast around them. Little Hope and

Mim and Thomas Myan and even Matthew, her most beloved friend. They stood in court and condemned her for her sins and she knew they spoke only out of fear.

And worse than this, the man she had seen so many times, who had invaded her dreams and set her body burning with feelings she could have never known. He stood before them all. Judge and jury and even executioner as he hung the rope about her neck and drew the knot tight beneath her chin. And even as she stood there, the rope pulled tight, forcing her head back and her feet losing their purchase on the solid ground, this man with the scarred hands and face, he touched her as a lover might. Caressed her as he had that night in her own bed, his hand moving between her legs until the pleasure-pain spread through her body and she woke screaming in her cell.

What if Prescott spoke the truth? What if he looked into her eyes and saw knowledge that no unmarried woman had a right to? What if this man who seemed real enough to give her pleasure and to cause such pain was in truth the devil or the devil's messenger? What if she worked such evil and did not know? Oh God help her! She no longer knew which way her heart should turn.

'Step forward, Master Jordan. The court will hear you.'

Matthew Jordan got unsteadily from his seat and walked the length of the courtroom. His footsteps sounded overloud on the wooden floor and the tap-scrape-tap of his walking cane echoed around the chamber.

'I come to speak for the defendant,' Matthew Jordan said. His voice shook and his old eyes watered with emotion. 'I know her to be innocent, my Lords. Katherine would do no harm. All her life has been spent in the care of others, she is a good woman, a God-fearing woman, and with the last breath in my body I will defend her name.'

His voice cracked and Judge Hale looked at him with concern.

'Master Jordan,' he said, 'the accused resided in your house these past seven years. She is a kinswoman?'

'Yes, she is. She kept house for me. Her father placed Katherine in my care and now, now I feel that I have failed her.'

'No one accuses you of neglect, Master Jordan, but you understand the charges which this court has brought? The seriousness of them. I would caution you, sir, that in choosing to defend this woman, you might also find yourself condemned.'

Matthew Jordan leaned heavily on his walking cane, the old man frail and alone in the hostile courtroom, but he looked boldly at Judge Hale.

'Sir, my life has been long and for all of it I have done my utmost to serve truth. I will not go to my grave knowing that I turned my back on one I have always counted friend. As God will be my witness, sir,' his voice once more breaking with emotion, 'as the good God is my witness, I will hold to Katherine's innocence until the day I die.'

Judge Hale regarded the old man sternly. 'I hear you, Master Jordan,' he said, 'but I ask you to consider your words and this woman's claim on your loyalty. Think of your family, of your friends, of the consequences that may come from your defence of something that all natural and God-given law sees as indefensible.'

'If I believed for one instant that these claims made against my kinswoman had a shred of credence, sir, then I would desist at once and let Katherine meet any fate that the court decides. But, in the name of God, I cannot stand by and see such wrong being committed against an innocent soul. I am an old man and I go to meet my Maker soon enough. I will not die with such a stain on my soul as would be left by my silence.'

Judge Hale nodded. 'Then so be it,' he said 'and God's will be done.'

Chapter Fifty-Five

The phone was ringing when Ray arrived back at the cottage. It was Helen Jones and she was very distressed.

'They came and searched the flat,' she said. 'They didn't find anything, there was nothing for them to find, but they warned me. Said I'd been accused of supplying drugs. But I haven't done anything. I've done nothing.'

Ray promised he would go straight over. He took Sarah with him and this time his driving rivalled hers.

The flat was in complete disarray and Helen was doing her best to clean up. Her eyes were red with crying.

'Where's Ian?' Ray asked her.

'At his friend's. Took him there after they'd gone. They've been really good but God knows what they think of me.'

Sarah had her coat off and was ready to pitch in and help. 'Do your lot always leave such a bloody mess?' she demanded of Ray.

'You're not police then?' Helen asked. 'Didn't think you had the look.'

Sarah shook her head. 'I'm an archivist,' she said.

'A what?'

'Bit like a librarian, but I look after historical stuff at the records office.'

'Oh. Look, you don't have to do that,' Helen protested as Sarah began to pick things up from the floor.

'Oh yes, I do. Can't let your little boy come home to this, he's seen enough already and you can't do it all on your own. I expect it took more than one of them to get it this way.'

'There were five of them,' Helen said. 'Trampling through my home, tearing everything about. It was worse than last time, somehow. I just got so angry I didn't know what to say to them. They didn't find anything, there was nothing to find, but they took the rest of the list I was putting together for you. Tried to make out it was some list of people I was selling to.'

'Hmm,' Ray said. 'We'll have to see what response that shakes up. Who led the search?'

'Some sergeant called Enwright. Reminded me of Halshaw. As he went out he told me I'd been lucky this time, but I should keep out of other people's business or I might not be so lucky next time.'

'That's a threat in anyone's language,' Sarah commented. 'You think this might be Walters' doing?'

Ray nodded. 'You said there were five of them,' he said. 'Do you think the others were in on it?'

Helen thought about it, then shook her head. 'They were all uniform,' she said, 'and I got the feeling they were just as put out by the way the sergeant was behaving. I'd guess they really thought I might be dealing or at least a user.'

'That would make sense,' Ray said thoughtfully. He wandered off to survey the damage in the rest of the flat, then came back into the living room. 'I'll make some tea, shall I? Then we'll give you a hand to straighten this lot up and then we'll talk.'

Helen nodded. 'Thanks,' she said.

It took more than an hour to restore some semblance of order, then they sat down together at the kitchen table and Ray made more tea.

'It's my fault,' he told her. 'I provoked Walters and I guess this is his response.'

'I don't understand,' Helen said.

Gently, Ray filled her in on what he had found out and what he suspected about Frank being responsible for his injuries.

'So he lied to me,' she said. 'He fucking lied to me. And he did this to you? Oh God.'

'It's all right, love. I'm past being bitter about it. Wouldn't do much good, would it, and Frank's the one that's dead. He tried to protect you, love. I think Frank must have realized straight away that he'd got the wrong man and I think Halshaw must have put two and two together very quickly.'

'But why did he do it? He knew there was nothing going on with me and Halshaw. The man was a bastard, I had nothing to do with him. Oh God, he must have been so scared.'

'I don't know what pushed him over the edge. Maybe we never will know but afterwards, I think that Halshaw must have cornered Frank and then introduced him to Walters. And yes, he must have been scared. He'd committed a serious assault on a serving officer. He was in deep.'

'And Walters took advantage of that. I'm sorry, Ray. I am so sorry. Frank wasn't a violent man, not really, but he was a weak one I suppose, and Halshaw wouldn't leave him alone. He couldn't have been thinking straight.'

Ray said, 'If Frank was drinking in Middleton, what pub would he use?'

She thought about it. 'The Mill, probably, or maybe the Full Moon. They're both along the towpath.'

'He didn't have a mobile phone?'

'Frank? No, he said they cost too much. Look, I'm sorry I dragged you both over here. I was just so gutted. I'm going to get out for a few days, Frank's mum says I can stay there for a bit.'

'We'll give you a lift over,' Ray told her.

She went off to get Ian. Sarah gave Ray a quizzical look. 'Phones?' she asked.

'I think Frank wanted out that night. I think he might have called Walters and demanded a meeting. There has to have been some reason for him trekking all the way to Middleton. If he called Walters he'd probably have done it from the pub. If the payphone in either of the pubs records a call to Walters, that would be enough to establish a link.'

'And reopen the investigation?'

'It would be a start,' Ray said.

'The thing I want to know,' Ray said as they drove home, 'is why Halshaw wanted me dragged into this.'

'Remorse?' Sarah suggested.

'Not Halshaw.'

'Maybe he wanted revenge. Maybe Walters didn't cut him in on his little business deal.'

'That's more like it. I think I should talk to him again.'

'That means another trip up there?' Sarah asked. 'I don't like this, Ray. You're playing against people who don't have any scruples.'

'I've been doing that for years.'

Sarah laughed uneasily. 'Yes, but you were getting paid for it then.'

There was a message on the answerphone when Ray got back. A DCI Bentham asking him to call and giving the number. Ray recognized the Manchester code.

'Halshaw?' Sarah asked.

Ray shrugged, he dialled and asked for DCI Bentham. It was about Halshaw. The man had been found dead at his home. They were assuming suicide at this stage, a combination of sleeping pills and alcohol.

'He left a note,' Bentham said. 'With your name on the envelope. We traced you through your phone number. It was written on a sugar bag and slipped inside the envelope.'

He was obviously puzzled by this. 'I didn't have any paper,' Ray told him.

They wanted him to go up, or if not, offered to have Bentham come to him. Ray said he'd drive up to them.

'Are you going to tell Helen?' Sarah asked.

'Not yet, when I know what's going on then I will. I'm glad she's not at the flat though.'

'Why?'

'I don't know. I just don't trust Walters.'

The following morning Ray left early. He had called George from a payphone on the way to ask about the

Jane Adams

phone records from the two pubs and tell him about Halshaw.

'I never took him for the suicidal type,' George commented.

'Is there one?'

'No suspicion of foul play?'

'Not that they mentioned. But they didn't tell me a lot. I'm eager to know what Halshaw wrote in that note.'

Driving up the motorway, Ray found that he was thinking a lot about Kitty. How did Kitty feel when she heard the news of Matthew's death? *If* she heard the news. It seemed such a waste that these two, who cared so much for each other despite the great difference in age, should not have become more than friends.

His own feelings for Kitty were so confused. The attraction he felt for her memory or ghost or whatever it was she had left behind, was so strong that it embarrassed him even to think about it. A short while ago, Ray thought, he would have been willing to make the cottage his permanent home. Now, he knew that if he was to have any future life with Sarah, this was an impossibility. So what was he to do with the place? If he sold, would Kitty be there for the new owners, to impinge upon their lives as she had upon Mathilda's and then on his?

The police station was not far from Halshaw's house. DCI Bentham was a youngish man – for the rank – with a direct manner that Ray immediately liked. He took Ray through to one of the interview rooms and apologized for the fact that only machine tea was available.

'It's good of you to come, Mr Flowers.'

'DI Flowers,' Ray corrected him, showing his ID. 'I'm

taking early retirement, but at the moment I'm only on sick leave.'

'I see,' Bentham said as though things began to fall into place. 'Well, I hope retirement goes a bit better for you than it did for Guy Halshaw.'

'I should have made it plain last night that we were ex-colleagues,' Ray apologized. 'But I was a bit shocked. I'd only seen him the other day and I'd never have thought he was headed for the pill bottle.'

'I don't know that you can ever tell. Why did you come to see him? Was he a friend?'

'No, no he wasn't. As I say, an ex-colleague and even then not close. He'd sent me something and I wanted to know why.' He took the clipping from his pocket and laid it on the table. 'The date is the day I was injured.'

'Your hands and face?' Bentham asked. 'I did wonder when you mentioned sick leave.' He read the clipping. 'Was he claiming that this Frank Jones was involved?' he asked.

'Exactly the conclusion I came to. So I came to ask him, but he wasn't telling. Seemed he'd changed his mind.'

'The suicide note,' Bentham said, producing a document bag from a folder lying on the desk. Ray noticed another one holding the envelope and sugar bag. He passed the note to Ray. 'Mean anything?'

Ray nodded. 'It might do,' he said. 'Walters was Halshaw's boss before he transferred.'

'Ah,' Bentham mused, as though that too filled in a few gaps. 'Didn't get on with him?'

'I'm not sure,' Ray hedged, 'but I understand there was a little friction.'

Bentham nodded as though satisfied. 'Well, I'm sorry to have dragged you all the way up here for that, but we have to check things out. I've got to admit it's the first time we had a sugar pack in a suicide note. You'd really got some of the younger officers going. We'd a probationer convinced it was some kind of code.'

Ray shook his head. 'Really I just didn't have any paper,' he said again.

'And that was it,' he told Sarah, calling her from the car park at the police station. 'They've decided it was a simple suicide. Retirement that didn't work out, his family breaking up and now this quarrel that Bentham's decided he had with his superiors. It all adds up and it's tidied up the paperwork.'

'And you didn't enlighten them?'

'Lord, no. I wanted to get home this week. Has George called?'

'Not yet. Has he got your mobile number? What time do you think you'll be back?'

Yes and about five, Ray told her. He was smiling when he left the car park and headed back towards the motorway. It had taken a little persuasion, but Bentham had copied the note for him. It contained only one sentence.

Ask Walters what he was doing the night Frank died.

*

Matthew had been dead for three days before anyone told her, it had taken that long for his nephew to be granted access.

'I knew that he was ill. I thank you, Master Stone, for bringing this news yourself. It is kind. My sympathies are with you.'

Thomas Stone hesitated, then he said quietly, 'His last words were for you, I thought you should know that. He said, "Let there be flowers for Katherine". It was as if he knew that he would die that day. That afternoon we left him to sleep and when we went to wake him, he was already gone. I know he cared deeply for you.'

She tried to thank him, but could not speak. Thomas Stone seemed to understand, and just nodded, satisfied that he had done his duty to his uncle. 'I must take my leave now, mistress,' he said, 'I wish you good day.'

She watched him go and heard the jailer bar the door. Tears filled her eyes and she felt the sobs rise in her throat. 'Oh dear God, take care of him. Oh dear sweet Lord, please keep him safe.'

Finally, she had lost everything and the only compensation she could find was that Matthew had not lived to see her hanged.

Ray was just pulling off the motorway when George phoned him. Ray hated using the hands-free set, the microphone always flummoxed him, but George's news made up for any amount of inconvenience.

'The Mill,' George said. 'The call was made from there at ten fifteen that night.'

Jane Adams

Despite his misgivings about the use of mobiles, Ray filled George Mahoney in on the details of Guy Halshaw's note.

'Is it enough?' he asked.

'Enough to get things moving,' George assured him.

Ray went to see Walters. His reception, after last time, was a little cool.

'Halshaw's dead,' he said.

'Yes, I've not long had a call. Suicide, they said.'

'That's what it looks like. They tell you he left a note? Mentioned you.'

Walters sighed. 'Get to the point, Ray.'

'Supposing,' Ray said, 'just supposing that someone in the force, someone with influence, hired Frank Jones as their informant, and suppose, for a moment, that they used what he told them to put pressure on the dealers.'

'What kind of pressure,' Walters asked him.

'The kind that says you pay me enough and I'll turn a blind eye when the merchandise arrives. I won't crash the distribution, or at least, I'll make sure most of it goes through. Just the odd seizure here and there to keep the public happy.'

'I thought you'd got something useful to say.'

Ray ignored him. 'What if Frank Jones wanted out? What if Frank Jones didn't want to be involved in the first place? What if whoever pushed Frank into the information game did so because they knew Frank was guilty of some other crime? Something he didn't want known because it would put him inside for a long time.'

'Like attacking you? Come on, Ray. You weren't the intended victim, Halshaw was. They wanted a witness out of the way before the Pierce thing came to court.'

'Then why not pay someone a couple of grand to put a bullet in his brain? That would sort him once and for all. A few burns, a stay in hospital, what would that do? Court cases can be adjourned until witnesses are well enough to testify. Prisoners can stay on remand for as long as it takes. No, this wasn't drugs, this was personal.'

'So? If you're right, if Frank Jones took it into his head to get his own back on Halshaw for fucking his wife, you think he'd mistake you for Guy?'

'I don't flatter myself,' Ray said. 'But you think about it. I was standing next to Halshaw's car. I'm the same height, same build if you ignore the belly, same colour hair and I'm standing with my back to you. Frank would be in a hurry, panicked, scared of what he was about to do and when I turned around and he realized I wasn't Guy Halshaw it's a bit late to stop. My face felt as though it was being eaten off the bone, but I can remember the way this man moved. It's about all I can remember clearly and I've spent a lot of time going through it. He just stood there. There were seconds when he didn't try to run, didn't move. Just stood there shuffling his feet as though he couldn't figure out what to do next. Any stupid bugger would have known that he had to run. But no. He's got the wrong man and he doesn't know what to do about it.'

Then, Ray recalled, he'd heard someone shout and the man had taken off, out of his consciousness, feet thudding on the pavement, then the sound gone altogether as others rushed to Ray's side. Halshaw among them.

'And if this was true,' Walters was asking, 'you're saying this was the leverage whoever it was used to recruit Frank? Anyway, what could he have known? Sure, he worked at the nightclub, but he was a man in a penguin suit standing on the door. He was nothing more than that.'

'And that's exactly why they wanted him,' Ray said. 'He was a nobody. A second-class doorman without even the qualifications it took to do that. He was invisible. He could go anywhere, be anywhere and no one would pay a blind bit of notice.'

Walters was losing patience. 'Ray, why are you telling me all this? It's bull and you know it. There's not a shred of evidence could be made to stick. I think the strain's been getting to you,' he said. 'The sooner you retire . . .'

Ray stood up and turned towards the door. 'I can't prove a thing,' he said, glancing back at Walters. 'Yet,' he added as he took his leave.

'He knows,' Walters said. 'No, I'm not certain how much but certainly enough to tie me to Frank and Frank to you and Halshaw.'

There was a pause on the other end of the phone. 'Sure he's not trying to wind you up? Look at it logically, what proof does he have? And with Halshaw gone that's one more know-it-all out of the way.'

Walters sighed. 'I know Ray. He says he has no direct proof, but in his language that just means he's not got the full picture. He could do us all a lot of damage just with his speculations so far if he talks to the wrong people. Believe me, Ray doesn't give a damn when he's got his teeth in.'

There was a further considered silence on the end of the phone. 'We've got his address, we'll take care of it.'

'What are you planning to do?'

'Don't be such a pratt, Walters.'

The phone went dead. Walters lowered the receiver and told himself that he should leave everything to Alex Pierce, but it couldn't change the fact that he'd been badly shaken. Couldn't stop him from wondering what more Ray already knew.

George had been concerned for his friend. He, too, knew Ray's propensity for hanging on no matter what. He'd got authorization for a watch to be kept on Ray's cottage. The local pub was just across the green and had rooms to rent. He'd had two men ensconced in the front since earlier that day and at three o'clock they called to tell him of Ray's return.

'Tell me if he leaves,' George told them. 'He's likely to head off for Edgemere later, I'll have him picked up that end.'

It was almost five when Ray went out again. He'd changed his clothes and driven off to meet Sarah out of work. Knowing his habits of the last few days it seemed safe to assume that he would be gone until late or perhaps not even return that day.

It was eight thirty when they got the call that Ray was coming home.

'Fallen out with the girlfriend, has he?'

George laughed. 'Not likely. No, it seems she had a prior engagement. They only met up to have a drink together, then her sister collected her and they went off somewhere. Uniform are keeping tabs. Ray's headed back your way. Should be back by nine fifteen at the latest.'

At eight forty-five the watchers saw a movement outside of Ray's house, but it wasn't Ray. Ray's cottage was the second in a row of four and access to the back gardens could be gained along a pathway that led around the block. Two men walked past the row of cottages and then around the back. At first, George's observer thought little of it. The men looked confident as though they belonged there and it was quite possible that they would continue along the little path and into the churchyard, which acted as a short cut to the other half of the village. But he continued to watch, lifting his camera and running a sequence of shots anyway.

'Anything?' Clive asked him.

'I'm not sure. Those two didn't look right. They were trying too hard to be casual.'

'Want me to get onto George?'

'Not yet. It might be nothing.'

Simons waited. It was still light but the sky was becoming overcast and full dusk looked as if it might come early.

'I think they've gone past and up towards the church,' he said. 'I'll give them five minutes and then take a look around. Maybe put in an appearance in the bar before someone wonders what the hell we're doing up here all day.'

'Wait until he gets in,' Clive said, 'then we can both go down. He's not likely to go anywhere else tonight.'

Simons nodded and gave his attention back to the front of Ray's house. There were no movements. Nothing different. He cursed the fact that the angle of view was set obliquely and gave no sight into the narrow windows, then glanced at his watch. It was two minutes before nine. To go wandering about now would be to risk running into Ray Flowers when he returned home. George had given word that he'd be a trifle touchy about what he'd see as patronizing overprotection and Ray was enough of a veteran to be able to spot Simons a mile off.

Ray was back by five past nine. Simons watched him park his car and open the cottage door, switch on the light and then Simons was running for the door, yelling at Clive to follow him. They shot through the bar and out across the green.

'Round the back,' Simons yelled to Clive as he himself headed for the still-open cottage door.

Inside, the place was a mess, furniture tipped over and books strewn across the floor. It had been Ray's sudden reaction as he had halted inside the door, hand on the light switch, that had alerted Simons. Ray had only just been visible, but he had seen him freeze, then run and that had been enough.

Simons slipped on a pile of magazines, recovered

himself, tore through into the kitchen. The back door hung open and he saw briefly that the ancient lock had been forced. Through the back gate and onto the path he heard the sound of shots being fired.

'Shit.' He drew his own weapon, the familiar weight of the Browning nestling in his hand, then ran for the gate.

Ray had seen the two men racing out of his back door as he had reached to switch on the light. Giving chase was an instinctive reaction not necessarily tempered with reason. It became very clear very quickly that both men were younger and a good deal fitter than he was. The slight lead they had on him had lengthened considerably by the time Ray had scrambled over the churchyard wall and fallen heavily on the other side.

Hauling himself to his feet Ray began to run once more. The two men were well ahead and in the distance, from the direction of the road, Ray heard a car engine flare into life.

Angry with himself, he tried hard to sprint faster, suddenly aware that other footsteps pounded after him across the churchyard grass.

'What the hell?' He half turned, wondering briefly if one of the locals had seen the men running from his house. His thoughts were cut short as one of the men he was chasing turned and fired.

'Shit!' Stupidly, it had never occurred to him they might be armed. He hit the ground, diving behind the nearest headstone, the second shot blasting a chunk from the granite block. A third shot fired, this time from behind him. Momentarily confused, Ray lurched to his feet once more.

'Get down! Down!'

Ray dropped heavily as a fourth shot rang out and suddenly a man was crouched beside him, reaching a hand to warn him to stay where he was, a second man giving chase with far more speed than Ray could have managed, sprinting towards the churchyard wall.

'You hit?'

'No, just too bloody fat. Who the fuck are you?'

Simons had run ahead of them still in pursuit and after assuring himself that Ray was OK, Clive followed. But they were too late. The roar of a car engine could be heard from beyond the churchyard wall.

Ray had propped himself against the back of a tombstone when they got back to him. 'You lost them?'

''Fraid so. There was a driver waiting and it took off too fast for me to get the full index. But they dropped this.'

Ray took the pages from him. Some of the arrest details from the file George had sent on Frank Jones. They must have fallen from the folder as the men made their escape.

'George send you?' Ray demanded.

Simons nodded.

'What were you doing while they were raiding my house? Drinking in the flaming bar?'

Simons winced, but let it pass figuring that he'd feel the same in Ray's shoes.

'We'd better call this in,' Clive said. 'Get some damage limitation in place.'

'Bit late for that,' Ray commented. 'This might be the sticks but they still watch television. It won't take a genius to figure out they just heard gunshots and even less of one to know the local press might be interested. Fuck, what a bloody mess.'

People were already gathered on the green when they returned to Ray's cottage. Many of them, Simons realized, had come from the local pub. Their exit through the public bar had hardly been discreet.

Ray closed his front door and pulled the curtains closed against curious eyes, many of whom must already have looked inside and seen that the place had been ransacked. He wondered vaguely what Evie would say if she saw it like this.

'Um, anything missing, sir?' Simons asked as Clive radioed in.

Ray sat down on the stairs and surveyed the mess.

'Right now,' he said, 'it's a little hard to say.'

Sarah Gordon arrived at Ray's cottage at half past ten, close on the heels of the local police and just ahead of the press. She found Ray still sitting on the stairs while SOCOs sifted through the remnants of his home and the local officers took his statement.

Sarah was reminded forcibly of the scene at Helen's flat. Ray looked up as she came in. She had Clive in tow, evidently that was how she had got through the police cordon.

'Sarah? How come you're here?'

'Well, that's a fine welcome. Lord, what a mess, more

of your lot, was it?' She shook her head as Ray began to answer. 'No, I know the story. George telephoned me at my sister's place. Really pissed her off, she's been ex-directory for years.'

She glanced around again, a frown creasing between her eyes. Then she reached for Ray's hand and jerked her head towards Simons and Clive. 'Come on, they can finish up here, it's about time they earned their keep. They probably know more of what went on anyway.'

Ray found himself being pulled to his feet and directed towards the door much to the consternation of the young officer.

'But sir, your statement, sir.'

'Tomorrow,' Sarah announced. 'Those two over there can fill you in until then.'

Ray shook his head, but decided he was too tired and too pissed off to resist Sarah Gordon in her present mood. She opened the cottage door and exited, scattering onlookers as she went. Ray barely had his seat belt fastened before she had accelerated away.

'I'm sorry,' he said, 'that George disturbed your evening.'

Sarah snorted rudely. 'Probably knew what I'd do to him if he hadn't,' she said.

Chapter Fifty-Six

For the next stage in her interrogation Prescott had Kitty
brought out of her cell and into the ante-room above. His
approach this day was different. He bade her sit down,
offered wine and sat opposite as though they were friends
about to discuss some trivial event. Kitty's head was
reeling. Just to be brought up into this well-lit room
confused her and the wine, which she accepted without
thinking, went straight to her head.

'Where is Master Randall?' she asked him.

'Gone to bring his wife here to give her evidence.'

'Martha?' Kitty's hand shook and the wine threatened
to spill. She steadied it with her other. 'Martha is wrong,'
she said boldly. 'She lied about me.'

'She lied about what she had seen? You, lying naked
on the ground, writhing in the mud and crying out for
your Lord to take you?'

'She misunderstood what she saw. I cried out, yes,
but not for the devil to come to me.'

'Who then? Some lover we do not know about?'

'No, of course not.'

'Hmm, maybe you have a point,' Prescott said, looking at her scarred face. 'Though, of course, there are
many men who do not look at a woman's face when they
seek satisfaction.'

Kitty swallowed hard, feeling the flush rising to her

cheeks. 'There was no one,' she said. 'I was alone. I have lain with no man and I have certainly never given myself to the devil.'

Prescott got up from his chair and wandered over to the window. It was open and Kitty could smell the freshness of the air. Flowers grew in the castle yard and the scent of them rose up through the open window and into the room. She longed to be outside. Prescott's words broke into her thoughts.

'It is easy enough to prove, of course?'

'What is?'

'Whether or not you have a lover, or have had one. I will arrange for a doctor to be brought here. If he finds you to be virgin, well, the charges still stand, but we will know the devil came to you in no human form and that maybe Martha Randall mistook a little of what she witnessed. If not, well, Mistress Hallam, you will have to find another tale to tell.'

He crossed the room and sat down once more, reaching to pour more wine. Offering the jug to Kitty as though she were his guest and not his prisoner. Numbly, she shook her head.

'You've not bled since you came here, mistress.'

'What?'

'They brought you here in June and it is nearly September and yet you've not bled. A woman's time comes each month unless she is with child. Do you carry a child, Mistress Hallam?'

Kitty stared at him, shock taking away her ability to reply. Then she shook her head. 'I have told you, sir, I have lain with no man, human or inhuman. No succubus

323

or demon has come into my bed and no one's husband crept in through my window or met with me in Southby wood. As to my not bleeding, any doctor could tell you that stress of the mind or body can cause such things to cease. If you must, then bring your doctors, let them examine me, but it would prove nothing.'

'Would it not? Well, I must arrange it then.' He leaned back in the chair and regarded her thoughtfully. 'I am prepared to be charitable in my dealings with you,' he said. 'But, you are a woman of education and I will not insult your learning. I am prepared to accept that some simple soul who has no knowledge of the world might mistake some devil's messenger and believe them to be simply a lover of human kind. But not you, mistress. You know too much. You embraced the devil and his works in full consciousness. I know it and so do you.' He leaned forward. 'When I studied in Prussia there was a case of a young woman, not yet married, who was troubled each night by dreams. A man came to her bed, spoke soft words to her, caressed her body and treated her in such a manner as only her husband should. She woke each morning in a fever and finally she confided in her mother who went to the church for help. We excorcized the demon, mistress, but we found the girl no longer virgin and, not only that, we found her pregnant.'

'Then she must have had a lover. When she realized that she was with child she made up the tale to try to cover her guilt. Perhaps to protect the man. The girl is to be pitied, not condemned.'

Prescott shook his head. 'I can hear your voice tremble,' he said. 'Does your lover come to you in dreams?

Has he seeded your belly? And when the months pass will you be delivered of a demon child?'

Kitty stared at him. He had come so close to speaking her own fears that at first she was struck dumb. Prescott noted her silence and the pallor of her face beneath the dirt.

'I think I strike close to the truth,' he said. 'Did he come to you in dreams? Did he possess you while you slept? If this is the truth, woman, then why did you not seek help? Much of this business might have been avoided.'

'What happened to her?' Kitty whispered.

Prescott shrugged. 'We excorcized the demon, but the child still grew within her. It could not be allowed to live, of course. We allowed it birth, then I myself took its life in God's name. Then we burned the woman. In Europe they know that fire cleanses.'

Kitty felt her stomach contract and the wine she had drunk come back up to burn her throat. She vomited, retching and choking while Prescott watched. He called for the jailer to take her back to her cell, looking with open distaste at the woman he had tortured, though, in accordance with the law, he had laid not even a finger upon her.

'Take her away,' he said. 'And send someone to clean this mess. We will talk further,' he said to Kitty. 'And you will tell me of your dreams. Oh yes, and the small matter of which friends have joined you in your wrongdoing. I will want a list, Mistress Hallam. A full list when we speak again.'

Chapter Fifty-Seven

George arrived at Sarah's early the next morning while they were still having breakfast. He had the early editions of the two local papers with him together with one of the nationals, which had already picked up on the previous night's events.

'Must have a stringer on one of the locals,' George commented. 'You only made it to page five, but my guess is that this is only the beginning.'

Ray's expression told him that he didn't like the sound of that.

'Tough, I'm afraid,' George told him. 'You're news and it's all the better for you having a back story.'

'Your compassion is overwhelming,' Ray said sourly. He'd had a bad night with very little sleep and George had arrived before he'd had his second mug of tea. He was feeling slightly less than human.

Sarah, on the other hand, had grabbed her reading glasses and was scanning the reports. 'Shots fired in village church,' she read. 'Hardly accurate, is it? MI5 stakeout in the Royal Oak. Are you MI5, George?'

He smiled. 'We've already had an official complaint about that one,' he said. 'We spooks have this aversion to being mistaken for one another.'

'Spooks,' Sarah repeated, laughing delightedly at the

sarcasm in George's voice. 'Oh, George, I shall never think of you in the same way again.'

'Glad you both think it's so bloody funny. I take a dim view of being shot at.'

'Sorry,' Sarah apologized. Ray's look told her he wasn't convinced. 'Do we know who they were?'

'Well, actually, yes we do.' George reached into his briefcase for a Manila folder and opened it to reveal the photographs his men had taken through the pub window the night before.

'Recognize either of them?' he asked.

Ray studied them, then shook his head. 'Pierce's mob, are they?'

'Good guess. This one, name of William Havers, worked the door with Frank Jones, but we know that was just a sideline. The other goes by the name of Leon Travers. Known user and dealer. Strictly small time, though he sees himself as the next Mister Big. Pierce encouraged that, made him feel important and gave him all the crap jobs.'

'Like shooting at Ray? OK, OK, I know. Mark it down to incipient hysteria. I admit it, I'm way out of my depth here. I like my history to be historical, Ray, I already told you that. I don't like the idea I might be involved in the making of it.'

Ray glared, but let it pass. 'I'll go back this morning, see what was taken,' he said. 'But I doubt it's more than the file you sent me or the list Helen Jones put together.'

Sarah looked worried for the first time. 'You think Helen might be in danger?' she asked. 'I mean, if they're violent enough to shoot at you . . .'

'Helen's being taken care of,' George assured her.

'Well, I hope it's not Clive and his sidekick. Real load of use they were.'

George shook his head. 'They spent last night giving statements to the local force and being debriefed by my people,' he told her. 'I've had two officers with Helen and her son all night. They were going to move her this morning. We've offered her a safe house, but she says she'd rather stay with Frank's mother.'

'You think she'll be all right there?' Sarah asked.

Ray snorted. 'Frank's mam lives on the Richmond estate,' he said. 'She's been there thirty years. They've got their own "home boys". Neither our lot nor the likes of Pierce so much as fart there without the locals coming down hard.'

'Sounds wonderful,' Sarah commented. 'Sorry, but I was a sheltered suburban child. The only Richmond I knew was tree-lined and in Surrey.'

'Bit different, love,' Ray said. 'But in a tight corner I know which one I'd prefer. Anyway, I'll go back home this morning, start to tidy things up. And I suppose I'd better catch up with constable plod and finish making my statement.'

'It would probably be appreciated,' George said.

'So what now?' Sarah wanted to know. 'What's the next move?'

'We turn the press coverage to our advantage,' George told her.

Ray groaned.

'The suicide note,' George continued, ignoring him. 'I think that might give us a little bit of leverage. I thought that if it were quietly leaked it might provoke a bit of a reaction.'

Ray looked suspiciously at him. 'And what favours did you call in to get that done?'

George just smiled. 'That would be telling,' he said.

Ray spent the day completing his statement and trying to make some sense of the chaos in his cottage. Visitors came and went, the most useful being Maggie and Evie, who at least helped to set things to rights; the most annoying the predictable run of journalists, and media folk who tried their best to get more than a no-comment response. In between were locals who wanted to lend a hand or just to offer sympathy. They were curious, but they were also genuinely concerned for the most part and more than a little disturbed at this interruption of their peace. He began to wonder if settling here was, after all, just a pipe dream.

He had heard victims of burglary talk about violation and tried to understand what they meant. He thought he began to now. It was the taking away of his sense of security and belonging that he found hardest of all.

Evie left at two and Maggie said she'd soon have to follow and fetch the kids from school. Hiding behind the net curtains like regular busybodies, they watched Evie as she meandered hopefully across the green, soon to be accosted by one of the local reporters. A second bore down on them and then another, this one with a camera emblazoned with the logo of a local TV news programme. After her first pretence at coyness they could see Evie begin to perform, her urgent mime clearly demostrating the mess that the raiders had made of Ray's cottage.

Ray laughed.

'She'll tell them everything, you know,' Maggie said. 'Will you mind?'

'Inevitable, but it'll keep them busy for five minutes. Might be a good time to go.'

Maggie nodded. On Ray's advice, she'd parked on the other side of the churchyard and come in through the back. 'Can I give you a lift anywhere? You could come to dinner. I don't think anyone knows about us. Well, they didn't until Evie.'

Ray grimaced. 'Sorry about that,' he said. 'I wasn't thinking.'

'That's OK, nothing we can tell them however much they ask.'

Ray's expression told her that he wasn't too sure of the truth in that. He scribbled George's number on a scrap of paper. 'If they do get to be a nuisance, give him a call, he might be able to help out.'

'Don't worry. We'll be fine. Now, do you need a lift?'

She dropped him in Edgemere and he wandered around the old town waiting for Sarah to finish work, ending up in the same cafe he had visited that first morning he had gone to the records office, when he had begun to look for clues to Kitty's story. He sat by the window watching the passers-by and musing over the events that had taken place since that day. There were trees lining both sides of the broad Market Road and the leaves were now well on the turn. When he had first seen them three weeks before they had still been a defiant summer green.

Kitty had been unable to see that last autumn, he thought, and that saddened him. She had loved the autumn. The fresh scents that came with frosty mornings and the gilded light that blessed sunny afternoons. And she had loved the activities of the season. The pickling and preserving and the satisfaction of being well prepared for the winter, and she had toiled hard, too, for the parish fund, ensuring that there would be food and warm clothes and medicines for those who fell on bad times.

That she should have died in the early autumn, at a time when she would have been at her busiest and her most alive, that seemed the final pain.

Ray shook himself. His mind had wandered, the sun, hot through the window, must have made him drowsy and yet the thoughts about Kitty that had filled his mind for that brief time had such certainty about them. He tried to think of something in Matthew's journals that might have given him that knowledge, but could think of none.

He sighed irritably and drained his coffee cup. Not enough sleep the night before and a difficult day, he thought. That was all.

He tried to concentrate on the view outside, looked at his watch to see if it was time enough to meet Sarah from work and toyed with the idea of ordering another coffee, but in the end it was Kitty that won. The scent of her perfume, rose and lavender, that filled his mind and the memory of her, lying in his arms. The feel of smooth skin against his own and the desperate need that he had felt, wanting to be inside of her, to share that pleasure . . . and the pain of losing, of knowing that this woman was about to die and there was nothing he could do to prevent that happening.

Shocked beyond measure, Ray, dragging himself forcibly back to the present, reached up and wiped the tears pouring down his face.

Chapter Fifty-Eight

Ray had made an excuse not to spend the night at Sarah's, telling her that he was tired and that he wanted to make an early start on the final clean-up. The truth was, there was little else to do and she must have realized that when she dropped him off. Sarah had made no comment, however, just kissed him and said that she would call tomorrow. She had gone, leaving Ray to stand in the living room of his unusually tidy house feeling rather foolish and wondering if he should run out after her, tell her that he'd changed his mind and would she please stay.

His mind was still full of Kitty. The way she made him feel, the way she flooded his mind with images at the most awkward of moments and the difficulty he was now having in judging her as history and not an ongoing event.

Did Mathilda ever feel like this? Her diaries gave no indication. Mathilda seemed to view Kitty as a visitor who drifted in and out of her life. Ray wished that he could adopt the same perspective. Kitty seemed to have a different effect on different people. Mathilda had come to regard her almost as part of the furniture. Ray himself was on the way to becoming obsessed. John hadn't even been aware of her. There seemed no rhyme or reason to it.

It would almost be easier, Ray thought, if Kitty had fulfilled the 'normal' role of the average ghost. If she'd specifically wanted something done, some wrong put right. But there had been none of that. Mathilda had no sense of her strange visitor having a mission and neither did Ray. It was simply as though their worlds briefly coincided and then drifted apart once again.

It was deeply confusing for a would-be sceptic to take on board.

He went to bed early, deliberately sleeping in Kitty's old room as though daring her to appear, but nothing happened. He slept soundly and did not recollect his dreams.

Morning found him in better mood and he was on his way downstairs when the post arrived. More redirected mail. A brown padded envelope with his name scrawled across in slightly uneven letters.

'Halshaw,' Ray said. Now what?'

He pulled the envelope apart in his hurry to get at the contents. Photographs of Halshaw's children spilled onto the floor together with a videotape.

Suddenly grateful that he had taken his video player out of storage, despite Mathilda's inadequate television, Ray set it playing.

It only took him a few minutes to know how important this was. Still watching the tape, he grabbed the phone.

'George,' he said, 'we've got the bastards.'

*

Walters was alone in his office when Ray arrived.

'Ray?' Walters was cautious. 'And what can I do for you this time? More daft theories?'

In answer, Ray crossed to the outer office and came back pushing a TV trolley used for viewing evidence. Halshaw's tape was tucked inside a Sainsbury's carrier bag, together with the photographs of Halshaw's family.

'It took a few days to get to me,' he said, 'on account of it having to be redirected, but Halshaw wanted me to have this and I thought I'd share it with you. Oh and a few others I thought might be interested.'

Ray played the tape. Walters watched and Ray scrutinized him.

'They had pictures too. Halshaw's wife and kids. A bit of a threat in case his conscience got the better of him.'

The scene was a basement. A man, blindfolded and gagged, was tied to a chair. The camera pulled in to tight focus, showing only the man's face as someone off camera pulled the blindfold aside.

'Michaeljohn,' Ray said. 'Though I'm sure you recognize him.'

The two men watched in silence as the camera pulled back to reveal Guy Halshaw, an automatic pistol clasped in a shaking hand. Michaeljohn's eyes widened and there was no mistaking the shock of recognition.

Then Halshaw fired, his hand jerking with the recoil and then he had moved in to fire again as Michaeljohn's body fell back, still bound to the high-backed chair. Halshaw emptied the full clip into the dead man and even then continued to try to fire, the hammer clipping emptiness until someone reached into shot and took the gun away.

'And you think this has anything to do with me? You're insane.'

Ray shook his head. 'I *know* this has everything to do with you,' he said. 'And I'm not the only one either.'

'You've nothing,' Walters said. 'Not a scrap of evidence. Ray, I don't know why you're choosing to do this, but I'll tell you now, you'll not be welcome here again.'

Ray ejected the tape. 'I didn't think I was all that welcome this time,' he said. 'Oh, and by the way. That list, or rather that bit of a list Enwright took from Helen Jones's flat. Your name was on the missing half. Though maybe your friend Pierce told you that already?'

'Pierce, what's Pierce got to do with it, he's on remand?'

'Mark might be locked away, but he had a brother and his brother has his best interests at heart. Though I don't need to tell you that, do I?'

Walters still looked blank and Ray wondered if that was a bit of the jigsaw Walters hadn't completely got to grips with yet.

'Oh come on, you must've seen the papers. My cottage was broken into. Made a hell of a mess and tried to shoot me into the bargain.'

'Of course I heard,' Walters snapped. 'What of it?'

'Well, it was Pierce's boys that did it and they took the list. Didn't even touch the TV and video, though I was kind of hurt that my hi-fi didn't attract more notice. Cost months of overtime, that did. Anyway, we've pretty pictures of them to prove it.'

'There've been no arrests.'

'Not yet, no. Why hang folk for a lamb when you can get them for the whole bloody sheep? See you around, guv.'

'He's left the station. He's headed left down Cranmer and just turned right into Openshore Avenue. I'm following.'

'Keep your distance,' George advised, 'this isn't an amateur.'

'Acknowledged,' Peterson said, unable to keep the irony out of his voice. He nodded to Josephs who eased out into the light traffic and followed Walters into Openshore.

For a moment they thought they might have lost him, then, 'There,' Josephs nodded. 'TK, right-hand side, outside the pub.'

'Got him.' Peterson keyed up. 'He's in a telephone box outside the Three Cranes Hotel,' he said. 'Pull over.' Josephs had already moved to comply.

They sat opposite the Three Cranes and watched Walters as he spoke animatedly into the telephone. It was less than an hour since Ray's visit. They had expected to have had to wait for much longer before he made his move.

'What the fuck are you doing calling me? I thought we had an understanding. Third party contact only.'

'Think I'm completely stupid? I'm in a call box.'

'And what if someone's watching? Your lot know

about you and it's only a matter of time before they wrap you up. I'm fucked if I'm going to be caught in the flack.'

'Bit late to worry about your image,' Walters snapped. 'You talk about stupid? What the fuck were you doing, sending your dickheads to turn over Flowers' place?'

'Your job. That's what we were doing. You should have paid more attention. Found out what he knew. Watched your own back instead of leaving it to other people and then squeaking about it.'

'You took a list—'

'Amongst other things. And before you ask, yes it had your name on it. Look, Walters, fuck off and keep your head down. Your lot are clutching at straws right now. What do you want to do? Give them your head on a plate? You want to do that, fine, but keep the fuck away from me.'

'Halshaw sent him the video. He showed it to me. Said he knew I was involved.'

Pierce was silent, then, 'And you did exactly what they wanted you to do,' he said. 'Act like he'd come in there and cut your balls off. Like you ever had any.'

He cut the connection leaving Walters staring at the phone.

Chapter Fifty-Nine

'Repent, woman,' Prescott said. 'For the sake of your soul, admit your guilt and ask God's forgiveness.'

'And for the sake of my life?'

'Your life is already forfeit. We have witnesses in plenty to your misdeeds, Randall's wife amongst them. And we will watch you, mistress. See what form the devil takes when he comes to you.'

'When the devil comes . . . Master Prescott, you talk of things I do not understand. I know nothing of the devil, nothing of his works. Before God, sir, I am innocent.'

She saw Prescott signal to men standing beside the door and she was seized. They sat her in a plain wooden chair and bound her hand and foot, the ropes biting into her flesh. She could move only her head.

'Don't struggle, woman,' Prescott said. 'The chair will only fall and none will come to help you. I am expert in the ways of your kind. The devil vows, when he binds your soul, he will come to you should your wickedness ever be found out and offer means of escape.'

'Escape? I am tied here. I can barely move. How could I even hope for escape?'

'The devil can take many forms,' Prescott said. 'A spider or a mouse. A rat, even a toad. He can take any form to slip into your cell. The devil keeps his promises.

Should we see any of these things we will know that he is
come for you.'

'A spider? A mouse? This place is overrun with such
things.'

'And any that approach you will be killed.'

'And you hope to kill the devil in this way? You think
that you can crush such power beneath your feet by
killing a spider?'

The man sucked in a satisfied breath. His nostrils
flared and his lips puckered in a half smile and she knew
that she had played this wrongly. 'So you admit it,
woman. You admit that the devil comes to you in such
forms.'

'You are twisting my words. I never meant to say
that.'

'You will condemn yourself. I have seen this before.
Again and again you will condemn yourself from your
own lips. We have only to watch and wait.'

He turned towards the door and one of the guards
gagged her with a rag that tasted of sweat. She almost
choked on the taste of it.

They left her then. A single light burning close by her
feet illuminating a small circle of floor and they watched
her. She could hear them when they moved, catch a
whisper of their talk as they waited for some small sign
of guilt. And Kitty watched too, staring at the floor until
her eyes hurt from gazing at the small circle of light,
suddenly afraid of the spiders she would once have swept
away with her broom.

Chapter Sixty

Ray had stayed with Sarah until late, arriving home in the early hours long after even the most persistent newshound must have filed their story and gone home.

After the excitement of Halshaw's tape, the remainder of the day had felt like an anticlimax. He knew that others would be taking a more active role – George amongst them – that arrests were imminent and he felt left out and . . . used, even, though he knew that was totally unreasonable. He had been distracted and depressed all evening and Sarah had noted his preoccupation but she had not pushed for explanations.

'Withdrawal symptoms,' she had commented. 'Very understandable.' And Ray was profoundly glad of her matter-of-fact acceptance. His feelings about the whole Halshaw–Pierce business, coupled with his confused emotions about Kitty left him feeling vulnerable and disturbed. Much as he felt he could confide in Sarah, to try to explain those unbidden feelings that he had for Kitty, well, that was a challenge he did not feel equal to.

She was disappointed when he decided not to stay the night and, really, so was he. But she said she understood that he needed to keep an eye on his place. Ray felt terrible, worried that she would read the signals wrongly and take it personally, particularly after his weak excuses of the night before. But he could not bear to lie in bed with Sarah when his mind and senses were still so over-whelmed by some other woman.

To his relief, he did not dream on this night either. He awoke to a morning that was already bright and promised to be unseasonably warm. More importantly, he woke without the oppressive melancholy that had pursued him the evening before.

Three of the national papers had been pushed through his front door. One of George's lot, Ray guessed. He sat in bed reading the account of Halshaw's death and staring with mild astonishment at the pictures George had somehow had released of the suicide note and the sugar bag with Ray's number carefully blotted out. Links were made, tentative but telling, to the Pierce affair and to the attack on Ray. Hints of expected arrests. He wondered what George's next move was going to be.

The phone rang before he was properly dressed and he clumped down stairs in just his trousers, glad it wasn't an Evie cleaning day. The caller was Maggie, wanting to know if he'd seen the national papers.

'Yes,' he told her.

'Your friend George doesn't pull his punches, does he? Anyway, that's only part of why I called.'

'Oh?'

'Beth's been dreaming again. No, not nightmares or anything like that, but she's very excited about it and wanted to call you before she went to school, but I told her she'd have to wait.'

In Beth's dream, something had been buried at Ray's cottage. Something that belonged to Kitty. It was buried close to the door in a little black box.

'She wants you to dig for it,' Maggie said. 'Like it's some kind of treasure hunt. Humour her, will you?'

'Of course I will and if I find anything I'll bring it over. Promise.' He hesitated and then he said, 'Give them both a hug for me.'

'Sure I will. See you soon.'

Ray put the receiver down, amused at the thought that Beth's dream might prove real. Though it would be a logical place to hide something, he thought. A large slab of weathered stone lay just outside the back door, very different from the modern slabs of the path. He wondered if, just possibly, it could have been there in Kitty's time.

Chapter Sixty-One

They were back in the courtroom.

Presiding were Judge Hale and his assistant counsel in the shape of Sir Martin Wyatt and Dr Thomas Skeffington accompanied by various serjeants-at-arms.

Of course, she had been given no defence counsel but, she had been told, she might question the witnesses herself should she so wish. Kitty found herself over-whelmed by the formality and the threat and she could not at that moment think what she might possibly ask.

The prosecutor was a Dr William Ames, a man of God, she had been told. It seemed that such beasts were plentiful. He had a stack of books lying on the table in front of him, which he consulted at odd moments, merely, she felt, to impress the others. Beside him sat Prescott, the inquisitor, the witch finder and burner of heretics.

'You have heard the charges,' Judge Hale said. 'How do you plead?'

'I am innocent, sir. Innocent of every one.'

Judge Hale regarded her with cold grey eyes, then motioned the prosecution to proceed.

'The first witness,' Dr Ames announced. 'Let Mistress Randall be called into the court.'

Kitty watched as the outer door was eased open and Martha Randall, eyes cast down, slipped into the court.

What would the woman say? Surely she couldn't lie

on oath? But Martha didn't even make it halfway across the room. She raised her eyes once to look at the judge and then swung around as though in terror to face Kitty. Then Martha began to scream, not ceasing until finally she fell breathless to the floor.

Chapter Sixty-Two

It had been too dark to dig the evening before, but Ray was up early trying to shift the slab of stone. He dug around it, trying to establish its depth and, for that matter, if it was attached to the house. It wasn't, it proved to be about four inches deep by about a foot by two feet six in size. Ray didn't think he could move it on his own, certainly not without a crowbar.

He stepped back and thought about it, wondering again how long it had been there. If he couldn't shift it then it would be no easier for anyone else to do so either. If something had been buried there, either it was beneath the stone and presently inaccessible or it was somewhere close by. Somewhere that could have remained undisturbed for a long time.

At each side of the door was a small flower bed, well planted. Surely, if there had been anything to find then someone digging in the garden would have found it long ago.

He told himself he was being stupid, that after all, it was just a child's dream. Then he went next door and asked the neighbour's son to give him a hand.

'And we found this,' Ray said, laying a plastic bag on the table and folding it back to reveal what was left of a wooden box, lined with what he guessed was lead.

'Oh wow.' Beth was astounded. 'You really found it there?'

'Just where you said I would.'

Beth's small fingers prised the top of the box open. Inside was a grubby cloth, part of which fragmented as soon as she touched it. And inside that, a locket, large enough to cover the palm of Beth's small hand.

Gently, Ray took it from her. He'd cleaned it up a little earlier. The locket was made in silver and clearly very old. He opened it carefully and showed them the curled lock of hair that lay inside.

'I think the cloth must have been oiled,' he said. 'And the box was lined with lead.'

'Is this our tape recorder?' Beth asked, remembering their conversation.

'I think it might well be,' Ray told her.

'So what do we do with it now?'

'Have you any idea where they buried Matthew Jordan?'

John shook his head. 'No,' he said. 'But it shouldn't be too hard to find out.'

They had been interviewing staff at the Video Wall when another piece of the puzzle fell into place.

The interviewee was a young cleaner who'd been taken on about two or so months before the club re-opened. She was never a suspect. It was clear from the word go that the main attraction of the job – after the above-average pay – had been the attention Alex Pierce had paid to her, giving her the eye, taking her home in his car and generally making her feel that maybe she was going up in the world.

'You like him?'

'Yeah, sure,' she giggled. 'My friend Jez, she works there as well, she reckons he was only after the one thing. But he'd always been really nice, never pushed for more than a bit of a kiss.'

She sounded rather disappointed, Josephs thought.

'He must be a busy man, Alex Pierce. Nice of him to find time to run you about. Did he ever ask you to help him out, like, when he was really busy?'

She frowned. 'Like what d'you mean? Extra shifts and that? Sometimes. But he knew I could do with the money. I still live with my mam and dad and I want a place of my own.'

'Nothing more personal? Little errands maybe? Seeing as how you two got on so well.'

She giggled. 'Well, I delivered a birthday card for him once, if that's the sort of thing. Look, I don't know what you want me to say, but Alex Pierce is good to his employees. Anyone you ask'll tell you the same. He's a nice man.'

Josephs ignored the mild attempt at outrage. 'This birthday card, who was it for?'

'It was for Ike's mam. Ike at the garage Alex always takes his car to. I mean, it shows what kind of man he is, still uses Ike even though he could afford to go anywhere. But Ike sold him his first car and taught him and his brother how to drive. Loyalty. That's what it is.'

'And the card, it was only a card, nothing more?'

'What? . . . I don't see what you're so interested in. It

was a birthday card with a little present tucked into the envelope all wrapped in purple tissue paper. The envelope was purple too.'

'And you just delivered it to Ike?'

'Yeah, that's right. I said I hoped his mam would have a happy birthday and he said thank you, I'm sure she will and then I left.'

'And was there anyone else with Ike when you delivered the card?'

She laughed. 'Haven't you lot got something better to investigate? OK. There was a man with him, a customer.'

'You know he was a customer?'

'They were looking at a bill.'

'And what was he like, this customer? Can you describe him to me?'

She sighed. 'He was . . . well, actually he was quite good-looking. Blonde, blue eyes. Looked tall, but it was a bit hard to tell, he was sort of perched on the desk. Nice body.'

'Age?'

'Oh, about thirty. Older than Alex. Anyway, he must have been quite well off. He had this soft brown leather jacket, you know, the sort that kind of clings. Not like a biker jacket or anything like that. This was new and soft and really nice. And he wore this flashy watch.'

'What, like a Rolex or something?'

She was shaking her head. 'No, it was a chronograph thing. Lots of dials and polish on a stainless steel strap. I've seen them in that expensive jeweller's in the market-place. Cost a fortune, but I don't remember the brand.' She screwed up her eyes in an effort to remember.

'It doesn't matter right now.' Josephs smiled at her. 'If it becomes important we can always take a trip down there and you can show me the ones you mean.'

She giggled again. 'You trying to chat me up?'

'Not while I'm on duty.' He went over to the filing cabinet and pulled out a Manila file containing a number of photographs. Others had been added that had no relevance to the case. 'I'd like you to look at these,' he said. 'Take your time. Tell me if anyone looks familiar.'

He spread the photographs on the table and then sat back, watching as she pored carefully over each one. Enwright's was seventh in the sequence and she pounced on it straight away.

'That's the man at Ike's,' she said.

'You're certain?'

'Oh yes, but he looked better in the leather.'

Chapter Sixty-Three

Randall had demanded that the village gather in the church, though he had sent Martha home, unable to cope with more of her hysteria. She had screamed and wailed and pleaded for God to help her all the way from Leicester and Randall had endured all that he could. Prescott, seeing her state of mind, had pressed the judge to order that she remain at the assizes. It is evidence, he said. And from this woman's mouth will come the names of others that have conspired with Kitty Hallam.

But Judge Hale had seen enough. 'I want her gone,' he had told Prescott. 'Katherine Hallam has been found guilty and will hang. Let that be an end.'

In vain, Prescott had tried to press the judge to change his mind, to allow him to question Martha Randall. Or, if that should not be allowed, then to interrogate Kitty further as he had planned to do in the belief that she would incriminate more of her fellow devil worshippers.

Hale had stood firm. Many other matters demanded his attention and Randall had added his voice to the appeal that this incident should be closed. Bad enough that his wife be dragged into court but Randall knew that if Martha was questioned then she would implicate Hope and he sought to avoid that almost at any cost. His daughter, he believed, was misguided and sinful and it would take a long time to purify her soul, but he had seen Prescott at work and the thought of allowing him to do to Hope what he had done to Kitty sickened him. Randall, for all his faults, loved his child.

He watched her now as she stood amongst his congregation, her head lowered so that he would not see that she had recently been weeping.

'Katherine Hallam has been tried according to the law,' Randall said. 'And the law finds her guilty. I have prevailed upon Judge Hale that this matter should go no further. There will be no search for others of her kind in this village. I do not believe that friends or neighbours of this woman were implicated in her crimes. But I tell you this, let there be found one shred of evidence to prove me wrong, one incident of such sinful disobedience and I myself will call upon the interrogator to come to this village and seek out those who commit evil in the sight of God.'

He felt the murmur of relief run through the crowd gathered before him. They had been afraid, deeply afraid that he might continue in his hunt. There had been too many incidences where one accusation had led to others. Where whole families found themselves condemned and communities were torn apart by suspicion.

'Go now,' Randall said. 'And do not ever again mention her name.'

Hope turned away, led from the church by Mim. Randall worried about the old woman caring for his child, but was uncertain as to what other solution he could find. Her mother clearly had no fondness for her. Not, Edward Randall thought, that she had ever truly had fondness for anyone. He had thought of sending

Hope away for a time and written to his brother with this in mind. Samuel was already there and he knew that his children missed one another. Though it pained him sorely should she go.

He finished his business at the church and walked slowly back home past Kitty's house. The little cottage should be re-tenanted, if any could be found to take over the home of a witch. Had it been separate and not part of this row of four, then he might have seriously thought of pulling it down and burning what was left.

Once home he enquired after his wife and then his daughter.

'We gave the mistress the draught you ordered for her,' he was told, 'and she is sleeping now.'

Hope had fled to her own room.

He would go to her, Randall thought. Speak with her about joining Samuel. The child would probably be relieved to be away from the gossip in the village.

Hope was startled as he opened the door. She sat by the window in her high-backed chair, looking out over the woods and she held some kind of bundle in her lap.

'Father!' Reflexively, she clutched the bundle closer.

He crossed the room. 'And what is that?'

Wordlessly, she handed it to him. He unwrapped the old shawl and stared at the dried remains of a wreath she had concealed inside.

'And what is that?' he repeated. 'Hope, where did you get this thing?'

'Kitty gave it to me,' his daughter whispered. 'I would have told you, truly I would, but everything had gone so wrong and I was so afraid. I did not know what to do.'

'She made this thing?'

Hope nodded.

'When?'

'On May Day. I followed her into the woods. I wanted to know what she did there and what the village had once done in celebration. I asked her about the May dancing and . . . and . . . she made this for me. She said that for the May dancing all the children would wear a garland. She said that I looked like a princess and I danced with her in the clearing.'

'The clearing?'

'There is a ring of oak trees and of birch and a glade with grass and wild flowers. She made the garland there and I wore it.'

Randall's silence was worse, far worse, than his outright anger. He rewrapped the bundle, concealing the withered garland inside. Then took the key from Hope's door and left her, locking it from the outside.

Chapter Sixty-Four

Randall came alone into Kitty's cell carrying the garland still wrapped in the old blue shawl.

He threw it at her feet. 'Open it.'

Slowly, Kitty bent and picked it up, she unbound the folds of cloth, drawing them back until the crown of flowers inside was revealed. It was so faded and dried and the delicate flowers so crumpled that at first she didn't realize what it was she held. Then understanding dawned. She remembered that bright spring day. Hope dancing on the sunlit grass with the band of flowers coiled around her soft hair.

'She kept this? I thought . . .' She had, in fact, given it little thought. The garland had been such a simple thing. Made to please a child. Nothing more.

'Don't punish her,' Kitty said softly. 'She did nothing wrong. I will take blame for this as for all other things of which I am accused but do not wrong your child by punishing her.'

Randall stared at this woman. He had gone beyond words. Because of her, his daughter was locked in her room, forbidden speech or intercourse with any in his household. Allowed only bread and water, and that only enough to sustain her until he could feel that she might be purified enough to beg God for mercy. Because of her, his child was at risk of condemnation both in this world and the one beyond.

'You will not tell that man, Prescott? He sees evil in all things. Think what he should see in this?'

It was as if she had read his mind, dragged his darkest visions to the surface and displayed them before the world. And suddenly he was afraid of something else. What if this woman should seek further mischief and herself tell Prescott of what his child had done? He felt the bile rise into his throat, aware that by coming here he might have played right into the devil's hands.

Angrily, he turned away. Then paused at the door. 'Should any harm come to my child because of this, woman, you will rue the day that ever you were born. I will make the suffering that Prescott heaped upon you seem tame. I vow this.'

Kitty laughed. As had happened that day in the churchyard, the laughter rose unbidden and she could do nothing to prevent it. She laughed until her lungs, already made painful by the fetid air, burned and choked. She laughed until she could no longer draw breath. And Randall watched her, his eyes wide and throat tight with horror. He fled from her cell and out through the prison yard to where his horse was tethered. It had little time to rest and usually Randall was so careful of the beast, but this time, he could think of nothing but Kitty's laughter as he had pleaded for the very soul of his child. He whipped his horse until its mouth and flanks foamed and it began to stumble, forcing him to slow down, but all the time, above the noise of hoofbeats, the woman's laughter echoed in his head.

Part V

Chapter Sixty-Five

Katherine Mary Hallam was sentenced to die on the morning of 23 September and Mim had arrived at the Southgates in Leicester at dawn that morning.

It had been a long walk, many lonely frightening hours of it and Mim wondered if it had been all for nothing. What could she do now that she was here? She had prayed that, should she be in the crowd, Kitty might know it somehow and feel less alone. Less betrayed.

People already lined the route to Gaeltree Gate. The crowd buzzing with gossip about the witch that was to die that day. Mim could not recognize Kitty in their accounts of her. She felt tears welling in her eyes and, drawing her shawl close round her face, moved to the edge of the crowd so that none might remark them.

The best that could be hoped was that death would come swiftly. She had seen folk hang and heard of many more, dancing to the hangman's tune for minutes at a time as they slowly had the life choked out of them.

She had been hesitant about coming because it meant that she must leave Hope behind, the child still closed up in her room with her mother still shrieking about the witch that would not leave her in peace. The decision had been made for her by Master Randall. He had returned from his errand in the town in the early hours of morning, his face white and his body shaking as though the devil himself had chased him home. Randall's horse had been blowing and sweating and had weals across its flanks where the man had beaten it into flight. The stableman had poulticed them, but the creature had grown fey and wild with Randall's treatment of it and it had bitten the stableman's hand for his trouble.

That was not like Master Randall, Mim acknowledged. Something had frightened him and done so to the extent that his reason had fled almost as much as his wife's had done.

Hope was to be dispatched that same day to join her brother at their cousins' home and Mim had not even been permitted to say goodbye. Suddenly, she was tainted by Kitty's friendship as never before and barred from the Randall house. Mim had packed a few belongings for her journey and she had left the village.

Now that she was here, Mim was uncertain what to do.

A sudden excited murmur rose amongst the crowd. The castle gate was open, the time had come.

For much of the day Mim had wandered, dazed and invisible on the busy streets not knowing what to do next. Nightfall found her by the castle gate, staring up at the place where Kitty had spent her last days.

A man emerged from a small side door and crossed the green towards her. He was in servant's garb, but comfortably dressed and his step was assured as he came towards her.

'Your name is Mim?'

She was completely taken aback. 'What if it is?'

'A friend to the witch.'

Mim stared at him, wondering whether to run or if he would call the guard.

'No, mistress,' he said, 'have no fear of me. She told me you would come.'

Mim gaped at him. 'I've done no wrong, sir. I came here simply on a whim. I did not—'

'Please, mistress, do not deny your friend.' He took a small leather pouch from his pocket and drew from it a small fold of cloth. 'She bid me give you this,' he said, 'and told me not to feel sorrow for her. She feels that God at least will judge her rightly.'

'Who are you, sir?' Mim asked him.

'Sad to say, mistress, I was her jailor. I witnessed all that was done to her and all that passed between the woman and those that set themselves to judge her. Go now, before someone sees and questions what you do here.'

Without another word, Mim left him and hurried away. Only later, when she paused in the light shed from an inn window, did she unwrap the twist of fabric that the man had given to her. Inside was a lock of hair and a brief note, scribbled on a scrap of crumpled paper.

Mim could barely read, but she made out two words. The name of Thomas Stone.

Morning found her curled asleep upon the doorstep of Matthew Jordan's kinsman and the servant that found her was more inclined to beat her for a vagrant than allow her entry.

Finally, Mim's cries attracted the attention of Matthew's niece. She remembered Mim from visits to her uncle's house.

Mim stood, watching the pair at breakfast as Thomas Stone took the note from her hand and read it, deep puzzlement in his eyes and Mim, not having eaten since dawn of the day before, stood almost fainting in the centre of the room.

'You say that she knew that you would come?'

'So her jailer told me, sir.'

'And yet, from what you tell me, you decided to travel here only on the morning of her hanging?'

'The feeling grew upon me, sir, and after the master returned in such a state, I had to come.'

Thomas Stone looked anxiously at his wife.

'You have read this note?' he asked Mim.

She shook her head. 'I could make out your name, sir, but nothing more. Mistress Hallam did try to teach me, but I was not apt.'

Thomas Stone fell silent. He did not speak for so long that Mim thought he must have quite forgotten her. Then he said, 'You were a good and faithful servant to my uncle, and I do not believe that you are tainted with evil because of your friendship with our unfortunate cousin.' He paused. 'She asks that we care for you and give you work in our house. What do you understand by that? When she left you were in full employ and in no need of help.'

Mim shook her head. 'I do not know.'

He sighed. 'It is true that since we moved within the town many of our servants have left to meet the call of war. You could be useful to us.'

'I would be faithful, sir. As I was to Master Jordan.'

And so it was arranged. Mim kept house and ruled the kitchen and Thomas Stone kept secret the second message in the note, as Kitty had requested, until the time that she had asked it to be told. And it crossed his mind more than once in coming years, that although he could not see the punishment as just, the charges against Katherine Mary Hallam might have been seen to be true.

James Eton stood at the back of the church and listened to Randall preach. He was already dressed for the journey that would take him to join the King's men, a decision taken less from conviction that Charles was right in what he did and more from fear of what pass a land left to the likes of Randall might come to.

He had arranged for his house to be closed down and given his duties as a tithingman over to Thomas Stone, suggesting that he and his wife come and manage the estate for him and live in the dower house, an establishment it would be easy enough to run with the few servants they had that the war had not claimed.

Thomas Stone had accepted readily, and taken on the obligation to collect the tithes. He had been eager to leave a town he saw would be drawn further into the conflict and it was no difficulty for him to take over for his business the stables and coach houses on the Eton estate. Boots and saddles could be made anywhere and in such a backwater as Oscombe, his skilled men and apprentices were less likely to be commandeered.

Eton himself had no wish for a swift return. His inability to be of real help to Kitty played upon his mind and he had made a will to the effect that the Stones were granted the dower house in perpetuity if he should die. They were his last link to Kitty and to Matthew, who had been his dearest friend. Eton had few kin and none close. He had no children of his own, though he would have been content if in time that could have been rectified by his marriage to Kitty. He had hesitated too long, knowing Matthew's fondness for her. As his wife he could have given her protection from the likes of Randall and he knew that he would spend an entire lifetime blaming himself for this fault.

From the pulpit, Randall met his eyes. 'God has meted out justice to this evil doer, this child of Satan,' he pronounced, 'and we must pray to the Lord that no others among us have been contaminated by such depravity.'

Eton waited to hear no more. He left the church and rode away at a gallop, never even looking back at Oscombe vale.

The war claimed him and he never returned.

Chapter Sixty-Six

The days after Walters and Enwright were arrested passed uneventfully and Ray had to admit that he was bored. The house sale would be going through, so at least there would be money in the bank. George had assured him that his retirement package would still be offered, but Ray was determined not to count on anything before it happened.

He felt as though he was just waiting for something to happen and it was frustrating in the extreme. He messed about in the garden, saw as much of Sarah as he could, made plans with George, but was painfully aware of the one last thread waiting to be tied. The little box containing Kitty's locket.

Then, John called with the news they had waited for. He had found Matthew Jordan's grave.

'I was looking in the wrong place,' he said. 'I assumed he'd been buried in Leicester, but I'd drawn a total blank. Then I began looking at the villages. Matthew was taken back to the place he was born and buried there, away from the fighting. The stone fell down years ago, but the parish records are complete and there was an inventory made in about 1820 marking all the graves.'

They chose a Monday morning to go to Foston, assuming that it would be quiet then, following the single track road and parking on the muddy frontage of the church.

Matthew's grave was right at the back of the churchyard and they took the locket there, Ray and Sarah, John and his family, and John cut a square of turf with his penknife, scooped out the earth beneath until he had a hole about a foot deep. Then they placed the little box inside.

Once the turf had been replaced nothing could be seen. John said the prayers for the dead over the grave and Beth placed a posy of flowers cut from Mathilda's garden close by, though not too close to the hole that they had made. 'Flowers for Katherine,' Maggie said. She smiled at Ray.

'We still don't know how she died,' Sarah reminded them.

'I'm not sure that it matters now. We know that she was innocent and Matthew knew that too. I think that was all she cared about.'

'Unless she escaped?' Ray said. The others looked at him. 'There was a war on. There might have been an opportunity.' He looked vaguely embarrassed. 'I don't know. I just want to think she did.'

'There's no record of her being hanged,' Sarah mused.

'No, and I like the idea that she got away.' He nodded to himself and walked away from the little group, determined to believe that, no matter what the odds, it was the way it should have been for Kitty Hallam.

Chapter Sixty-Seven

It was nine years since Kitty's arrest and much in Mim's world had changed.

King Charles had been tried and executed in the January of 1649 and a month later his son had been proclaimed King in Scotland, though the leaders of the Commonwealth had declared this illegal and of no consequence. The proclamation had been followed the next year by the young Charles being crowned at Scone and the Scots marching south to restore him to the English throne.

Only a few days previously, the Scottish army had been defeated at Worcester and their men scattered and pursued. Mim pitied any that might be captured by Cromwell's men. Death would not be swift in coming. There had been rumours of torture and brutality.

The worst news brought out of this time, Mim thought, was Master Eton's death. He had followed his King and then his King's son, but Worcester had ended it for him.

Mim had been amazed that he had survived that long, knowing the privations that the army had suffered and the troubles of exile. Much of Eton's land had been sold and only the fact that it had been under Master Stone's protection, and he having a skill to change his coat with fortune that left Mim amazed, meant that the rest had not been seized. Thomas Stone was clever in his dealings with others and even Master Randall had no ill word to say.

And now this new turn of events. That morning Master Stone had called her to his chamber. He had Kitty's final letter on the table at his side and he spoke to her gravely.

'She left these words for you and I must confess, I have been in two minds about speaking them. She bid you go to her old home on this morning and to take with you the lock of her hair. She claimed in her letter that Mistress Hope Randall would return today and would come to you.' He shook his head. 'I would not speak ill of Kitty, Mim, but sometimes I do wonder about her. Hope has not visited her family these many years and I did not look for her to come . . .'

'And now the summer fever took her mother. You believe that Kitty knew. That she foretold these things.'

Thomas Stone rose and took the letter in his hand. 'Mim, you should go because this was the last of your friend's wishes and, for Matthew's sake, I feel we should respect them. But if this should come into the wrong hands, the whole vile business could begin again.'

Mim nodded. 'You should burn the letter, sir,' she said. She took a wooden splint from the jar above the fire and lit it. She had wondered at his insistence upon a fire on a day that was not really cold, but he had pleaded a touch of the ague and his wife had said to humour him, as indeed they always did. She lit the taper from the fire and touched it to the letter that he held in his hand. Together they watched the flame eat the last of Kitty's words and then he dropped the final fragments into the fire and used the poker to break them into dust.

'I have arranged errands for the Farrants that will take them from home most of the day,' he said, speaking of the family that now lived in Kitty's house. 'Go now, Mim, but I do not wish to know what passes.'

Mim had not seen Hope Randall since she had left her father's house, but there was no mistaking the young woman who stood uncertainly at the gate to Kitty's garden.

'There's no one home, Master Stone has made certain of that.'

'Mim!' The girl sprang forward to hug her. She looked pale in her mourning clothes but she had grown beautiful and her eyes were bright and kind. 'How did you know that I was here?'

'What would have kept you away? You have not changed that much, for all you've grown.'

'I wanted to bring her something,' Hope said softly. 'Stupid, I know, after such a time. I wanted to bring flowers, but someone would have seen.'

'She had all the flowers in life that she could ever need.'

'But I brought this. It was my mother's, but I know that I could never wear it and that my father would not notice whether I did or no.'

She held out her hand. In her palm lay a silver locket, heavily engraved with twining columbine and wild roses.

Jane Adams

Silently, Mim took it from her and placed the lock of hair inside.

'Is that hers? Oh, Mim, could I . . . ?'

'No, my sweeting, you should know the dangers in keeping remembrances.'

They buried the locket in the little box that Hope's mother had kept it in. She rarely wore such things, seeing them as frippery. It was easy to decide where the hiding place should be. A stone slab lay outside the kitchen door and it was easy to scrape away the earth beneath and excavate a hole big enough to hide the box and then pack the earth back with little sign that anything had been disturbed.

And then Mim hugged her and they parted for the final time.

Epilogue

The morning of 23 September was bright and clear and as Kitty was led from her cell the light almost blinded her. She had been moved in secret the night before, from her cell beneath the castle, and brought to the makeshift prison where she and the others had been forced to make grenades. Kitty guessed this place must be closer to the gallows.

Outside, beyond the courtyard gate, stood a cart. On this they would take her to the gallows. They had tied her hands behind her back and a cloth over her mouth to prevent her cursing them. She was still dressed in the clothes that she had worn when they arrested her and Kitty knew she must stink. The prison filth scabbed her skin and her hair was stiff with dirt and full of lice.

She went peacefully enough through the prison gate, escorted by a single guard. A musketeer stood beside the gate, another already in the cart. Further along the route there would be waiting crowds. God-fearing men and women waiting to see the witch hang.

James Randall himself sat beside the driver. Kitty looked at him as they led her forward, but could not bring herself even to hate any more.

She had not planned what she did next, but as they made to help her into the cart, Kitty broke away. She swung around so violently that the man who'd held her fell back and let her go. And then Kitty ran. The air was fresh and sweet and the sun was warm and she tasted freedom, her mind not even registering the shouts of the men behind her or their footsteps in her wake.

'Stand clear!' She heard the shout but it made no sense to her. The man pursuing threw himself aside and the shot rang out, the ball hitting her squarely in the back. She fell beside the Angel Gateway.

'You bloody fool! She was meant to hang.'

James Randall's voice reached her, but she knew that there was nothing he could do. She was going to die.

She heard his footsteps, running, then he knelt, turning her onto her back and she registered the stab of pain. He pulled the cloth from her mouth. 'Ask forgiveness, woman,' Randall said. 'Pray God be merciful and save your soul.'

And then she smiled at him. 'I do forgive you, Master Randall,' Kitty said.